A BRIDE'S GUIDE TO HAPPINESS AND HOMICIDE

KRISTEN BIRD

Storm

Ebook ISBN: 978-1-80508-899-8
Paperback ISBN: 978-1-80508-901-8

Cover design: Ghost
Cover images: Adobe Stock, Shutterstock

Published by Storm Publishing.
For further information, visit:
www.stormpublishing.co

Dakota Green

A Beauty Queen's Guide to Murder and Mayhem

An Heiress's Guide to Death and Diamonds

The Night She Went Missing

I Love It When You Lie

Watch It Burn

To Ruby, the one who loves stories.
Keep dreaming new worlds.

Mr. and Mrs. Abbott
together with Mr. and Mrs. Swanson
cordially request your presence at the wedding of

Lacy Hope Abbott
and
Anthony David Swanson

at 3 p.m.
on Sunday, December 28

at the Rose Palace
Aubergine, Virginia
Reception to follow

ONE

SATURDAY

9 p.m.

If the newly fallen snow wasn't enough to put me into the holiday spirit, then a dead body in the holly bushes at the base of the Rose Palace certainly wouldn't help.

It was two days after Christmas, and I didn't know it yet, but with every mile Savilla drove us toward our now-shared ancestral estate, I was headed straight for my third investigation of the year, one that would fall squarely on my shoulders this time.

"You cold?" my half-sister asked, handing me a scarf that she tugged from around her own neck. "It's fracialish out here tonight."

By this, I assumed she meant some combination of "frosty" and "glacial", but I was too angsty to ask and took the scarf without protest. I'd grown accustomed to Savilla's unique merging of the English language, so much so that it had now become a kind of personal game for me to figure out which words my half-sister was pushing together.

It was only my second Christmas and New Year's without Momma, and for whatever reason, the week sandwiched between the two holidays was particularly daunting. I wasn't a crier, but I'd cried at least three times in the past forty-eight hours: on the airplane as I touched down in Richmond; as soon as I stepped foot into Momma's house with my weekend suitcase in hand; and a few minutes ago in the bathroom at the Pheasant Inn, the swankiest restaurant in town that happened to be hosting the classiest rehearsal dinner in Aubergine history.

Lacy and Savilla had truly outdone themselves with this weekend's planning, and in spite of Anton's family and friends trying to ruin it every step of the way, in less than twenty-four hours, Lacy would wed her intended.

Savilla had found me in the bathroom between the third course and dessert. She'd caught me crying, despite my best attempts to appear like a normal, happy maid of honor.

"Aw, sis, what's the matter?"

"Missing Momma." A few minutes earlier I'd happened to look out the restaurant window to see that the first snow of the season had begun to fall in a thick blanket. Like Lorelai Gilmore in Stars Hollow, my mother always loved the first snow. She would pull me out of bed in the middle of the night to catch flakes on my tongue, keeping me wrapped in my purple comforter—covered in a design of cowgirl hats and lassos—as she carried me from the warmth of our generations-old house to the back garden, where she'd point out the camellias, hellebores, and snowdrops covered in a downy white. The look of wonder on her face never changed from year to year no matter how many times she'd seen the white landscape. Years later, when I was away at college, she called me at 2 a.m. to announce the first Aubergine snowfall of the year.

In the bathroom, I sniffled and rubbed at the mascara that was surely lining my eyes. I caught Savilla's expression and remembered that she too had people to miss this year, but instead of reminding me of the fact, she leaned her head toward mine and touched my chin gently.

"Have I messed up my face?" I asked, already knowing the answer.

Savilla wrinkled her nose even as her eyes pitied me. "You're just a bit Rudolph-ish." She pulled a compact of powder and a makeup brush from her purse as she led me to the mirror and sat me in front of her. Her touch was comforting, and I felt the crease in my forehead relax as she worked her magic.

"Better," she said after standing back to study me. Then she thought of something. "I was actually looking for you because I need to pick up another case of wine from the house. Anton's family can pour it back." Because our county was dry, the restaurant wasn't allowed to serve wine, but we could bring our own. Her eyes narrowed as if she was thinking of something in particular, but then she shook it off. "Why don't you tag along?"

That would give me a few more minutes to process without having to put on a smile, so I agreed, grabbed my winter coat, and hurried toward her car.

The pre-wedding festivities, along with the town of Aubergine—backlit by the moon and the Blue Ridge Mountains—were putting forth their best efforts at driving the Scrooge-ness from my personality. My favorite decorations—the greenery molded into the shapes of candles, candy canes, and wreaths—lined every light pole on Main Street, and a forty-foot-high evergreen with gold and silver orbs of every size sprouted from the gazebo in the town square.

"Have you noticed anything strange about Anton's family?" Savilla asked after we were settled inside the car, the heater blowing against our hands. She glanced at me quickly before turning back to the road.

"I think the word 'strange' is embroidered on their family crest," I said. Anton's mother and her much-younger boyfriend, as well as an MIA father, were enough to give any wedding attendee pause, but the array of extended family who hadn't actually been invited but showed up anyway topped it all. "Lacy says that after this weekend, she understands why he was so willing to leave Texas without looking back."

"All families have their things, I suppose," Savilla mused, likely thinking of our surprising reveal this past year. My down-to-earth Momma and Savilla's self-absorbed, multi-millionaire father having a one-night stand nearly thirty years ago had been a shock to both of us, but we were making the best of it. Having a sister was even starting to grow on me. "But as a whole, the Swansons seem..." Savilla hesitated, not being one to speak ill of most people, probably because she'd learned what it was like being the target of speculation and gossip by growing up in the sprawling Rose Palace. "They seem like dysfunctionaires."

While my sister certainly had her own way with words, I'd learned to understand her most of the time.

"Dysfunctional millionaires?" I queried.

"Exactly." Savilla nodded eagerly as we drove down a country road that wound toward the estate. There were no lights lining the road, and the darkness, broken only by the headlights, fell thick around us.

Bing Crosby's "White Christmas" sounded over the radio's airwaves, and I sniffled back a fresh set of tears. This tune just happened to be one of Momma's favorite Christmas songs, and as I wiped at my eyes, I blamed the moisture on the ridiculous cold rather than sentimentality. Without a word, Savilla put a hand atop mine as we rounded the long drive to the main entrance of the estate. Say what you want about my newly discovered sister—and I had—but when she attached herself to you, she wouldn't let go, come hell or high water.

We pulled up in the grand drive in front of the house, and I prepared myself for the brisk air before opening the door. "It's freezing. You keep the car running, and I'll grab the wine," I said. "Remind me the fastest way to get to the wine cellar?" I tried to envision the blueprints that I'd finally taken time to study. At least I knew it was in the basement—not the sub-basement, where the Vampire Room had stood untouched since the fake séance we'd hosted there to uncover a killer in October.

"Take the first set of stairs past the vestibule, and when you reach the landing, take a sharp right down the long hall," Savilla answered. "Do you have your key card?"

I patted at the pockets of my coat and realized they were empty. "I left it in the room."

Savilla gave me a motherly smile. "You know, this place is half yours now. You should probably keep a key to it on you."

I knew the words were true even though I still didn't feel like an heiress. Her father's will had guaranteed that I owned half of the sprawling and impressive estate, which would soon be struggling to maintain itself unless it became a profitable venue. Still, I hadn't really accepted my right to The Rose yet.

Savilla handed me her key card. "There should be a dolly right inside the cellar door. Take the staff elevator so you don't have to carry it up the stairs."

I closed one eye, which Savilla rightfully took to mean that I didn't remember how to get to the elevator.

"Go back down the same hall but this time take a right and then a sharp left." Savilla tapped at the steering wheel. These directions were rote memory to her, and I think both of us were aware of the strangeness of me not knowing how to navigate my own home. "You sure you don't want me to come with you?"

"I got it," I tried to reassure her. "I'll call you if I get confused."

I climbed out of the car and clenched my hands together, blowing warmth into them in the frigid night air.

I started toward the short staircase that ascended to the grand entrance—but then I spotted something in my periphery. It was in the bushes, and the shape of the thing made me pause.

I peered over the stone balustrade, letting my eyes adjust to the darkness below. I blinked several times as I stared at the lump in the holly bushes that the landscapers had planted for the holiday season, and as my eyes adjusted, a figure came into focus.

This was a man in a priest collar, the very person who was supposed to marry Anton and Lacy tomorrow: Reverend Todd Anderson, as he'd introduced himself, with a thick Boston accent. At thirty-something, he was much younger than the woman he was dating, which just happened to be Anton's mother, Patty Swanson.

All of these details rushed at me at once as I tried to fit the fact of this man's body in the bushes into the puzzle of this weekend, which was supposed to be such a joyous occasion.

My first thought, one that I would later find ridiculous, was how odd it was that he would take a nap in the snow. His eyes were closed, and I could almost make out a film of ice already coating his eyelashes. His head of dark black hair was sprinkled with the newly fallen snow.

I blinked, trying to recall whether or not I'd seen the man at all during the rehearsal dinner. I was sure I had—at least at the beginning of the night. Yeah, that was right. He'd started the evening by reading a blessing that Anton's mother had insisted on, and then he'd sat beside her, rubbing the back of her hand with his thumb, the gesture seeming obscene for many reasons: their age difference; the fact that Anton's parents' divorce wasn't yet final; and his, well, supposed priestliness.

Then, after dinner had been served and the toasts had begun, Todd Anderson was... Huh, I couldn't remember. But we'd been sitting at opposite ends of the table, and as soon as Aunt DeeDee had finished her toast, the one that Momma would've given, I ended up sobbing into a wad of toilet paper in a bathroom stall. All of that meant that the last time I'd really noticed him must've been two hours ago, at the start of dinner.

I stared down at the body, realizing that regardless of whether or not I remembered seeing him leave, he was definitely here now, and he wasn't sleeping peacefully. Nope, he was dead. Dead as a doornail, as Dickens had once written in his holiday morality tale.

I shook away my scattered thoughts. I needed to focus.

I crouched down to study the figure and take his pulse for confirmation. The new perspective allowed me to notice for the first time that he was contorted at an awkward angle, suggesting he'd fallen from a height: one leg was bent in an unnatural direction and the head was twisted to the side as if he'd turned to respond to someone calling his name. An arm was outstretched as if the man were about to wave it up and down to make a snow angel, but his face was blank, the thin lips set in an unremarkable line. Thankfully, his eyes were closed, though one appeared to be creeping open, the fixed pupil visible. His white clerical collar peeked from beneath a navy winter jacket—a tailored one, from the look of it.

I stepped even closer, into the snow cushioning the mulch around the red holly bushes, and I almost lost my footing as the toe of my boot caught on a stem. The Rose Palace had been named for the swamp rose bushes that grew wild around the property, and over the years the Finches, the owners, had tamed the plant, showcasing the pink petals on most of the branding for their home and the annual pageant they hosted. But every December without fail, landscapers lined the front of the house with festive greenery, the Finches spending a small fortune to switch out the plants for holiday visitors. With the wedding festivities this winter season, and with the impending reopening of The Rose as a hotel, Savilla had splurged on the old tradition.

In the freezing cold, I bent closer to move the clerical collar and feel the man's carotid artery. I counted for thirty seconds. I waited a full minute. I placed a hand in front of his nose, his mouth, waiting for any kind of breath. Nothing.

I glanced around the body. I didn't immediately see any blood, and at first there seemed to be no visible marks on the skin. But when I bent even closer to his face, I saw a two-inch bruise along the right side of his jaw. I would've assumed it was from the fall, but mottled yellow and purpling had begun around the injury, reminding me of how I'd watched my boyfriend and our local sheriff, Charlie Strong, pummel him to the icy ground about twenty-four hours ago during the bachelor party.

Oh Lord, this does not look good.

As I crouched, Savilla left the running car and started toward me. She'd been unable to see what I was doing from her vantage point in the car and, anyway, was likely scrolling Instagram videos of babies. Something must've caught her attention because now as she stomped forward, blowing warmth into her hands, she frowned at me from the driveway. "What in the world is going on?"

I poked my head above the plant line and pointed down at the body that had landed face up on the holly bushes, noticing again the layer of snow was coating the man's clothing. In a few hours, he would be part of the unblemished white landscape.

Savilla hurried forward and gasped as she reached my side. "Oh my God!" Her eyes darted, her words coming out haltingly when she finally spoke. "Is that... is that the priest?"

"Reverend Todd," I confirmed. "That's what he said to call him."

"But I don't understand," Savilla said, struggling for words. "How did he get... *here*?"

I heard a noise and glanced up to see Charlie poking his head over the railing of the balcony.

At first, the image didn't compute.

Without thinking, I shouted up, "What are you doing here?"

"The security company called me," he yelled back, before shaking his head in exasperation. He didn't have time to explain. "Hold on. I'll be right down."

In what seemed to be seconds later, he raced out of the front door of the house, breathing hard.

"I came to check the house and while I was making my rounds" —Charlie was looking all around as he rushed toward us—"I heard someone screaming inside his room. His door was locked, so I busted it down. Is he okay?"

"He's... he seems to be... very... dead."

Not taking my word for it, Charlie got on the ground and moved through the same routine I'd just performed: feeling for a pulse, a breath, any kind of hope. He went one step further and slipped a hand underneath the body, feeling along the head and then down to the spine when he stopped suddenly, a look of horror overcoming him as he pulled his hand away and lifted it to the moonlight.

Sticky and red. Blood.

Charlie froze and blinked twice as he processed the information, and his hand went instinctively to the holster he always wore on his hip. "This is an active crime scene. Do you have any gloves? Something we can use so we don't contaminate the evidence?"

I did actually. Since undergrad, I'd always kept a bag of latex gloves in my purse in case I came across an animal in crisis. I hurried back to the car, grabbed them, and made my way back to Charlie and Savilla, handing them over as I slipped my hands inside my own pair.

After gloving up, Charlie felt inside the man's jacket and then lifted the body only enough to get a quick look. "It's a gunshot wound from behind. Into the chest, near the heart, maybe even lodged in the sternum since there's so little blood and there doesn't seem to be an exit wound." He narrowed his eyes, thinking. "I parked around the side of the house, but I didn't see or hear anyone else around."

I tried to order my thoughts to ensure I didn't overlook any details before an entire team of officials arrived. I turned to Charlie. "Can you check his coat pockets?"

He hesitated a moment before beginning to rifle through each of the man's four pockets—the two on the outside and the two concealed pockets on the inside.

Charlie pulled out a phone, a wallet, and a piece of paper that he unfolded and held up to the light. As my eyes scanned the words, the ground dropped from beneath me.

On it was written two words: *blame Charlie.*

TWO
FRIDAY

7 p.m.

Welcome, wedding party!

*Please enjoy our Friday evening schedule before settling into your rooms
for the night.*

Cocktail reception in the Carriage House at 8 p.m.
*Respective bachelor and bachelorette festivities from 9 p.m. to
midnight*
(or until we party ourselves out!)

Lacy stood in front of the mirror in the Sweet Briar suite at the Rose Palace, wearing a Jenny Yoo dress with large, dark blue peonies splayed across it. She'd thrown a knee-length white satin jacket on the back of her chair, and though it appeared to be a simple outfit, I was certain it had cost more than I would make in a month as a vet tech.

Lacy clutched her stomach and hurried to the bathroom, calling as she went, "Oh God, I feel like I might be sick."

Savilla and I stood in the room, helpless to intervene.

"Is she okay?" Savilla whispered. "I hope it's not the flu. That's been running rampaviously through the staff."

Rampaviously? I guessed "rampage" and "pervasive", with a "ly" thrown in for fun.

Savilla and I listened, relieved when we didn't hear any awful sounds coming from the bathroom. A moment later Lacy emerged, pale but put together.

I went to her and put an arm around her shoulders. "You okay?"

"Maybe." Lacy's words and her expression were both uncertain. "I didn't think wedding nerves would hit me like this." Her eyes widened. "Do you think Anton's feeling this way? Do you think he might change his mind?"

"Never." I led her to the chair in front of the vanity and sat her down so we could both see her reflection. "Look at you. Radiant inside and out." Because of the late December season, the sun had already set and she was relying on the LED lights of the armoire to prep for the night ahead, the evening of her bachelorette soirée and Anton's bachelor party.

"More like wrung out." Lacy laughed before picking up a mascara wand and reapplying it to her already thick lashes.

"All you need is a bit of bronzer and you're as good as new," Savilla said, picking up a brush and moving in to apply it with expert precision.

We were in a suite in the old wing of the house, but with a substantial life insurance policy that had come through a week after her father's will reading, Savilla had already started renovating the space for a more modern look.

One of her—our—father's pieces, an abstract portrait of Miss 1984 in hues of purple and gold, hung in this very room. On the opposite wall was a piece on loan from the Aubergine Art Collective & Retreat Center, our small town's attempt at high society, a lovely snowscape with the familiar mountain ridges of the Blue Ridge Mountains in the background.

"I've borrowed some of the paintings from the Collective especially for this weekend—put them all over the estate," Savilla had said proudly when I'd noticed one upon my arrival. "This one was actually painted by a former pageant winner. Miss 1926, I believe. What do you think?"

Our town's picturesque beauty had not only drawn the eyes of the wealthy Finch family more than a hundred years ago; it had also become a haunt for American artists, trying to pin down their muse long enough to create a masterpiece. The Finches had finally supported these artistic endeavors, all in an attempt to bring culture to our small town.

I moved toward the Impressionist-style painting Savilla had selected for this room. I didn't know much about art, but something about the colors—the grays and blues and purples against so many shades of white—had a calming effect on me. The subject of the painting—my mountains—also brought up a surge of affection in me.

"It's lovely," I found myself saying as I stood in front of the painting. Suddenly, I realized that the Finch side of my family tree, dysfunctional as it might've been, had funded beauty like this. Surely that was something noble.

"Good," Savilla said, though she was more interested in applying finishing touches to Lacy's brow. "Because I had two similar pieces hung in this room and the Salon, where the bridal party will get dressed on Sunday before the ceremony, and I borrowed a few more modernist ones for the Billiards Room and bachelor quarters." Savilla lifted a shoulder. "If we like them, the Collective told us we could borrow many more. I feel works like these add a bit of, I don't know… elegastication."

I closed one eye, trying to parse out this one. Elegance and sophistication perhaps? Either way, I appreciated her attention to detail.

Savilla spun Lacy to see her reflection, and my friend smiled gratefully at my sister's handiwork.

"Well, then," Savilla said, "I'd best get down to the Winter

Garden and make sure they've set up enough heaters to keep us toasty as we admire the stars."

"Don't go to too much trouble," Lacy said. "We're just meeting Anton's parents."

"But, I thought..." Savilla pursed her lips as if she was about to disagree but then seemed to think better of arguing the matter. "No matter. We want *everyone* to be comfortable."

With that vague comment, Savilla practically skipped out of the room, reminding me once again how in her element she was as mistress of The Rose.

Three of Lacy's suitcases—and one of mine—lined the wall of our suite, and several dress bags hung in the closet. On the vanity was a row of makeup and hair products, as well as the familiar sight of Lacy's signature scent, *Jasmine.*

"I want you—and only you—staying with me," Lacy had said when she'd booked the suite. "I'm fine with a ton of people at the wedding and reception, but I want everything leading up to that day to be small and intimate."

That made sense. Though Lacy had always been more of the party type, never meeting a stranger, she also liked to cocoon with those who knew her best before or after any big event.

· It was Friday evening, and in less than forty-eight hours, my best friend would be a married woman.

The evening would be a night down memory lane, visiting all of our old Aubergine haunts with her bridal party in tow. The bridesmaids included me, Savilla, and Jemma Jenkins. Lacy had known Savilla forever, and recently with the disclosure of her as my half-sister, Lacy had generously welcomed her into the fold of our makeshift family unit. As for Jemma, she'd grown on all of us since the pageant we'd competed in this past summer, and Lacy had been spending a lot of time with her as she booked her for events in between her off-off-Broadway shows.

Anton would be enjoying a more stationary celebration in the Billiards Room with the handful of guys he'd selected as his groomsmen. He still didn't know people in Aubergine well, and the one friend he'd kept in touch with from home couldn't make it on such short notice.

Lacy had suggested he ask three guys from town: Charlie, who would hopefully become a good friend going forward; Will Hurt, who was recently unemployed and also a new dad needing to get out of the house; and Joe Larson, a former classmate and all-around pretty decent guy.

Now, I laugh, thinking that I could've actually kept the bridal party celebration small and intimate, but at that point, I hadn't yet met Anton's very extensive, very intrusive family from the great state of Texas. My fantasy of a quiet-but-festive walk down memory lane was about to be turned upside down.

"How's my makeup?" Lacy lifted her chin so I could take in the full view. "I got a new lipstick, but is this red too whore-ish?"

"You're beautiful." I placed both of my hands on her shoulders, turning Lacy away from the mirror. "Just the right amount of whore."

I hadn't seen her this nervous since the day she pitched the proposal for her event-planning business to the bank for a loan, but to be fair, she was about to meet Anton's parents in person for the first time. We were scheduled for a quick meet and greet in the Winter Garden before the evening got underway. Apparently, they'd just flown in on a private jet from a ranch town in East Texas.

"They're *really* conservative, you know? Like, donate to every Republican politician they can find," Lacy said, holding her stomach again.

"Oh no," I said, trying to lighten the mood with mock horror. "Don't tell them about the time you got elected for fifth-grade class president by running on a 'Girls-rule-and-boys-drool' platform."

"Ha-ha." Lacy swung back around to face the full-length mirror and prodded gently at her hair, which was pulled into a bouquet of tight curls. "They've already asked why we're getting married so fast."

"And the answer is...?" I'd wondered that myself, but I also knew that Lacy was stubborn and she knew her own mind well enough to make her own decisions. I hadn't even dared to bring up the question until now.

"It's *not* because I'm pregnant," she said, putting a hand to her stomach. "This is all nerves."

"I figured." I laughed. "Lest you forget, we share a period tracker. I'm alerted with a little chime every time your cycle starts over." We'd downloaded the app together when we were thirteen, and we'd both kept up with it ever since, jokingly referring to ourselves as blood sisters.

"Anton's the one," Lacy said, suddenly serious as she stared back at me in the mirror. "So, I guess I thought... I don't know, why wait?"

I tilted my head, taking that in. The accelerated timeline was impulsive, which was something that I loved about her. Lacy's ability to seize the day, to trust her gut, to grab life by the balls—that was always something I'd tried, and mostly failed, to mimic.

"And you know I've always wanted a holiday wedding," Lacy said, dabbing her scent on her wrist and neck. "I love the cold weather and the evergreens and the coziness. If we waited, it would be another entire year, and I'm almost thirty. Maybe I'm ready to settle down, to start a family."

"A family? As in two-point-four kids and a picket fence?"

That had never been the future I'd envisioned for my friend, who seemed more like a cosmopolitan traveler than a domestic caregiver.

Then, I remembered something Momma had once told me when she was trying to help me be a less rigid, less set-in-my-ways twenty-year-old: *Sometimes we don't know that we really want something until we try a bunch of other things.*

Lacy had dated at least a dozen guys, most of them very short-term relationships. She'd traveled for a year after college before getting an MBA and starting her own already profitable business. Maybe she knew what she really wanted because she'd tried other things, and maybe I should've taken that advice back when Momma had offered it to me, because I still had no idea what I would do next May, after graduating from veterinary school.

At the end of the fall semester, I'd accepted my professor's nomination for a prestigious fellowship program in San Diego, and the recent interview had gone well. In fact, it had gone so well that at the end of the call, they'd told me I was their top pick and that I would hear from them very soon, adding that they would want an answer fast—within forty-eight hours after the official offer was made. I hadn't told anyone yet.

Lacy noticed the frown before I realized it was on my face. "What? You think we're moving too fast?"

"It's not that," I said, shaking away thoughts of the uncertainties about my own future. This was Lacy's weekend. "You'll be a fantastic wife—and mom, if you want, although last I remember you referred to a summer nannying job as 'the kidpocalypse.' You called the two-year-old the 'Demogorgon,' and his mom had to explain why you couldn't leave him in bed and go for a run while he napped."

"I get the point." Lacy waved a hand. "But I learned a lot, and besides, people say it's different if the kid is your own. That has to be true—otherwise, no one would procreate." She gave me a knowing half-grin. "And I plan to practice a lot of procreating in... Fiji?"

Anton had planned the honeymoon, keeping the location a surprise for Lacy. He'd asked for my input along the way, and I'd accidentally leaked that it was an island destination. I shook my head, adamant that I wouldn't give away more.

"The Caymans? Hawaii? Thailand? The Amalfi Coast?"

I side-eyed Lacy as I clasped the necklace she'd handed me. "I'll be sure to tell Anton's mother that you plan on lots of sex wherever he's taking you."

My friend's face fell, and immediately, I regretted the joke.

"Oh no, Lacy, I was totally kidding." I wrapped my arms around her and swayed slightly from side to side. Lacy relaxed into me, releasing more tension than I'd realized she'd been carrying. "What's really wrong? You're not having cold feet, are you?"

"No, of course not. I mean, not about Anton," Lacy said, starting to tear up. She wasn't one to cry easily, but when she let them loose, the tears streamed down her face like she'd turned on a faucet. She blinked rapidly and fanned herself, trying to ward them off before her emotions made her face blotchy.

I handed her a box of Kleenex.

"It's stupid," Lacy said, dabbing delicately under her eye with a tissue. "I just have this feeling."

That put me on alert. "What kind of feeling?"

Lacy wasn't prone to premonitions, but when she had them, she was often spot on. We'd laughed about the time that she'd dreamed Brandi Lucher would get bangs in seventh grade and the next week the girl had come to school with a new look, but we hadn't laughed at all when she'd called me right as I was picking up the phone to call her about Momma's cancer diagnosis. As soon as I'd said hello she'd asked me what was wrong. She'd had a feeling I needed her that day.

Lacy tilted her head. "Yeah, I know it's weird, but I feel like— or maybe I'm just afraid—that something is going to mess up this weekend; maybe even keep me and Anton from getting married."

"What could possibly—" I began, before she cut me off with her list of possibilities.

"Maybe one of his exes will show up. Maybe his family will hate me. Maybe Anton will get cold feet. What if he waits until the bridal march is playing before he realizes the terrible mistake he's made?"

It was nonsensical, which was much more my go-to state of mind. I tried a technique we'd always used when our—or, mostly, my—anxieties veered in a ridiculous direction.

"Okay, let's play out The Worst," I said, sitting on the edge of the bed. "What if Anton's family doesn't like you and he decides he actually wants to go home and live with his mommy for the rest of his life? Or, what if his ex shows up and it's actually his cousin and she asks him to run away with her?" I stood up and untwisted the right strap on her dress. "What if your wedding has to be canceled because the Demogorgon shows up and rubs peanut butter and jelly all over your dress?"

As my questions grew stranger, Lacy's face relaxed more. "That kid is eleven by now, so he's more likely to show up and shout nonsense gen alpha words during the ceremony," Lacy said, but with a soft smile rather than potential tears. "But I hear you."

"The point is that you're gonna be okay, so don't think like me, always waiting for the other shoe to drop. My brain is not always a fun place to be."

Lacy leaned into me again. "Is this what you mean when you say you're spinning?"

"Yep."

Lacy tipped her chin back to look up at me. "Your brain is exhausting."

"It's a wild ride." I smiled, trying again to reframe things for her. "But listen, after the past few months at The Rose, anything short of a murder this weekend will be great."

THREE

A rapid series of knocks sounded at the door to our suite, and when I opened it, Anton was standing there with a wide smile above his cleft chin. His curly, dark red hair was gelled into a more formal look than he usually sported. He peeked around me like a little boy who'd waited and waited for his favorite day of the year. "Is she ready?"

From the vanity, Lacy called that she was almost done and hurried to the bathroom one more time.

I moved out of the way so Anton could pass, but he stayed put. "Lacy doesn't want us in each other's rooms until the wedding day."

"Ah," I said, finding the rule silly but refraining from saying so. Whatever my friend wanted this weekend, she would get, especially with all of her feelings already on edge.

Since I'd returned to my veterinary program, Anton and I hadn't had the opportunity to spend much time together, so we were still getting to know one another. We stood awkwardly waiting for the woman we both loved to appear.

When Anton resorted to getting his phone out of his pocket, I tried to make conversation. "Have you seen your family yet?"

Anton's eyes flitted from his phone to me and he took a

moment to refocus them, obviously running my question back through his mind. "Uh, no. Mother just texted that she's just got to the Winter Garden."

"Are you nervous?" I asked, before I stopped myself. I didn't want to pry, but Anton did seem rather distracted.

Anton took a beat too long to decide, which answered the question for me. "Nervous? Um... not really. Although, my family can be"—he searched for the right word—"challenging."

I waited for more.

Anton checked his phone one more time before looking up at me. "My parents separated a year ago, but they still live in the same house. Just in different wings."

I squinted one eye, trying to envision how this might work while also noticing the reference to his family's home having "wings".

"It's a big house," Anton clarified.

"Like The Rose?" I asked.

"No, but..." His head bobbed as he considered. "Maybe a quarter of the size?"

That would put it at twenty-five thousand square feet, which was still pretty dang big. But still, living in the same house—even if it was ginormous—after you'd technically separated had to be a recipe for madness.

Anton held up his text messages as another one appeared on-screen. "Looks like they didn't travel together this time, which was probably for the best." He hesitated, studying the message again before thinking out loud. "Although, it is strange that my father didn't just fly in tonight too. Maybe business stuff came up." His eyes jumped back to me as if he had just realized I was listening. "I never know if my parents will be on good terms, or pecking each other to death."

The image of parents with beaks stabbing at one another was not a pleasant one. No wonder Anton was on edge. Having grown up without a father, I had no idea about bickering parents. The closest I'd ever come was listening to Aunt DeeDee and Momma argue over which movie to watch on Friday nights.

Thankfully, at that moment, Lacy appeared, her face smooth and devoid of any tell-tale signs of worry.

"Hello, beautiful." Anton beamed at Lacy and leaned in for a kiss. "My mother and the priest just got here. You still good to meet them in the Winter Garden?"

"Yep." Lacy raised her eyebrows and grabbed my arm. "Especially since Dakota is coming with us."

Anton's face registered surprise for a split second, but then he nodded. "Sure. The more the merrier. Just remember that my parents can feel a bit overwhelming at first, especially my mother."

I patted Lacy's arm to remind her I was here, and Lacy pasted on a smile for Anton. "As long as this weekend ends with me married to you, I'll try not to care about anything else— deal?"

Anton smiled and gave her a quick kiss. "Deal."

Soon after the engagement, Lacy and I had talked for three hours one night, laying out all of the wedding possibilities. She'd considered everything from eloping to Las Vegas or a Caribbean destination wedding to a ranch-style wedding in Texas, but when I'd finally asked her what she really wanted, down deep, she'd admitted that she'd always seen herself having a winter wedding at home, in Aubergine. That's when she'd decided to make it happen sooner rather than later, pulling together a wedding in eight weeks.

I hadn't contributed much, what with finishing classes in New York and preparing my application for the fellowship across the country in San Diego. Still, I'd done what I could from afar, and I'd promised myself that this weekend would be all about Lacy.

Being on the estate now, with the holiday décor, and my friends and family coming and going, did make me wonder how I might feel about being almost three thousand miles from home in sunny California. It was a thirty-eight-hour drive without stops, or a seven-hour flight without check-in or inevitable delays—not exactly a drop-in-for-the-weekend kind of distance.

I tamped back the thought, trying to focus on what really mattered right now: Lacy.

As we reached the main floor, a hum of anticipation was already in the air. The Rose looked different from when I'd been there two months earlier. It was brighter and sleeker, with a cool ambience that still kept the history of the estate at the forefront.

Occasionally, a laugh filtered out into the long hallway as we made our way through the Color Gallery, featuring a few of the Finch family gems that had been reclaimed, as well as more art, from the town's collective.

Lacy halted and took a deep breath as we rounded the corner and spotted the full, tented-over garden through the windows. Thankfully, no one noticed us standing in the shadows and out of earshot. "How many people did you say we were meeting?"

Savilla's expression as she'd left to check on final preparations came to mind, as well as her parting words: "We want everyone to be comfortable." She must've thought Lacy was being her usual unfussy self, but I wished that Savilla had said what she'd already known—that a bunch of Anton's family and friends had shown up early. With Lacy's nerves already on edge, she didn't need any surprises this weekend.

Anton's brow knit, his concern deepening into a frown. "Oh Lord." He sighed. "It's all of them—well, except for my father. Mother just texted and said that he's not arriving until tomorrow."

"All of...?" I asked on Lacy's behalf.

"A couple dozen Swansons and a few old friends," he breathed, obviously as shocked as Lacy by the news. He peered out the window again. "Looks like thirty or so people."

Lacy turned to me, her eyes wide and pleading.

"You can't run now," I said, answering her unasked question. "It'll be all right."

"This is just like my mother, springing something out of the blue on us." Anton closed his eyes for a handful of seconds as if steeling himself for an onslaught, and then took his future bride's hand. "It's all right. They'll love you. They have to."

The words, sharp and commanding, didn't exactly settle Lacy's nerves, but the kiss he placed gently on her brow and the look that passed between them did seem to strengthen her resolve to meet the many Swansons head on.

"Let's do this," Lacy muttered almost to herself, before taking my arm with her other hand and pulling me into the Winter Garden alongside her. The invasion of the Texas Swanson family at the Virginia Rose was happening, ready or not.

FOUR

We walked outside, into the Winter Garden. The air was chilly, but heaters stationed around the plants were keeping us warm. Orchids of every size and different colors—magenta, purple, and orange—had been brought from the solarium just for the evening, and they were displayed in pots along the walkway.

Two dozen or so heads turned to us as we approached the canopy of the wide tent, and voices quieted until we could hear the sound of our footsteps tromping across the paved pathway.

The Winter Garden had been designed with foliage that could withstand the cold. Yellow witch hazel, purple Christmas roses, and pink winter-blooming camellias provided color, and the yellow lights that had been strung through the trees and tent canopy set everything and everyone aglow. Though I could barely make them out, I knew my Blue Ridge Mountains loomed in the distance, which was always somehow reassuring. A constant in the midst of chaos.

Seating had been stationed under the tent in circles and squares. There was a bar with drinks at the end, and Savilla was currently pouring. Though Lacy and Anton had planned to meet just his parents for drinks out here, I suddenly realized that Savilla must've shifted things last minute to include the twenty-five or so more guests. She was good.

Nearest us, at a cocktail table, was a thirty-something-year-old priest and a fifty-something woman, boldly dressed. I caught something in her eyes that matched Anton's and realized that this must be his mother.

Lacy squeezed my hand as she noticed the same thing.

Anton cleared his throat as we approached the two of them, absorbed in one another.

Mrs. Swanson looked every inch the Texas elite in a light pink skirt that ended right above her knee and a quarter-length-sleeved jacket. She had long acrylic nails painted the exact same shade, and her hair was big and blond, sprayed in a way that had come back to haunt us from the early nineties. She'd obviously had some work done because her forehead was smooth and her eyebrows couldn't quite ascend as she laughed riotously at something the priest said.

The priest was handsome, though perhaps not age-appropriate for whatever was going on between him and Anton's mother. He wore a collar, even though I was fairly sure he wasn't currently on duty, but perhaps collars were an all-day, all-season fashion statement. I cringed when I saw Anton's mother caress his arm and then pull him closer. Then, the priest's hand was low on the small of her back. Another inch, and he definitely shouldn't have been wearing that collar.

Anton coughed lightly, and his mother jumped as if she'd been caught in the act of something forbidden.

Putting a manicured hand over her heart, she leaned forward to kiss Anton's cheek. "Oh, hey there, darlin'," she drawled in a thick East Texas accent. "You about scared me to death." She glanced around at the crowd with the confidence of a woman used to having all eyes on her. "If you'd been a snake, you would've bit me."

At that, the rest of the party chuckled. Anton did not.

Perhaps he would've laughed too if his mother hadn't obviously been flirting with the priest before Anton's approach—or even if the age difference between the priest and his mother hadn't been so pronounced. Maybe it would've even been fine if Anton had already been told about the two of them, but his shocked expression said that he'd been completely in the dark.

"Mrs. Swanson, so lovely to finally meet you in person," Lacy said, generous and composed as ever, her earlier nerves seeming to have fled in the face of Anton needing her steadiness now.

"Yes, uh, Mother, good... good to see you," Anton finally stammered, swallowing back his surprise before glancing around at the other guests, who were nodding and smiling at them.

With the greeting, some of the tension in the garden eased, and attendees returned to their separate conversations, though I did sense that more than one eye remained on us as we talked.

Lacy turned to me and lifted an eyebrow in a way only I could read. She was hoping I would jump in and act like everything was normal.

I took the cue and extended a hand, trying to keep my tone light. "Dakota Green, maid of honor and all-around gopher for this weekend."

"Nice to meet you," the priest said, startling me with his accent —it was far removed from the South. A New Englander, maybe. Boston, perhaps? He extended a hand even as his eyes lingered on Anton for a half-second longer. "I'm Todd."

"Reverend Todd Anderson," Anton's mother clarified. The priest touched his collar as if just remembering, and Anton's mother grinned proudly. "He's my beau. What do you think, hon?"

Her beau? It was an antiquated word for such a modern affair. Anton was obviously speechless.

"It's great to meet you, Reverend," Lacy said, coming to Anton's rescue again. She spoke with a warm smile that deserved an Emmy nomination. I wondered suddenly if Lacy wished she'd decided on a Vegas elopement after all. Still, her words were kind as she continued, "I'm so glad you both could join us, Mrs. Swanson."

"Call me Patricia. Patty, for short," the woman said, grabbing

Lacy and pulling her close. "Oh, come on, we're practically family. Let me give you a hug, doll." After a squeeze that lasted a few seconds too long, Patty pushed Lacy away and examined her before looking back to her son. "My goodness, you two will make pretty babies."

Anton's eyes widened. "All right, Mother, I think that's enough for now."

"Me too," Patty said, releasing her grip from Lacy's arm while planting a kiss on Anton's cheek and leaving a lipstick stain behind. Someone nearby caught Patty's eye and she motioned the person over.

The woman was a brunette with a flawless, dark complexion and green eyes, her loose curls draping down her back. Two women moved in lockstep behind her.

"You remember Bella, don't you, darling?" Patty asked, motioning from her son to this other woman.

At first the name caught me off guard. "Bella" was the name of my beloved horse, my faithful partner who'd spent countless hours carrying me around the Blue Ridge foothills. While I would've been happy to introduce any of these people to her, I pretty quickly realized that this wasn't the creature Patty Swanson was referencing.

Anton coughed and swallowed hard, obviously surprised to see this person there.

"I'm sure he remembers *all* of me," Bella said, her voice full of a double entendre. She wore an off-the-shoulder, A-line dress with a slit up the side, which was much too formal for tonight's festivities.

It's almost as if she's the one celebrating her nuptials, I thought, suddenly.

Lacy's eyes roamed from the young woman to Anton, a million questions contained in a single glance; but like a coward, Anton looked away.

Bella put out a delicate hand and waited for Lacy to take it even as her gaze remained locked on Anton's wriggling form. "I'm Bella Rivera, one of Anthony's oldest... friends." The last word was said in a way that conveyed far more than friendship. Bella lifted her heart-shaped face over one shoulder and then the next, introducing the ladies behind her. "These are Anthony's cousins, Charlotte and Myrtis Swanson."

Myrtis put out a limp hand, and Charlotte stepped forward, eyeing Lacy with a single raised brow.

"Nice to meet all of you," Lacy managed.

"We wouldn't miss this for the world," Charlotte Swanson said.

"Not for the world," Myrtis repeated.

I was fairly certain that the cousins had been invited as family, but Bella Rivera had obviously not been on the guest list for this weekend. As soon as Lacy touched Bella's hand, the other woman yanked it away as if she'd been scalded.

"When Bella told me that she didn't get an invitation, I knew it must be a mistake," Patty crooned, putting a hand on her son's back and pushing him toward Bella. "You two go way back. My God, I have photos of you both in a bubble bath together when you were three years old," Patty guffawed as if the memory of the pair of them naked together was just too funny. "We went to that god-awful lodge in Big Bend and it rained all week. We finally gave up and let you two loose in the mud. Had to practically hose you down afterward."

Patty cackled again, waiting for Anton to join in the hilarity, but he didn't seem to remember—or, if he did, he certainly didn't want to talk about it.

"Any-hoo," she continued, all smiles, as if totally unaware of the emotional slings and arrows she was hurling at the bride and groom, "I was sure you wouldn't want Bella to miss such an important weekend. Her invitation must've been lost in the mail."

The last few words were said with an innocence that belied the smile on Patty's face, which was beginning to appear more forced. The cousins, Charlotte and Myrtis, were hanging on every word, as if they couldn't wait for the family drama to unfold.

I chewed at my bottom lip, nervous about the cloud I saw overtaking Lacy. If I had to guess, I was pretty certain she'd never heard of Bella Rivera, much less seen bubble-bath photos of her.

Still, I had hopes that Lacy could let it go. She wasn't the jealous type, never possessive or manipulative. After she'd ended her dysfunctional high school romance with Brett Brinkley, she'd turned over a new leaf, vowing to only date high-functioning men from that day forward. Since then, Lacy had always said that if someone chose to be with her, she might as well trust him to be with her—until he proved otherwise. I admired her ability not to worry, particularly when I'd had to confront my own green-eyed monster when Charlie's deputy had started working so closely with him. I suddenly wondered if this weekend might put my friend's mettle to the test.

"Of course. It's good to see you, Bella," Anton finally said, definitely on edge.

Bella lifted her cheek for him to kiss, and he hesitated long enough for all of us to know that he felt awkward and unsure of the dynamics at play. When he finally did lean forward, Bella moved an inch to the right, so their lips almost touched. That would've been the last straw for me, but Lacy's cheeks only reddened. She was keeping herself in control despite Anton's family's best attempts to destabilize her.

I was about to tell Bella where she could plant her kisses when the woman turned as if she'd heard someone call her name. "We'll catch up later," she said, leaning toward him absentmindedly, almost as if he was the one who'd come to see her. "Maybe after the bachelorette party tonight?"

Lacy's eyes darted from Bella to Anton to his mother.

Patty gave Lacy a quick pat on the arm. "I knew you wouldn't want Bella left at The Rose all night, even if it is a fancy little hotel."

Somehow this woman was managing to insult my ancestral home as well as my best friend. I kind of hated her.

Then I thought about the alternative to having Bella join our party tonight. Having her with us was probably best. I could keep a close eye on her.

"Of course," Lacy managed to say to Patty and Bella, clenching her jaw as she smiled.

Bella waved her long fingers, reminding me of spider's legs, before she gave Patty and the cousins a quick wink and turned away. As Momma would have said, this lady was trouble with a capital T.

FIVE

Those who couldn't read my friend would never know the effort it took for Lacy to keep herself in check as she stood in the Winter Garden. We had no need of the heaters any longer, what with the rising temperature of the situation we were finding ourselves in. I was proud of her for remaining cool and collected, but a part of me wanted her to explode, to put these people in their place.

Anton was avoiding Lacy's gaze, which was probably a good idea since, as the seconds passed, her stare was growing sharper.

"I'm glad you're here," Anton said, turning back to his mother and trying to find his conversational footing. "But where is Dad?"

"Oh, you know, entangled in some new business opportunity." Patty waved as if such things didn't concern her before placing a possessive hand on the priest's shoulder, giving it a squeeze. "I told Todd that he would definitely want to be with you, get to know you, tonight."

"And I told her that would be terribly inappropriate," Reverend Todd responded, with a tight smile that was difficult to read. I couldn't tell if he didn't want to attend the bachelor party or if he was waiting for Anton to extend an actual invitation.

Either way, Anton wasn't having it. His eyes flicked between the priest, his mother, his cousins, and Lacy, but Anton decided to deal with the instigator first. "Can I speak with you alone, Mother?"

Patty let him lead her to the farthest edges of the Winter Garden and onto the back lawn, toward the rose hedge maze.

Lacy and I stood awkwardly, with Anton's watchful cousins and the priest, who was only a couple of years older than us. Would this man become Lacy's father-in-law? Would he expect Anton to call him "Dad"? If so, I could hardly imagine the level of awkwardness that would permeate their future holiday gatherings.

Lacy shot me a look that said she needed me to jump in.

I turned to the collared man still standing with us. "So, how did you two... you and Mrs. Swanson... meet?"

"At Sully's," he said, before catching himself, seeming to remember that I was an outsider and thus had no knowledge of their Texas town. "It's a... a homeless organization that I—and the church, of course—run. In downtown Swanson."

Lacy saw my confusion. "The Swansons founded and live in the town of Swanson," she clarified, her raised eyebrows telling me that she realized how pretentious this fact sounded. "Three brothers were running everything for the past few decades, but now Anton's father is the only one alive."

"That's right. My dad and Myrtis's father died a few years ago, but we carry on their legacy," Cousin Charlotte interjected, obviously proud of her roots. "Great-great-grandfather Swanson worked his way up from cattle hand to land owner, and every generation since then has improved our little corner of the world."

"With a little help from a wealthy widow who took a liking to him," Myrtis added, causing Charlotte to frown at her. Myrtis's shoulders slumped under her cousin's gaze.

I thought of a documentary I'd watched during one of my agricultural animal science classes about King Ranch, a Texas cattle ranch in the southern part of the state. Larger than the state of Rhode Island, and while not incorporated as a city, it generated revenue of more than $600 million a year. Were the Swansons this level of rich? And was this young priest dating the matriarch of the family?

Several things clicked into place at once as I realized that Anton had grown up in the same kind of town as Aubergine, but there, he'd been the royalty. He was already familiar with how small towns worked, how outsiders were always and forever "the other."

Charlie had dealt with this issue a lot over the past year: citizens who asked to speak with officers instead of the sheriff because they didn't trust him yet; drunks who yelled profanities punctuated with "You ain't even from around here" when he hauled them into the station to sleep it off in a cell. Aunt DeeDee and I told him to just give it time, but Charlie was often frustrated by his inability to make inroads with the people of Aubergine. At least Anton had known what he was getting into by deciding to settle down here with Lacy.

As I processed all of this, I took a step back and bumped into a tall planter filled with winter jasmine. I hit it just right, and the table wobbled, the pot falling too quickly for me to catch it. As it broke, dirt flew around us, causing Myrtis and Charlotte to scowl and scoot away as a staff member hurried over to assess the damage.

"Are you all right, Ms. Green?" a young man in the standard black-and-burgundy Rose uniform asked as he knelt to swipe at the dirt on my dressiest white boots. I wasn't used to being called "Ms." anything, and I certainly wasn't familiar with being fawned over by an employee, particularly one who was technically *my* employee, since half of my inheritance funded the maintenance of this estate.

"I'm fine," I said, stomping the dirt off my boots.

Lacy, in her fancy heels, jumped back and, startlingly, Reverend Todd began to curse, his calm expression twisting into irritation.

"Watch it. Shit!" he muttered, stomping his feet before bending to wipe at his shoes before remembering he had an audience and putting out a hand apologetically. "Forgive me. They're suede," he said, pointing at his shoes and composing his features into a more neutral expression as he addressed the young man. "Boy, do you have a suede brush?"

The worker glanced behind him to see if the priest might be addressing someone else as "boy." He was not.

"A soft-bristle toothbrush will do." The priest stared pointedly at the staff member. "Do you think you can handle finding that at least?"

The young man nodded rapidly and hurried away, and I wondered if he would be brave enough to return. The entire exchange was so rude and so unlike any priest or preacher I'd ever seen that I didn't know what to say.

I could tell that seeing the slight against a worker had emboldened something inside of Lacy, and she was preparing to put the priest in his place. She narrowed her eyes, studying the priest's shoes. "I would guess Santonis from the looks of them? That's a pricey brand for someone of your occupation."

Reverend Todd's jaw moved mechanically as if he didn't want to admit to his expensive taste. "I got them at an outlet. On sale."

As he knelt and meticulously attempted to flick the remaining dirt away, Lacy looked at me over his head. She put up nine fingers before pointing at the shoes and mouthing, "Nine hundred dollars."

Even a half-off sale meant that the priest was wearing four-hundred-and-fifty-dollar shoes. It seemed strange for a priest to be able to afford such luxury unless... the longer Anton and his mother were out of sight, having their private tête-à-tête, the more I began to wonder if Mrs. Patty Swanson was this priest's sugar momma. Aunt DeeDee always said that the Lord will provide, but this was a whole new level.

After another minute of swiping at what now seemed to be invisible dirt, the priest stood, looking for the worker, who hadn't returned. Reverend Todd tugged at his collar as if it was choking him.

"It was rather stressful, traveling with Patty from Texas to... here." Reverend Todd glanced around as if the Winter Garden were unimpressive. It was true that a few of the plants were dormant and a couple of the pots were currently simple mounds of dirt, but the blooms that were growing were vibrant. "Patty has, let's say, mixed feelings about this weekend, if you know what I mean."

I didn't know what he meant, and I only hoped that it had nothing to do with Bella Rivera, the woman who'd almost kissed Anton. If Patty planned to stop the wedding this weekend by reminding Anton of an old flame, she could shove it. I silently begged Lacy to throw out another one of her sharp quips and put this man in his place, but she remained silent, too dumbstruck by the past half-hour to come up with solid repartee.

"The only feelings that matter this weekend are between Lacy and Anton," I said, meeting the priest's eye. "Any other agenda or plans can... well, they can go to hell."

It was the best I could come up with in the moment, but the words did seem to surprise the priest.

"Actually," Reverend Todd said, "you're totally right."

Even though the words sounded agreeable, I didn't trust them.

"In fact, Patty mentioned on the flight that it might be good for the four of us—me, Patty, Anton, and you..." Here, he pointed to Lacy as if to clarify I wasn't invited to this little gathering. "Well, it might be good for us to sit down and talk through what exactly you're hoping to get out of this... relationship?"

The way he said the last word made it sound like Lacy and Anton had enjoyed a one-night stand rather than a nearly two-year romance.

"What we're hoping to get?" Lacy asked, her voice rising the teensiest bit.

"Don't be offended," the reverend added, though his tone suggested that he very well meant to offend. "Patty and I just want to make sure that both of you have thought everything through. You know, Anton does have certain family responsibilities and obligations. We'd hate for anything or anyone to derail him from his future. To that end, Patty has taken the liberty of drawing up a prenup to ensure—"

"A prenup?" I nearly shouted. Every person turned toward me, the sound of conversations fading into the background.

My blood was boiling. The suggestion that Lacy would be marrying Anton for his money was grating, but the idea that the two of them couldn't make decisions for themselves about prenups or future plans made me even more furious. Bella Rivera's uninvited presence and this priest's veiled threats sealed my righteous anger. Aunt DeeDee had taught me to respect the Church, but I had a feeling about this guy and would bet that he knew as much about the Bible as I did.

I moved within inches of the priest and lowered my voice. "I realize that you don't know Lacy, but she is kind and honest and fair. She and Anton have a whole lifetime ahead of them, and the two of them get to call the shots about how they navigate their future. If you think for one second that the best woman in the world is marrying Anton for his family connections, then you can take that thought and shove it up your holy—"

"Language, my child," the priest said, eliciting raised brows from the cousins. He glanced around, noticing the attention I was drawing, and gave me a pitying and beatific smile, his forehead furrowing as he patted my arm, like I was a hysterical little lady. "I hate to start the weekend with anything except celebrations, but if you insist on behaving like a—"

Lacy put a gentle hand on my shoulder and shot the priest a look that made him stop speaking mid-sentence. "That's enough." Her tone was even and assertive, and she spoke loudly for everyone to hear. "Feel free to let Anton know your fee for performing the ceremony, but otherwise, we have no other use of your guidance this weekend."

At that, Lacy spun on her heel, motioning for me to follow her. I was happy to let her lead the way.

SIX

Lacy guided us back through the open doors. As soon as we were out of eyesight, the voices in the Winter Garden rose again, likely gossiping about Lacy and the angry friend who had the nerve to mouth off to a priest. In that moment I didn't care. I was grateful to step away from the heaters and into the cool night air. I needed to get away from that awful priest, and maybe the frigid weather could bring me back to myself.

We went a hundred yards past the Winter Garden and Lacy turned left. A minute later we found ourselves on the stone portico overlooking the rose hedge maze and the wide back lawn leading to the residential cottage. As we surveyed the mountains backlit by the moon, the sound of Anton's raised voice caught both of us by surprise.

"I don't think you're hearing what I'm say—" Anton practically shouted.

"You're one to talk," his mother cut him off. "I told you that this was all too fast, but you wouldn't listen."

Lacy's frame stiffened beside me, and when I turned to her, she was frozen in place, her eyes fixed on some point in the distance.

"I've been seeing Lacy for two years, Mother." I could barely make out the figures beyond us, but I was fairly certain I saw Anton's hand lifted in exasperation. "Two years!"

"You've known Bella for your entire life. She is the one we all wanted. She's the one who will take our family and the business into the next generation. She's the one we trust. Lacy is practically a stranger."

"I know her, and I trust her. That's what matters—not to mention the fact that I don't want Bella," Anton said. "I'm in love with Lacy."

I raised my eyebrows and gestured with my head that maybe we should head inside. This seemed like a positive note on which to end our eavesdropping, but Lacy, her expression wounded, didn't budge. I followed her gaze and realized that my eyes had adjusted to the darkness. I could see Anton and his mother clearly now, standing only a couple of feet from one another, engaged in a verbal sparring match.

"We had hoped for better things for you," Patty said.

"Who is 'we'? You and Dad? He's not even here, so I doubt he cares one way or another about who I marry."

The voices went quiet, presumably as Patty collected her thoughts. "Your father had a large shipment that he needed to get to a client."

Puzzled, I glanced at Lacy. She seemed just as confused. After all, Anton's family were ranchers, right? One didn't exactly ship cattle, and even if they did, surely the boss wouldn't need to travel with the cows.

"What does that even mean?" Anton asked, his voice tiring now.

"It means that your inheritance is at stake."

"I don't want to inherit the ranch, Mother. I told you both a long time ago that ranching isn't in my blood."

"That's not what I mean, and you know it." Patty sighed.

Did Anton know it? He seemed as oblivious as us.

"Regardless, you don't get to choose what is or is not in your blood, Anthony Swanson. You come from a long line of Texas entrepreneurs. They worked hard to get you to the place where you could choose your life's direction. That's a privilege that you shouldn't squander."

"Mother, do you hear yourself? Talk about privilege to choose! You left your husband and you're dating a man half your age."

"He's not half my age, and your father was the one who first decided to have a dalliance outside of our bed," Patty Swanson responded as adamantly. "Besides, we are making it work. He stays in his half of the house, and I stay in mine."

"With a priest?" Anton's voice was high-pitched, as if he couldn't stress the strange fact any further.

"I'm in love with Todd," Patty said.

"Love?" Anton laughed then. "That man-child is obviously after your money. It's..." Anton struggled for the word before spitting out, "It's inappropriate."

"And you're one to talk about inappropriate?" Patty threw back at him.

"What the hell does that mean?" Anton shouted.

I shivered and put an arm around Lacy, whose skin was cold to the touch. She shuddered, though I wasn't sure if it was from the night air or from the conversation we were overhearing.

"Lacy seems like a lovely girl, she really does," Patty said, her voice not nearly as loud but still carrying across the garden. "But, Anton, you're our only child. Things are expected of you."

"This isn't the 1800s, Mother."

"I'm aware," Patty said, with a sigh.

I hoped to God that the next words out of her mouth weren't something about how Lacy wasn't a fitting partner, a good woman for the role of Anton's wife, because I was ready to barge in on their conversation and slap Patty Swanson across her lifted face, mother of the groom or not.

Lacy was the best person I knew. She was loyal and kind. She had business acumen, the ability to laugh at herself and with others, as well as a natural sense of decency that let her know when to speak and when to simply sit and be with someone. Lacy had always been the best of friends to me, and a stalwart in the year after Momma died. Though I wanted to remember that Anton's mother didn't know all of these wonderful things about my friend firsthand, fury was rising in my chest. If I had my way, Patty and the priest—along with the rest of the Texas party—would leave tonight and never return.

When voices rose above the garden again, they were heading toward us, and instinctively, Lacy and I crouched behind the stone balustrade.

"We were fine with you gallivanting off to find yourself, taking menial jobs at restaurants and bars," Patty said, less aggressively but still as eager. "We were even fine when you moved halfway across the country and started working at a little stable even though you always said you didn't want to be a rancher. But, my dear boy, it's been long enough. We need you back home. We need you to help with our new direction." Patty's voice grew quieter. "Have you even asked Lacy if she's willing to move back to Texas? If she's willing to give herself to our community? Hundreds—no, thousands—of people depend on our family for their livelihood, and if you throw all of that away for a pretty face... then you're not the son I raised."

"I'm not throwing anything away," Anton said. "I could give you a list of people who can take over, and I know Dad has a dozen hired guys who would love to be in charge."

"They aren't *family*. We can't trust them with our next steps. Your wedding was supposed to be you and Bella tying the knot, starting a life together, coming home to run things. It was always supposed to be the two of you." Patty paused for a beat. "Tomorrow, when everyone arrives, you'll see. You'll understand how beloved you are in Swanson, how much people want you to come back and be one of them."

There was a long silence as Anton and his mother headed back into the garden. Lacy started sniffling next to me.

"Come on," I whispered, still bent forward at the waist so we wouldn't be spotted. A tear ran down Lacy's cheek as I said, "Let's go inside. We'll swing by the restroom and get you sorted out. I may even be able to swipe one of those travel-sized bottles of liquor from the maid's cart."

Lacy was more than willing to let me take the lead, and together we wound through the halls, past the Solarium and the doors to the Primrose Ballroom, through the Color Gallery, and into the large guest restrooms near the vestibule.

I considered taking her back upstairs, but she was supposed to make an appearance in the Carriage House to meet the girls for the bachelorette party in a few minutes. If I let her go back to the suite, she might not come back down, and I was hoping that seeing the handful of other women who were there to celebrate and support her this weekend might remind her why she'd decided to get married in Aubergine after all. I would just have to deal carefully with Bella Rivera's presence.

When we were inside the restroom, I handed her a Kleenex box before grabbing a wad of paper towels from the counter, wetting it lightly, and gesturing to a wingback chair in the entryway for her to sit. I dabbed at the edges of her eyes, where only a very small bit of her makeup had run.

"This waterproof mascara holds up well," I said, assessing her before beginning my ministrations: the primary skill I'd taken away from winning the Rose Palace Pageant six months earlier.

While Lacy sat staring at her hands in bewilderment, I took her purse and rummaged through it to find her emergency powder and lipstick. As I dabbed it on her lips, I tried not to let my own anger show, and reminded myself that there was something soothing about tending to another's beauty needs.

Lacy blew her nose and examined herself in the bathroom mirror. "Does Anton want me to move to Texas?" She hardly noticed her reflection though, as she spun around and tried to reason with me or herself—or the universe. "I have a business here, and he's never said a word about wanting to live there, much less work on a ranch."

"It didn't sound like they wanted him on the ranch," I replied, before quickly realizing that Anton's family's vague business prospects weren't the primary concern here. "Either way, it sounds like his mother is the one who wants him home." I dabbed a brush into her shadow, a shimmery nude, and motioned for her to close her eyes. "Anton wants you to be happy."

"But what if moving back home would make him happy?"

"So he can run a business with his obviously dysfunctional family?"

The question was genuine. I was still getting to know Anton. Him arriving on the scene after my mother's death hadn't exactly been great timing for me to become chummy with anyone, but I'd been coming out of the worst of the grief fog in the past few months and I'd found that I genuinely liked the guy. When he looked at Lacy, there was admiration and protectiveness—and laughter. I couldn't wish for more for my friend.

I bit my lip, wondering if I dared ask the next question. "Did you know about Bella?"

Lacy's eyes went to the ground as she thought back. "I think he mentioned her name, but you know how I am. I don't ask a lot of questions about the past. My motto, ever since Brett, has been to let the past lie, to focus on the future."

It was true. Brett's jealousy had made Lacy totally uninterested in being possessive of, or being possessed by, any man. Until now.

A stricken look crossed Lacy's face and her bottom lip trembled as she added, "I didn't know that they'd been bathing together as toddlers. Or that she was the chosen one for him to marry. He failed to mention those details."

"Because she doesn't mean anything to him," I suggested, though this didn't feel quite right. After all the drama with Lacy's high school sweetheart being murdered at our class reunion in October, I would've thought that the subject of former flames would've been on their minds.

Lacy started sniffling again, and tried to open her eyes wide to avoid undoing the work I'd just finished on them. The expression made her appear manic, and when both of us caught her reflection in the mirror, she laughed and groaned at the same time.

"Weddings are supposed to be happy," she breathed.

"No, they're not." I scoffed. "Please recall every bridal show we've ever watched on TLC."

Lacy chuckled softly. "But *mine* is supposed to be happy."

I lifted her chin. "Hey, you're marrying the man you love. Nothing can take that happiness away. And besides, The Countdown has begun."

Just like we referred to The Worst, as in the worst-case scenarios, to put things in perspective, we also used The Countdown, a shorthand way to remind ourselves that for better or worse, an impending event would pass. Over the years we'd used it to reference unwanted things like the SATs, Pap smears, and competitions. Using The Countdown to talk about Lacy's wedding ceremony wasn't ideal, but if the weekend was destined to be filled with family drama, then perhaps it was more than appropriate.

"Listen." I checked my watch. It was almost 8 p.m. "In about twenty-four hours, your rehearsal dinner begins, and in"—I calculated—"forty-three hours and twelve minutes you'll be walking down the aisle."

"We want a short ceremony," Lacy reminded me. "Twenty minutes tops. That's what we emailed the priest."

The mention of the priest made both of us pause.

"I didn't expect him to be quite so..." I wasn't sure how to finish the description of Reverend Todd Anderson.

"Dick-ish?" Lacy finished, one eyebrow lifted.

"That seems appropriate."

"Me either." Lacy blinked. "And to think that he and Anton's mother are... sleeping together? Without being married? Is that even allowed?"

I cringed, thinking about Anton's reaction to the news of his mother's love life, and Lacy put her forehead in her hands. She seemed to be trying to find the motivation to get herself through this weekend.

I wanted to tell Lacy that I would fix things, that I would drag Bella and Patty and the priest out to the backside of the property and keep them locked up until after the wedding, but I'd learned—was still learning—that I couldn't promise happiness or peace of mind or even a good eventual outcome. I could only be there for whatever came next.

"Regardless of the background noise this weekend, you're gonna be surrounded by people who love you. Not only do you have your family, you have me and Aunt DeeDee, Savilla, and Jemma." I listed the two other bridesmaids off on my fingers. "The three of us will form a little triangular shield around you this weekend. Patty Swanson and friends will not pass without our say-so." I winked at Lacy. "Aunt DeeDee and Charlie can be our bodyguards—a kind of first line of defense."

Lacy managed a smile. "I'm glad you're my friend, Dakota Green."

"Ditto," I said, putting my forehead against hers before taking a tiny bottle of gin I'd grabbed from the storage room and waving it in front of her. "Now let's get smiley so we can greet the bridal party and get you as drunk as you want."

"I'm not sure The Rose has enough liquor for this wedding."

"Then we'll find some more."

SEVEN

The Carriage House was almost unrecognizable in its new modern splendor. The groomsmen and bridesmaids were meeting here for a celebratory glass of champagne before going our separate ways, and I hoped it would serve as a good distraction for Lacy.

Savilla had hired workers to clean out the space and scrub it from top to bottom. The walls gleamed, and the cement floor had been painted a shimmery gold, glazed, and then covered with ivory rugs that looked soft enough to fall asleep on. She'd installed thousands of small circular bulbs that hung from the high ceiling, and just for that night, she opened the floor-to-ceiling door that had once been used to allow carriages and vehicles in and out. From inside the doorway, the mountain view was framed like a giant landscape painting.

I noticed that even in her jacket, Lacy shivered as we entered, but I was pretty sure it was from the nonsense she'd just witnessed. Perhaps the room, already buzzing with the excitement of the evening ahead, would help calm her nerves and remind her of the other, more sane people excited to celebrate her nuptials.

My heart did a little flip when we walked in and I saw Charlie, his head turned halfway to the door as if he was on the lookout for me. Unaware of the drama of the past hour, he winked at me as soon as I stepped inside, and then I noticed his eyes trail along my body. Heat traveled up my neck.

"You want a drink?" I asked Lacy, trying to set aside my own desires.

"Sure," she said, her voice strained, even though I could tell she was trying to rally.

"I'll be right back with libations," I said with a playful smile.

I tried to readjust my own expectations for the evening as I approached the table holding rows of filled glasses and the ice buckets of champagne—which just happened to be right next to Charlie. My heart beat more rapidly and I could practically feel my cheeks glowing as a wide grin spread across my face. I was so stinking happy to see him, and if it hadn't been my best friend's bachelorette party, I would have pulled him into a room and had my way with him right then. The look he was giving me said he would like to do the same.

I'd never had this kind of craving for another person. Something about Charlie's arms around me let me lay down my worries about what came next. Shyly, I'd told him as much after I'd arrived in town for the holidays two weeks ago, when he'd picked me up at the airport.

"I feel like I can finally breathe when I'm with you," I'd mused aloud in a moment of vulnerability, as he'd driven us toward the highway for the hour and a half drive to Aubergine. "Like, something unknots in my stomach."

"So, you're saying you like me?" Charlie had teased, raising an eyebrow playfully as he glanced at me.

I must've been caught off guard by his cheeky smile because in that moment I'd laughed and, without thinking, declared, "*Like* you? I *love* you!"

As soon as the words were out of my mouth I'd wished that I could rewind to ten seconds earlier. I would've made a joke, maybe some kind of innuendo about how I liked *every* part of him. Alas, it was too late. My real feelings had sprung out of my mouth and into the car to sit with us for the rest of the drive.

Gone was Charlie's amused expression as he used his blinker and veered past a slow eighteen-wheeler. In an instant, he'd turned inward, and I'd had no idea what was going on in his head.

My feelings for Charlie had been growing fast, and knowing an offer for the fellowship was coming had really made me consider our future together. Though it went against all of my feminist tendencies, Charlie was a factor in my decision. He'd already told me back in October that he was all in. At first I'd been taken aback, but over the next weeks, a realization had dawned: I was all in too.

I'd stepped a toe into a couple of relationships in the past, but I'd never given my heart and soul to anyone. Maybe it was because I'd never seen Aunt DeeDee or my mother in an actual long-term relationship. Sure, Aunt DeeDee had kept a few men at arm's length, but Momma had never let a man so much as cross our threshold. The times she'd gone on a date—which I could count on one hand—she'd either met the guy at a restaurant or made him honk in the driveaway like a teenage boy. She'd told me once that she never wanted to bother me with a potential new father without a long vetting process first. Apparently, no one had made the cut.

In the car on the way home from the airport, I'd tried to backtrack, even if it was disingenuous, even if I did actually love this man. "I didn't mean to imply that I..."

"I love you too," Charlie had said, cutting me off before I could take back my words.

"You can't love me," I'd said too quickly, my eyes wide with fear.

Not only would it make my decision about where to live much more complicated, it would also mean that Charlie and I were serious.

"Why not?" Charlie had chuckled. "You love me, so I get to love you back."

I hadn't known how to answer that. He was right. I did love him, but I hadn't meant for him to know that... at least not yet.

"It's too soon," I'd protested. "We've only been dating for six months."

"Ah." Charlie had nodded, keeping his hand steady on the steering wheel. "And what is the appropriate length of time for love to blossom?"

"A year," I'd suggested. "Maybe two?"

"Two years?" He'd frowned, but there was a playfulness about his lips. "And if I just so happen to find myself head over heels before then, what should I do? Keep my big mouth shut?"

"Preferably," I'd said, realizing that I'd done just the opposite. I sounded ridiculous. I should have been happy that this sharp, witty, sexy man loved me. He loved me! And I loved him! Why wouldn't I be happy? Thrilled? Ecstatic? Once again, I was being my own worst enemy.

"I love you, Dakota Green, and if you'd like me to set my calendar to tell you that in another six months, I can pretend you didn't just let your true feelings slip." There was traffic up ahead, so Charlie had slowed to a near stop, allowing him to reach over and wrap his hand around mine. "But just know: I don't plan to go anywhere between now and then, so I can wait."

Except for the tears I'd shed over Momma's diagnosis and eventual death, I'd never been a crier. Like, once every six months, I would have a good seven-minute sob and then carry on, but the gentleness in Charlie's voice—and the willingness to stick it out with me even if I was too pent up to tell him on purpose that I loved him—had brought tears.

I'd taken my hand from under his and wrapped it around his neck, leaning into his shoulder. I couldn't make eye contact quite yet, but this time I said it for real. "I love you, Charlie Strong."

He'd kissed my forehead and smiled so peacefully that, even though we had another sixty miles to Aubergine, I already felt like I was home.

Now in the refurbished Carriage House, Charlie handed me a glass of champagne as if he'd been waiting just for me.

"I'll need two," I said, grabbing another from the makeshift bar as I lifted my chin in the direction of Lacy. Savilla had come to her side and was handing her a steaming mug of something. Good. If anyone could be a conversational distraction for Lacy, it was Savilla.

Charlie wrapped a hand around my waist. He wasn't always one for public displays of affection, but he was off duty this entire weekend—or at least as much as one could be when serving as sheriff for a county comprising three small towns.

I was grateful to feel the solidness of his hand on me.

"You look ravishing, Ms. Green," he said, as his eyes fixed on mine.

I tilted my head and let my gaze linger on his. "Thanks, Sheriff. I was hoping one man in particular might notice."

He leaned into my ear and whispered, "That dress seems rather tight though. If you'd like me to help you out of it later, I'm at your service."

Tingles ran down my neck, and my lower belly pulsed with an anticipation that I could do nothing about for at least the next twenty-four hours. Unless I found a way to slip away after Lacy fell asleep tonight. But no, I couldn't leave her alone after tonight had gone so awry.

I inhaled deeply and tried to fix my mind on the evening ahead. I was the maid of honor. I had responsibilities, and Lacy came first. I gently nudged Charlie away, lifting my glass and clinking it against his as I said softly, "To a few minutes alone together. Later, much later."

"To sooner rather than later," he said, as I reluctantly pulled away from him.

"Are you excited about the wild night ahead?" I teased, knowing that "wild" wasn't exactly in the sheriff's vocabulary.

"You know me," Charlie said easily. "I've planned for the jet to get us to Vegas and back in the next twenty-four hours."

I laughed at the idea of Charlie, Anton, Joe Larson, and Will Hurt living out their own version of *The Hangover*, much less Charlie stepping foot in Vegas. That city wasn't made with my man in mind.

Regardless, Charlie and I had both found it strange that Anton had asked him to be the best man, and thus plan the bachelor party. For whatever reason, Anton hadn't seemed to want to pull in friends from earlier years, but after that sampling of his Texas hometown, I thought I might now understand why.

"Cigars, brandy, and pool, as we discussed. Oh—and I ended up hiring that professional dealer for a few rounds of poker."

I feigned shock at the suggestion that Charlie would do anything so scandalous. "Gambling? Isn't that… *illegal?*"

"It isn't illegal to play in a residence as long as that residence isn't typically used for poker."

"Did you look that up to double check?"

Charlie raised a glass to me, indicating that I already knew the answer and should celebrate his meticulous planning rather than make fun. "Speaking of which, have you seen the groom?" he asked, looking over my head toward the door.

"A few minutes ago. He was in the garden with his mother, discussing"—I wasn't sure how to finish the sentence—"discussing the weekend."

Charlie could tell by my intonation that both the location—outside in the cold darkness—and the "discussion", had not necessarily been pleasant.

"Well, I'm sure things will figure themselves out, and tonight will be great." He gave me a lingering kiss on the cheek as he squeezed my waist. Then, he turned to Joe and Will, the other two groomsmen.

"Gentlemen," he said in a cheerful voice, "looks like we need to go find our groom."

Will's face was drawn and stubble dotted his jaw, as if he hadn't slept in some time, but Joe was freshly shaven and smiling. Joe put down his champagne glass while Will refilled his to the brim, and then the three of them started toward the door, Charlie giving me one last longing look before he trailed behind them.

With a sigh, I made my way back to Lacy.

EIGHT

"I'm on duty this weekend, so don't worry about a thing," I heard Savilla say to Lacy as I approached. She'd brought the two of us piping-hot hot toddies. The cups had Anton's and Lacy's names and their wedding date scrawled in a cursive font across the front. "I had these made for this weekend, and when I realized how hard it is to heat the Carriage House, I decided to offer hot drinks too."

I set aside our champagne in favor of the warm mug and gave Savilla a grateful nod, pleased that our combined efforts were keeping Lacy's face from showing signs of her earlier distress.

"This place is transformed." I smiled, turning to Savilla. "I'm really impressed with what you've done with it."

"Who knew that a dusty old garage had so much potential?" Savilla surveyed her handiwork proudly and then she pointed above us. "I'm thinking about turning the storage space up there into a loft apartment. And it would be the perfect size for a gal who wants her space but also wants to live near her sister."

She gave me a fixed smile, and I laughed. Savilla's hints about me moving "back home" were no longer subtle. Every other day she texted me an article about thriving businesses in small towns, about the need for veterinarians in rural areas, and the best parts of country living. Though at first I'd struggled with the idea that

Savilla and I could possibly be related, my sister had definitely become a part of my daily life with her random texts about updates at The Rose and her FaceTimes, which kept me up-to-date on town gossip.

"I haven't decided yet," I said, hoping to keep this conversation from becoming about me. "But I'll keep that in mind."

"Can't you see turning this into the cutest little veterinarian office ever?" Savilla asked Lacy, looking around. "This could be the lobby where owners drink coffee and chat with other animal lovers while their pets have their"—Savilla struggled to find the word and waved her fingers vaguely toward the wall—"their surgimacal things Dakota does to make their furry little lives better."

Lacy glanced at me with a half-smile. She'd come to appreciate Savilla's unique phrasing as much as I had.

"Didn't you just have this space upgraded for parties?" I asked, as I took in the plush seats gathered into little clusters.

"No, silly. I had it upgraded for you," Savilla said, staring at me as if this should be obvious. "For your thriving practice."

"You think horses and puppies need room for coffee and conversation?"

"No, but their owners do." Savilla chuckled. "I took an unofficial poll of at least a hundred residents. They would love a practice here. Imagine: they relax and catch up while they wait for Rover and Spot to get their shots. Or they read a book while their horse gets their annual check-up. People would pay a premium for that kind of service from one of their very own."

I laughed, marveling at how Savilla could conjure realities out of thin air. She was the perfect person to run the Rose Palace.

"We could build three enclosed exam rooms along that far wall, and over there we could put a small surgical space," Savilla continued, her eyes glistening in the light as she visualized the possibilities. "And now you have plenty of resources to hire techs and assistants—ooooh, and in a year or two you could bring on another doctor."

I tried to see what Savilla had described. I'd always planned to be a small-town vet, but that was when I hadn't known there could be more, that I could work with some of the finest animal doctors in the nation, learning specialized procedures on creatures of every size. The only problem was that this opportunity was far from Aunt DeeDee, Lacy, Charlie, and Savilla. Was I willing to sacrifice home-cooked meals, coffee runs, late-night movies, and dinners out with them for a chance at a bigger life? The question made my heart beat faster, and I noticed I was gripping my mug tightly.

My sister, misreading my angst, made a pouty face. "Or you could move across the country and sell out to... I don't know... to the big vet."

I raised my eyebrows at my sister's abrupt change in tone as well as her use of "big vet." I was about to tell her all the ways she was misrepresenting the San Diego fellowship when Lacy caught our eyes and lifted her chin to silence us.

"Or," Lacy interjected, trying to mediate, "we could let Dakota make her own decisions."

It was generous of Lacy to take this approach since I knew that she too wanted me back here in Aubergine with her.

Savilla stepped closer and threw an arm around my shoulder, squeezing me tight. I could hear the hint of tears in her voice as she said, "I know, I know. It's just... I only found out about you. I don't want to lose you so soon."

"Whatever happens, you won't lose me," I reassured her. "We're blood."

At that moment Jemma joined us, swigging back a glass of champagne. "Hey, bitches, what naughtiness are we getting into tonight?" She was already tipsy, and though it was definitely amusing, we had a whole night ahead. She needed to slow down.

"Have you had anything to eat? Or water?"

Jemma narrowed her eyes at me. "I thought this was a party, Mommy dearest."

I shook my head as I laughed lightly. Jemma would be a good distraction from all the family nonsense if nothing else.

"Let's just try to pace ourselves, darling," I said, in my best mothering tone.

"I'm just saying," Savilla said, still on the subject of me and my future as she took a sip of hot toddy, "you'll have everything you need right here." She hesitated, catching Lacy's glance and adding almost as an afterthought, "if that's what you want."

I appreciated the last sentence, and wondered if Aunt DeeDee had also sat down with her for a chat about laying off the pressure just a smidge.

Savilla took a deep breath, and her smile settled easily back into place. "Okay, so we need to get to our first stop soon."

I'd planned a schedule that would take us to our old haunts in town when we were teens, and I'd written each stop in the form of scavenger hunt clues that Lacy could solve before we moved on to the next place. Since Bella Rivera hadn't yet shown her face—blessedly—I thought we might sneak out without her tagging along. I was about to pull out the first clue when four other women walked into the Carriage House, startling us all.

It was Patty Swanson along with Bella Rivera and the cousins, Myrtis and Charlotte.

"Lacy, we found you," Patty exclaimed, having fully recovered from her outdoor conversation with Anton.

I watched as Lacy peered around them, hoping to see Anton trailing along behind them—and leading them right back out the way they'd entered.

"Anton's off with the menfolk," Patty said, answering Lacy's unasked question. "But he told me where I could find you. Of course, I figured that you'd all want to get to know each other since we're about to be family."

After hearing Patty argue with Anton about how she didn't actually want Lacy to be in her family, I had the urge to tell her off and send all of them packing back to Texas.

"This is a closed party," Jemma said, her head to one side as she studied the other ladies before pointing at Bella. "Except for maybe you." She walked over, picked up a handful of hair from the woman's shoulder, and inhaled. Jemma's eyes glowed as she stayed only inches from Bella's face and she said seductively, "Yes, *you* can stay."

I'd assumed that Jemma only dated men, but once again my stereotyping of beauty queens was all wrong. Jemma was obviously smitten with Bella, who was backing away, worry lines deepening on her face with every inch.

"Don't be silly," Patty fluttered. "I don't plan to stay! I wouldn't want to be a buzzkill if you gals are getting up to something... illicit."

Lacy shook her head at her future mother-in-law, and I could see in her expression that despite Patty's awfulness, Lacy still cared what the woman thought. "We weren't planning anything like—"

"—but I knew you wouldn't want Bella or Anton's cousins to miss out," Patty interrupted, speaking over Lacy.

Bella glanced around the room, likely trying to find Anton, while Myrtis grabbed a drink and took a long swig.

That's when I spotted Will Hurt sneaking in the back door, his eyes fixed on a jacket he'd left behind.

As Patty prattled on about how everyone should be welcoming this weekend, Will went to grab the long coat. And I saw Charlotte fix her gaze on him and move toward him. He gave her a slight smile, and she took his arm easily, pressing into him and whispering something in his ear.

The entire interaction was ten seconds, maybe twenty, but it was long enough to notice a connection between the pair.

I frowned at the sight of the two of them—Will was married to one of my childhood peers, after all—but when I glanced around, no one else seemed to notice that Will and Charlotte obviously knew each other. But how?

I had the urge to scurry over and tell Charlotte to take her long-nailed paws off of him— which was strange. Although I'd grown up with Will's wife, Valerie, and although they'd both been guests at the homecoming reunion that turned murderish last October, I had no particular interest in the two of them. Still, married is married, and Charlotte had no right to flirt with Will. He was a family man.

My instincts had no time to play out though. A moment later, Will and his long coat were gone and Charlotte was slyly grinning to herself.

"So, I'll just leave the three of them here," Patty said. "And you can show them what a good time Aubergine has to offer." She began to back out of the Carriage House, calling the last words out almost like a threat. "Who knows? Maybe we'll all decide to settle down here someday."

As Patty Swanson gave one final smirk before exiting, I noticed Lacy's expression— which told me all I needed to know. She needed to see Anton. Now.

"I'll be right back," I said, excusing myself. I caught Savilla's eye and motioned for her to stay close to Lacy.

The three additional women—Myrtis, Charlotte, and Bella Rivera—seemed unbothered by Patty Swanson forcing them to be an addition to the wedding party's festivities. Or perhaps they'd seen her manipulate enough situations that they knew the drill: Fall in line or get left behind.

I started toward the place Anton was supposed to be that evening: the Billiards Room. I calculated the fastest route, taking a staff elevator, and as I stepped onto the second floor, I almost ran straight into him. He was pacing back and forth in the hallway, his face both surprised and bothered.

I could list off the things that might be troubling him, starting with his mother at the top.

"Thank God I found you," I said quietly, looking around to make sure no one else was nearby as I pulled him toward the balcony overlooking the gardens, a place where we would be assured of privacy.

"You were looking for me?" Anton asked distractedly, before realizing that if I was seeking him out, then something must be wrong. "Is it Lacy? Where is she?"

"She's in the Carriage House with the bridal party... and three extra ladies that we did not plan on hosting this evening."

"Oh God." Anton's hand went to his brow as he groaned. "I'm sorry. My mother is..." He couldn't seem to find the words at first. "She's... persistent."

"She's definitely that. She dropped off those extra guests to crash the bachelorette party."

Anton grimaced, but there was a look of hope in his eyes. "If it makes you feel better, Charlotte and Myrtis will probably keep to themselves and gossip about nonsense back home."

I gave him a pointed look. "Would they maybe gossip about, I don't know, you and Bella Rivera?"

Anton's eye twitched.

"Yep, she's there right now, making herself comfortable," I confirmed. "Apparently, Patty wants us to treat her like one of the family, and if I had to guess, I'd say she's hoping that you'll trade Lacy in for Bella before the weekend is out."

Anton grabbed his stomach as if I'd just punched him in the gut before recovering enough to say, "Lacy knows I only want her."

I frowned at this man. If he truly believed that anyone, even our bold and confident Lacy, could stand up against his mother without any insecurities or vulnerabilities showing, then he didn't realize the subtle cruelty Patty Swanson could inflict. I'd known her for maybe an hour, and I could already tell she was like a spider with a bite that goes unnoticed until the poison has already set in.

Anton cowered a bit under my disapproval and slumped back against the wall, reminding me of his drunken state two months earlier, when he'd been the one insecure and pining for Lacy after the death of her high school sweetheart. "Bella and I... we... it was never serious, not to me."

"And to Bella?"

He let out a heavy sigh. "I don't know. She probably expected... something."

"Something round and shiny?"

He lifted a shoulder as if to say, *Maybe.*

I still couldn't tell if he was playing dumb or if he was actually this dense, and he seemed to sense as much.

"We grew up together," Anton said, trying to explain. "Same grade level, same Sunday school classes, same kickball team—the Swanson Swans, if you can believe it. My parents always joked about me and Bella getting married someday, and when I was in my listless phase after college, trying to figure out how to tell them that I didn't want to run the family business, she was there and... I don't know, she was familiar."

"How familiar?" I asked, although I already knew the answer. They'd obviously dated, and she'd hoped it would end in marriage. His mother had hoped for that as well.

"We dated for three years, but I never asked her to marry me. In all that time, I didn't even bring up the idea." His expression said he was at a complete loss to explain the appearance of this woman.

"Did Bella talk about marriage?"

Anton nodded as his cheeks reddened. "Mother took her to Houston to look at rings, and she gave me a list of the settings Bella liked."

My irritation with Anton was growing by the second. "And you didn't stop either of them then and there?"

"I did," Anton said, hands outstretched as if to prove his innocence. "Eventually, I broke things off."

"Eventually?"

"It took me some time." His face crumpled.

I crossed my arms, waiting for him to continue. There was something he wasn't saying.

"A year, okay? It took me a year. I wrote her a letter, telling her things were over, then I packed a bag and left for Houston. I stayed on a college friend's couch. I got a job as a waiter, and a few months later, I met Lacy while she was there for a conference."

"So, Bella hasn't seen you since..."

"Since the day I left, I swear." He cringed at his own words.

"That must've been almost two and a half years ago now. I know how it sounds, like I'm some kind of…"

"Coward?" I finished for him.

"I've never been good at letting people down," Anton admitted. "It was easier to leave."

He wasn't wrong. Leaving was easier in a lot of ways, but it was something I'd never even thought about doing. Not when Momma got sick, not when my aunt shoved me into a beauty pageant, not when Savilla needed to know she had a sister. These were the moments that one had to rise to the occasion.

I would've never expected Anton to be the kind who would do a woman dirty like that— skipping town without a glance behind. It made me suddenly nervous for my friend.

"I've learned a lot since then," he said, trying to reassure me. "But my past is my past. Either way, I didn't invite Bella this weekend. I swear."

Despite my frustration with Anton, I believed him. If he hadn't even wanted to break things off with Bella in person, he certainly wouldn't have wanted her celebrating his nuptials.

"Is this why you didn't want the rest of your family arriving until tomorrow? Did you think something like this might happen?"

"Not *this*." He sighed. "Never *this*. My mother can be overbearing, but I never thought she would interfere to this extent."

"She doesn't want you marrying Lacy," I said as directly as possible, mainly because in less than forty-eight hours he was supposed to marry my friend and I did not want her heart broken by him or his mother—or anyone else. "How are you going to address that?"

Anton swallowed and lifted his head, trying to find his courage. "I'll talk to her."

"To your mother? To Bella? To Lacy?"

He nodded fervently. "All of them."

"And what will you say?"

"I'll tell my mother that I love Lacy and she needs to stand down."

I raised an eyebrow and lifted my chin, prodding him to continue.

He swallowed hard. "I'll tell Bella that I'm sorry that I wasn't brave enough to end things face-to-face."

"She deserved closure," I said, feeling very much like some kind of life coach that I had no desire to be.

"She did," he nodded. "That's what I'll say."

"And Lacy?"

To his credit, Anton's face softened at her name. "I'll tell her that she's the only person I've ever felt this way about. That when I imagine myself at eighty years old, I see the two of us sitting on a porch swing and watching our grandchildren play in the yard, the mountains hovering behind us."

That answer sounded like a good one, but it wasn't me he had to appease.

At that moment, I heard a step behind us. It was Lacy, her face mottled as if she'd been crying.

"Savilla released me so I could find you two," Lacy said. Her eyes brightened when she looked at Anton, who rushed forward and scooped her into his arms.

"I'm so sorry," he breathed into her. "I had no idea that my mother would be so..." He seemed unable to finish the sentence, which made sense when there was really no good way to describe how his mother had behaved up to that point.

Lacy and Anton held each other for a full minute, and I wondered if I should head back to the Carriage House.

Just as I was about to turn around and leave the two of them to talk, Lacy pulled back and wiped at her eyes, addressing Anton. "If you promise me that you had no idea what your mother was up to, I'll believe you," she said, more generous than I might've been under the same circumstances. It was a credit to how much she loved Anton, I was sure.

"I swear, Lacy, I had no idea my mother was dragging along almost my entire family two days early—much less inviting extra ladies to the bachelorette party," Anton said, staring into her eyes.

"And I swear I'll take care of everything so she won't interfere anymore." He hesitated. "I didn't invite Bella either, so I can talk to her, ask her to leave."

Lacy bit her lip and studied her fiancé. "No," she decided. "If you tell me that you didn't invite her—and that you don't have any lingering feelings for her—then I'll believe you. She seems off-putting, but I don't think it's Bella who's pushing herself on to you."

The implication was that any pushing was coming from his mother, which seemed accurate.

"I love you," Anton said quietly, his forehead pressed against Lacy's. "Only you."

As they shared a quiet moment I scooted back to give them privacy, catching a flash pass by in my periphery, a quick shadow that flittered away as fast as it had come.

I stepped toward the darkness, a tingle running up my arms to my neck. Someone had been at the edge of the corridor, listening to us.

NINE

I left Lacy and Anton talking in hushed tones and made my way into the darkness of the hall. Within a few seconds I heard a crash coming from a room at the very end of the corridor, one that I was pretty certain I'd never set foot inside up until now.

I'd memorized the layout of the mansion by this point, so I knew that straight ahead was the Salon, a room specifically designed for cultural conversations, although I would be very surprised if Mr. Finch had ever participated in one himself. From what I understood, the room—like so many others—was rarely used, though Savilla, with her artistic leanings, hoped to change that. For this weekend, it would serve as the bridal suite, where Lacy could change into her dress and take photographs on her big day.

With the shadowy figure that had flitted past still in mind, I was hesitant to barge into the room; instead, I ever so carefully opened the door, peeking my head inside.

Darkness was all that greeted me.

The soft tap of footsteps sounded in the room, and I tried to size up the person that I might encounter. A lighter frame, I thought at first, but when a loud sound of shattering glass came from a corner of the room, I wasn't so sure. This person was like a bull in a china shop.

I felt around the wall for a light and, thankfully, I found a switch quickly. My eyes had to readjust momentarily to the yellow light from the chandelier, but I quickly saw where the sound had originated: On the ground was an overturned Christmas tree that must've been ten feet tall, glass ornaments broken and scattered across the floor.

Savilla had told me she was going to decorate every room of the house, but I hadn't believed that she actually meant *every single room*, even ones that were barely used. I shouldn't have doubted her.

I heard a sound coming from behind a low couch—where visitors were encouraged to sit and talk and, I assumed, admire the art that was all over the walls. Moving toward it—ready to leap out of the way depending on who it was—there was Bella Rivera, in a crouched position and with both eyes closed, as if she was hoping I couldn't actually see her.

She was the shadowy figure from the hall, and I let out a breath I didn't realize I'd been holding, relieved to see that it wasn't someone larger or fiercer. If push came to shove, I stood a chance against this woman.

"What are you doing down there?" I asked, as much for something to say as anything else. I'd not yet spoken directly to this woman, and I hadn't planned to start, but there we were.

Bella pursed her lips, looked up at me and didn't speak for several seconds. When she did finally say something, her voice was quiet but each word was crisp. "I was looking for something."

"In here?" I narrowed my eyes as if to communicate that I wouldn't tolerate nonsense.

Bella blinked several times, but I couldn't tell if it was an effort to stall while she came up with some kind of lie or if she was merely trying to get her bearings and decide how much to share.

"I'm trying to get into the art world," she said, as if this should be the answer to what exactly she was looking for.

"I see." I frowned at the pieces all around us. The Christmas ornaments left on the tree seemed to match the décor—or at least the ornate gold frames around the room: All the pictures were portraits, ranging from Mr. Finch's abstract paintings of former beauty pageant queens and deceased, dour-faced members of the Finch family, to a regal but nameless horse and rider. My favorite was certainly the horse.

"What do you think?"

Bella lifted her head as if she was just noticing the selection around us. Then she dropped the façade and let out a long sigh. "I was hoping to have the chance to talk to Anthony, so I trailed Lacy." She said the name as if it was bitter on her tongue. "I was hoping to find him and maybe speak with him as soon as you two were finished with whatever it was you needed to say to him."

The words raised the red flags I'd already been mentally holding, largely because she was confirming what I'd been fearing all along. Bella was still in love with Anton, and she'd come uninvited to this wedding for God knew what reason. Speculating would only make me angrier.

"Look," Bella said, standing to her full height, which wasn't that impressive, and brushing tiny shards of glass from the ornaments off her dress. For the first time I noticed that a cylinder tube was tucked under her arm, and there was something in the angle of her lifted chin and the piercing look from her eyes that exuded a confidence I didn't appreciate. "I know nothing about your friend, so I couldn't possibly have anything against her."

"I don't believe that for a second," I said, growing more defensive of Lacy with every breath.

"It's true. She could be Joan of Arc's cousin or St. Theresa's niece, but I still know one thing."

"Which is?"

Bella stared straight at me as if I should know the answer already. "Regardless of how I feel, Lacy is not the one who should be marrying Anthony this weekend."

"You're wrong," I said, my voice rising. "Lacy wouldn't settle for just any man. She's stubborn and strong-willed in the best way, and she wants Anton. And he, he..." I tried to find the words. "Every day, he looks at Lacy like she hung the moon."

While I yammered on, Bella's eyes trailed from me to the floor, and she suddenly started up on her tiptoes as if she was afraid she might step on something she'd dropped. Then, she was on her knees, feeling underneath the couch where she'd been hiding when I arrived. She'd obviously lost something.

"What are you looking for?"

Bella's head popped above the back of the couch, and she frowned at me, her voice distracted. "A bag—or a purse. I had it when I came up here, I'm sure."

I glanced around but didn't see anything. Lacy had tried to explain to me years ago some women's relationships to their purses, but Bella's frantic reaction was a bit much. I rolled my eyes, realizing that I wasn't going to be able to reason with her until she found her stupid bag.

I retraced my steps while skirting the broken glass at the base of the felled tree, lifting branches. There at the base of the tree was a bright pink bag, not easy to miss. I picked it up and then watched Bella, who was almost manically overturning the couch cushions. Surely she wouldn't notice if I took a quick peek inside just to see what all the fuss was about?

I debated for all of two seconds before turning my back to Bella and crouching down as if I was still searching. With my right hand I opened the bag, expecting to see a wallet, lipstick, maybe a breath mint or two. I tried not to gasp at what I saw instead.

Inside Bella's purse was a mini arsenal, complete with a box cutter knife, pepper spray, a steel nail file, a long circular object, and the most compact gun I'd ever seen—not that I'd seen many. Aunt DeeDee had kept one in a safe in the loft—*for emergencies that might arise with a woman living alone*—but even though I'd heard it existed, I'd never set eyes on it.

"That's not mine," I heard Bella say from behind me, her breath coming fast as she extended a hand. "But I need it." She paused and took a deep breath in an attempt to keep calm. "Please. Give it back."

Somehow she made each word sound like a threat, but I could hear something under her words as well: A shakiness, a fear of discovery. Bella was denying that the bag was hers, but she'd brought it—and the deadly contents—with her to meet Anton... and presumably Lacy. What was Bella planning to *do* this weekend, with her fashionable assault toolbox?

"I said give it back. Now." Bella spoke with a venomous tone that also reeked of desperation. Just then, something fell from the purse, and I reached down to pick it up. It was a tiny button, covered in ivory fabric. It only took me a second to place it.

"I didn't... I mean..." Bella stammered, even though I already knew where it belonged.

I watched her turn toward the back of the room, my eyes following hers to where the button must've come from. Bella was lying to me about something—perhaps many things—that much was clear.

"I didn't mean to do it," she finally finished.

Lacy's wedding dress was hanging from a bar along the back wall. Since I'd been in New York when Lacy had gone dress shopping with her mom, I'd only seen it in pictures, but those dozens of photos had been taken from every possible angle. The design was timeless—long and flowing—and Lacy had particularly loved the seed pearls hand-stitched into the train, and the long row of buttons running down the back.

I stepped forward quickly, knocking into Bella with my shoulder as I passed her. Something wasn't right, and as I neared the dress, I could see what was bothering me. There were torn buttons and a slash along the back of the gown.

Someone had ruined the dress.

I swallowed hard and clenched my fist, my nails sinking into my palms in an effort to contain the explosion inside of me, but when I turned back to accuse Bella of destroying my best friend's dress, she was gone.

With a deep sigh, I turned back to the dress. Perhaps it could be fixed in time? It was only then that I noticed three additional buttons on the ground, below it. Instinctively, I stooped to pick them up. As I bent down, I also noticed a swatch of fabric on the ground. I picked it up too, and although at first I'd assumed it was from the dress, as soon as I touched its coarse threads I knew that wasn't right.

I ran a finger across the fabric, noticing for the first time a speckle of off-white paint around one edge. This was canvas torn from a painting. But when I quickly scanned the room, all of the art seemed perfect and in place; no random, torn edges gaping from the frames.

I had no idea what the fabric meant, so I folded it and tucked it into my pocket, along with the buttons.

I'd deal with Bella Rivera later.

TEN

The interaction with Bella in the Salon had been strange, to say the least. Finding a mini weapons kit and discovering she'd slashed my best friend's wedding dress had left me reeling— and I knew I needed to tell Lacy about the latter as soon as possible. The former could wait for now.

I met Lacy as she came around the corner of the darkened hallway toward the elevator. I reached out a hand to steady her so, as Momma used to say, I didn't scare the living daylight out of her.

"It's me, Lacy," I told her, hoping she wouldn't scream and bring all of the men running.

Despite my calm voice, Lacy jumped, hand over her heart. "Dakota Green, are you trying to frighten me to death?"

"That wouldn't be a great way to kick off your wedding weekend," I tried to tease. "I was coming to make sure you were okay. Did Anton head back to the bachelor party?"

Lacy nodded and took a deep breath before she looked at me with a raised eyebrow. "You're being my lookout, huh?"

"Lookout. Bodyguard. Whatever you want to call it, I'm here for you," I said, putting on a smile that I hoped would temper what I had to tell her.

Lacy beat me to the punch, narrowing her gaze as she read my expression all too well. "What is it? What's wrong now?"

I swallowed hard, not knowing how to inform her that her dress might be ruined—and that Bella Rivera was likely the person who'd cut it wide open.

"Tell me," Lacy practically demanded, her hand reaching out to clench my arm.

"It's your dress," I said, biting my lip. "Some of the buttons are torn off and there's a... gash."

"A gash?" Lacy repeated, inhaling sharply. "I only just hung it up, this afternoon, when I got here. Who would've done...?" But her question was lost as she rushed toward the Salon.

I followed behind her as she crossed the threshold into the place that would be her bridal suite in a day and a half. Lacy's breath caught in her throat and her eyes filled. She'd always been more of a crier than me, but this weekend had to be some kind of record with how many times I'd seen her tear up.

"I'm sure we can fix it," I said, and then, in sudden inspiration, I took my phone from my pocket and called the only person I knew who might be able to do any kind of repair.

Since Aunt DeeDee was planning to see us later that evening at the store on Main Street that houses her designs, she answered with a festive hello. I dampened her enthusiasm with my explanation of our situation before handing the phone to Lacy. Though I could only hear one side of the conversation, I was certain that Aunt DeeDee's soothing reassurances were the reason that Lacy wasn't going into full-blown panic mode.

As Lacy spoke into the phone, she ran a hand over the dress she'd selected for her big day. "It looks like six—no, seven—of the buttons are gone, but the bigger problem is the tear." She paused, sniffling. "Maybe a foot long? And not along a seam. It looks like someone just took a knife and cut at a diagonal." The tears started again. "You can? Are you sure?" A heavy sigh. "I can send you a picture... A sash might work, but it would have to be pretty big... Uh-huh, as long as it's tasteful." Lacy let go of the dress and wiped an eye. "Okay, thanks, DeeDee, I appreciate it." She handed the phone back to me and her shoulders released.

On the other end of the line, Aunt DeeDee caught me up quickly. She was going to stay at the shop for tonight—"Because you can't let this ruin the whole weekend"—but she was going to make a call to a friend in Richmond who was an even better seamstress than her. First thing tomorrow morning, they would meet at The Rose while we were still sleeping and fix the dress.

"You tell her not to worry about a thing," Aunt DeeDee said right before we hung up. "And you keep an eye out for more trouble."

"Hold that thought," I said, before pressing the phone to my chest and turning to Lacy. "Give me one sec, okay?"

Lacy's expression was confused but, too tired to argue, she agreed and sank into the couch that Bella had been hiding behind.

I made my way into the hall and checked around the corner to make sure no one else was around. When I was sure I was alone, I spoke again.

"I know who did this," I whispered into the phone.

Aunt DeeDee inhaled sharply.

"I'm almost positive that it was Anton's ex. Her name is Bella, and she arrived uninvited." I stopped and reconsidered my phrasing. "Actually, Anton's mother invited her, but he and Lacy had no idea—and everyone showed up a day early. And now two of Anton's cousins and this Bella lady are part of the bachelorette party, and I'm supposed to entertain them and somehow hold this night together so Lacy doesn't have to worry. This is such a mess."

I could almost see my aunt's mind quickly piecing together the information I'd just handed her.

"Okay, baby doll. Here's what you do: you and Lacy head out to tonight's planned festivities, and I'll make sure that each of the places knows to expect three additions to the party."

"But—" I started to protest, to say that I didn't want these other women anywhere near Lacy, but Aunt DeeDee anticipated my concerns.

"You remember what your momma always said about enemies?"

The words came back to me in a flash, Momma standing in the doorway of my bedroom, leaning against the doorframe, a hand on her hip, as she gave me advice on how to handle the upcoming Future Farmers of America competition. I was in tenth grade, and I'd been whining about how hard it was to work with some of the other girls on our biggest project of the year—hatching and raising chicks from egg to full-grown chicken. The three other girls—who I suddenly recalled had included Will's wife, Valerie—and I had been fighting from day one about everything, from the exact temperature for incubation to which seed to feed them.

"Those girls aren't your enemy, Dakota," Momma had said, her head tilted as she looked at me with a smile that said she wished I could see what she saw in me. "Just pull them in a little tighter, and I bet you'll see that they want the exact same things you do. You're just going about it different ways."

I'd considered her logic. I supposed that my group members did want to raise healthy chickens that we could present at the show. I supposed they didn't want to fail. I supposed they did want to win first place.

"At the end of the day we have more in common with each other—even with people we think are our enemies—than we can imagine," I mumbled into the phone now, remembering Momma's words with the exact intonation she'd used. She'd been right about the competition, too—though we'd taken second place, that was pretty good out of ten other competitors.

But I didn't have the same faith in human nature this time around. Maybe I'd seen too much.

"That's right," Aunt DeeDee said.

"But this woman slashed my best friend's dress. How in the world could she—or Anton's mother—have the same goals as Lacy and me? I want Lacy to get married. They want to ruin the wedding."

Aunt DeeDee was silent and all I heard across the line was the click of her tongue as she thought for a long moment before finally speaking. "But why would they want to ruin the wedding?"

I narrowed my eyes, trying to follow her line of thinking. "Because they hate Lacy," I said, before remembering what Bella had said—something about not even knowing Lacy. In her mind, this wasn't personal. I changed my answer. "Because they want to be happy."

"Exactly," Aunt DeeDee said. "You may just need to convince them that there's a better way to find their own happiness—without involving Anton or Lacy."

"That's an impossible mission."

"Your momma always did love the impossible." Aunt DeeDee chuckled down the line. "She was a better person than me, even though I sit my booty in the church pew every week. So if all else fails, you can follow my advice: Love your enemies to death—even if it kills you."

ELEVEN

Lacy and I started back down the hall, both of us relieved that Aunt DeeDee was on the job.

"It sounds like Anton is trying," I said, hoping my tone was optimistic enough, even though it came out more like a question. I supposed I wanted Lacy to say whether or not she felt like Anton was really hearing her concerns. Even as a bystander, I could see all of the dysfunction of his family. It was like a neon sign flashing: PASSIVE AGGRESSIVE, MANIPULATIVE, INSECURE.

"He told me that his family is complicated," Lacy said, as we reached the closest stairs. I realized that they were the same ones that we'd taken to the secret room a couple months earlier. Part of me wanted to step inside and hide away from the rest of this weekend's drama, but the better part of me wanted to forge ahead, trampling Anton's family nonsense as I pushed Lacy all the way down the aisle. "I just didn't realize that he meant *this* complicated."

We wound down the stairs, through to the main floor, and out the front door into the darkness of the night and toward the Carriage House. "Is his father more... sane?" I asked. "Do you think his arrival tomorrow will help calm things down?"

"I don't know, but it doesn't sound like it." Lacy's eyebrows dipped as she thought back. "A few weeks before we got engaged,

Anton mentioned something vague, something about how his dad had gotten into some shady stuff in recent years. At the time, Anton said that was why he didn't want anything to do with his family's business."

"Shady stuff?"

Lacy blinked as if trying to remember the full conversation. "He said that his father had begun 'transporting items.'" She put air quotes around the last two words. "Anton doesn't say much about his family, and now I see why." Lacy shivered under the cold moonlight, and I put an arm around her. "Maybe that should've been a red flag."

"Or maybe he's trying to make a new family, a new future for himself." I was proud of myself for the remark, particularly because I wasn't the kind of person to see the best in others. Still, until this weekend, Lacy had never doubted Anton or his love for her, even when I'd done so during the murder investigation two months ago.

I reminded myself that Anton had been a steady presence for Lacy for almost two years now. When he first moved here, he didn't push for them to move in together, even though he knew no one else in town. Instead, he'd got a little apartment and a job as a short-order cook at the diner, in part so he could get to know the town and the citizenry. He'd even met Charlie before I had the chance to do so. Even after Anton and Lacy had moved in together and started having little tiffs about things like who should cook and who should load the dishwasher, he always seemed to emerge from those conversations as a reasonable guy.

No wonder Anton wanted nothing to do with his family.

I said a few of these things out loud, and although I wasn't trying to defend him, I did want to remind Lacy that his family wasn't him. If that was the case, then my discovery of being related to the Finches this past year would've sent me spiraling. Savilla was becoming a fabulous sister, but the rest of the enormously wealthy side of my family was questionable at best—murderous at their worst. Maybe that's why Savilla had latched on to me and

Aunt DeeDee so tightly since the revelation of our biological connection.

"You're right," Lacy said, breathing in the night air. "Anton isn't his family, and his family isn't him." She spoke the words with the cadence of a mantra.

"You're keeping your last name anyway, right?" I said, nudging her. "That way you won't officially be one of them."

"I certainly am keeping it now." Lacy laughed. "Maybe Anton will want to take my name too."

She was smiling by the time we walked back into the Carriage House, which was the most I could expect, and she kept the smile on even as we spotted the added three participants—Cousin Charlotte, Cousin Myrtis, and Bella Rivera—in tonight's party, standing at the bar, conversing among themselves.

I was shocked that Bella had deigned to return to the party, and when she caught my eye, I noticed that she kept a possessive hand on that bright pink bag. Trying my best to channel Momma, I moved toward the Texan additions as Lacy peeled off toward Jemma.

"Long time no see," I said, taking a champagne glass and forcing a smile.

Bella's face remained neutral, almost as if she hadn't heard me —even though I was only two feet away from her. Myrtis turned a listening ear toward us, and Charlotte narrowed her eyes as if studying me. I ignored the pair of them for now.

"Given your handiwork on Lacy's dress," I said, lifting the glass to my lips as I attempted to appear friendly, "I'm surprised you didn't go straight to your room, pack up, and leave immediately, out of pure shame."

Bella spoke this time, her eyes wide as they darted between me and the cousins. "You don't know what you—or your friend—are getting into."

"Why don't you tell me?" I asked, my voice low.

"That's not how this works," Charlotte said, inserting herself into the conversation as she inched closer to us. Her voice was light even though her words were heavy, but then she composed her face and glanced around the room. "Is Valerie Hurt joining us tonight?"

"How do you know Valerie?" I asked, surprised.

"Todd—" Charlotte seemed to catch herself. "Reverend Todd introduced us."

I couldn't keep the confusion from my face. The priest didn't know Will, did he? Or had they become bosom buddies in the past few hours? Perhaps Will knew Todd the same way that he obviously knew Charlotte. There was some connection here I couldn't quite put together.

"How's their baby?" Charlotte continued, obviously unconcerned about what I did or did not know about this family and their connection to Will. It was difficult to tell whether she was trying to change the subject or was genuinely interested. Maybe it was both. "I know it was a difficult labor."

"Are you and Valerie... are you two friends?" I asked, trying to get the missing information.

"Tangentially," Charlotte said, the vague response raising more questions about Anton's family and their interest in this town and the people in it.

Since I was certain that she wouldn't answer any of them, I tried to read her body language, her expression, her voice. Charlotte's posture was erect and her face stoic; her tone was distant, almost to the point of being disdainful.

"Are you talking about Valerie and Will?" Myrtis asked, stepping forward. "I heard they've been on the rocks ever since the baby arrived and he lost his job."

My mind swarmed like a beehive. I felt as if I'd stepped into an alternate reality, one in which I was the stranger at this enormous estate. It was true that I'd been at college for the past few months but, even so, I was confident that besides Anton, no other Swanson had stepped foot in Aubergine. "How do you both know about...?"

"Recently, Will has become a friend," Charlotte finally admitted. "He mentioned that the baby's medical bills have become a bit overwhelming."

At that moment, Savilla hurried over, interrupting the interrogation I so wanted to conduct. She handed me a spoon, signaling that I should clink it against my glass to call everyone to order.

"We're running behind schedule," Savilla whispered. "You don't want to be unpunctuated."

Bella frowned at Savilla's word choice, and a sudden protectiveness coursed through my veins. I was the only one allowed to question exactly what my sister meant, but, once again, I understood right away. Savilla wanted to make sure we were going to be punctual and that the evening would run according to schedule, or perhaps as... anticipated?

Reluctant to leave the conversation with Charlotte but also fairly certain I wasn't going to get more out of her, I did as Savilla bid, dinging the spoon until everyone's eyes turned to me.

"Ladies, ladies, may I have your attention?" I asked, not quite knowing what else to say.

Thankfully, Savilla stepped behind Bella and the cousins and with a smile, prodded all of them toward the center of the room until the seven of us stood in a malformed circle with drinks in hand: me, Lacy, Jemma, Savilla, Myrtis, Charlotte, and Bella, whom I needed to watch like a hawk.

"I wanted to officially welcome everyone to Lacy's bachelorette party," I said, clearing my throat. "Tonight, I've organized a scavenger hunt to take us to some of Lacy's favorite Aubergine hangouts. The proprietors have agreed to open late so we can return to our old haunts."

Lacy's face lit up in delight for the first time that evening, and I knew I'd chosen the right direction for her bachelorette party. By contrast, I just had to ignore the three intruders: Myrtis stared on with a sort of grimace; a distracted Charlotte took yellow-tinted glasses from her hair and tucked them into a pink bag hanging off her arm; while Bella kept her eyes fixed on Lacy.

The night was already going great.

"I have a clue for each place we'll visit, and"—I dropped my spoon in the champagne flute and pulled the clue from my cleavage, where Aunt DeeDee had taught me by example to keep important things—"here's the first clue."

From Archibald to Viola
we've seen them all.
Now, tonight, we'll share
your favorite Law.

"Archibald?" called Jemma. "Is that the stripper's name? Is he hot?"

"No strippers," I corrected. I'd been relieved when I'd asked Lacy if she wanted me to hire one, and she'd scrunched her nose, complaining that they were too sweaty for her liking. "But," I continued, chuckling at Jemma's question, "Archibald was considered a heartthrob... in the 1940s."

Lacy took the paper from my hand, and I could see that she was enjoying having her mind on something frivolous as she explained the riddle. "Archie—that was the real-life first name of Cary Grant. And Viola, as in Davis, so a modern actress." Her eyes roamed across the second line again. "My favorite Law... It's capitalized, so... oh, I know! Jude Law."

Jemma jumped in. "He was soooo handsome in that Christmas movie. I watch it every year. It has Kate Winslet and that chubby guy."

"Jack Black," Lacy added.

"*The Holiday*," Bella said with lifted brows, simultaneously stopping the fun of discovery and shutting down all conversation with her abrupt tone.

"That's right." I tried to rally again. "We're watching *The Holiday* at The Reel."

The Reel was the only movie theater in town. It had opened sometime in the seventies, and when Lacy and I were in elementary school, we saw every Disney movie from the creaky seats.

Years later, The Reel had become the most popular Friday night hangout for most of the high schoolers in town, including me and Lacy, primarily because they served refillable popcorn and sodas—and because it was a parent-approved space since the owner, a notoriously gruff guy who tolerated no nonsense, ran it.

"To the theater," Savilla chimed, while also taking everyone's glasses and lining them in a row for the staff to more easily clean up.

Within a couple of minutes, we were heading outside, this eclectic pack of gals.

TWELVE

With the doubling of our bride's night out, we had to take two cars into town. I was one of the few who'd had no more than a sip of champagne, so I decided to play nice and offer to drive the Texas crew. The fact that I could pepper them with questions on the fifteen-minute drive may or may not have been the primary motivator. Not that I was particularly interested in their lives, but I was very interested in this weekend proceeding without any additional surprises from them.

Charlotte and Myrtis wordlessly took the back seats, their eyes locked on each other, communicating their distaste for my decades-old car. Despite my new standing as an heiress, I had yet to overhaul my entire life, car included, and I had no plans to change things up anytime soon.

With the cousins settled in the back, that left Bella up front with me. Good.

The CD player's eject button hadn't worked since Momma put in Coldplay in 2003, so it was either that or silence. I turned up "Green Eyes" to put my companions at ease enough to disclose information I needed—namely, why exactly Patty and the Swanson clan wanted to stop this wedding. It couldn't be just because they liked Bella better, surely.

As we drove out of the gates of the estate, Bella reached out a hand and turned the volume down, startling me. When Aunt DeeDee had taught me to drive, she'd also taught me about the sanctity of the driver's control of the music.

Bella must've noticed my expression because she touched her temple and gave an excuse. "I have a headache."

Myrtis spoke up from the back. "Must've been the cheap champagne."

Heat rose to my cheeks despite the cold. I really tried not to hate people, but these ladies weren't making it easy. Turning to Bella, I decided to start with the most awkward question I could think of. "So, you and Anton in the bathtub, huh?"

"I call him Anthony," Bella quipped back. "Always have. Anton is so..." She wrinkled her nose. "So *abbreviated*."

"That's how a nickname works."

"He calls me Arabella," Bella said, with an air of nostalgia that I neither appreciated nor believed. Every time he'd said this woman's name in my presence, it had been "Bella". Plain and simple.

"I love the name Arabella," Myrtis fawned, leaning forward from the back seat. "Always have. The first time Anton brought you to that family dinner years ago, I told Charlotte, 'Arabella is the perfect name.' Didn't I, Charlotte?"

Charlotte didn't answer, staring out the window as if she was above all of this. I did think I saw her nudge Myrtis ever so slightly.

Myrtis scooted away from her cousin and situated her head like a bobbing balloon between the two of us in the front seat. "I know Aunt Patty and Uncle Michael would love to do more business with your family."

I assumed Myrtis was referring to Patty Swanson and the man who must be her husband. Michael Swanson. Good to know.

"That's entirely up to my father," Bella answered, though she glanced over her shoulder quickly at Charlotte.

The tension in the car was humming with things unsaid, a history I couldn't begin to unravel.

"But I thought this was a test run," Myrtis said, all innocence.

Charlotte leaned into her cousin's ear and whispered. I watched as Myrtis's face went blank, her eyes wide, before she composed herself and nodded sharply.

A moment later, Charlotte deigned to speak. "We didn't come here this weekend to talk business, much less conduct it. We're here to celebrate Anton and..." She paused, as if she'd forgotten Lacy's name, but I wasn't about to help her.

"Lacy," Bella offered.

"Yes, Anton and Lacy." Charlotte smiled in a way that was much too fake, and then her eyes fixed on mine in the rearview mirror. "Are you here with anyone this weekend?"

Surely she'd seen me with Charlie in the Carriage House? But the way she asked the question seemed like she wanted me to admit to something more. I willingly took the bait this time.

"I'm dating a man named Charlie."

Her head tilted, but her face remained unreadable. "The sheriff?"

"The very one," I said lightly, even though I wondered how she knew this information. "Why? Do you need to confess to a crime?"

The car went silent at that and, for a moment, I relished it, feeling I'd gotten the upper hand. I decided to return to Myrtis's earlier comment. "You said that this weekend was supposed to be a test run? For what?"

No one answered.

I tried again, this time with a different question. "Is Will working with your family on a project?"

Bella's eyes went to the rearview mirror then, and I could almost feel the meeting of the minds in that car. I wanted to scream at these three women, command them to tell me what they knew and why my best friend's wedding was turning into some kind of hellish networking opportunity. I pressed my lips together, trying to keep myself from overreacting.

"I know Will is from up north somewhere," I said, trying to

recall what Momma had once told me. "D.C.? New York? Boston?"

Bella lifted a shoulder, suddenly mum.

Now, at the most inopportune time, the three of them had decided to go for radio silence. Frustration buzzed in my chest, and I had the urge to stop the car and demand that all three of them get out and go home—all the way back to Texas. Instead, I tried to channel Aunt DeeDee's desire never to cause a scene unless absolutely necessary, but Momma's straight shooting was definitely winning out.

"Look, I have no idea what kind of business opportunities you're talking about, but Anton has moved on from both his family's expectations and from... you," I said, catching Bella's eye as we took the road that would lead us to Main Street. "He's made a life with Lacy, here in Aubergine, and this weekend he's getting married. I get that moving on is hard, but it's time."

Bella crossed her arms but didn't say a word. Myrtis was suddenly tight-lipped as well, and I was beginning to get the sense that I'd originally misread the power dynamics at play here.

It wasn't Bella on top. Though Myrtis still seemed eager to please Anton's old flame, it was Cousin Charlotte deciding what could or couldn't be said.

"I understand that Patty Swanson took you ring shopping and that mothers can be"—I struggled for the word—"they can be persuasive, but Anton literally left town to get away from you and his family."

Bella spoke again. "How do you know about ring shopping?"

"Anton told me," I said, my knuckles white as I gripped the steering wheel. "At the same time that he told me that it's over between the two of you—and has been for more than two years."

"It's not over." Bella shook her head, and when she spoke next, there was a quiver in her voice as if I'd broken through her hard outer shell for the first time. "It can't be."

"Watching someone marry someone else is a pretty surefire

signal that they're no longer interested," I said more gently this time.

"We talk at least once a month," Bella offered as a kind of defense.

That information did catch me off guard, as I was sure Bella expected that it would. Anton had failed to mention that tidbit, but it still didn't mean that he was interested in her romantically.

"He never mentioned Lacy by name," Bella said, her voice low. "I didn't think it was serious. I thought that with all of the changes... I thought he would be back home any day now."

"What changes?"

Myrtis leaned forward again, whispering conspiratorially. "Patty thinks that if Anton comes home, then the business will be more profitable. Then Uncle Michael will start behaving himself again."

"Behaving himself?" I asked, recalling how Anton had mentioned his parents' separation even while they continued living together.

"Aunt Patty told Uncle Michael to leave," Myrtis added. "But he wouldn't. Stayed put in the same house, and they basically all but drew a line down the middle. It was around the same time that Anton ran off and the ranch started bleeding money."

This time Charlotte didn't silence her cousin, but I did catch the look she shot at Myrtis. *Be careful*, it silently commanded. I had a feeling that Myrtis was now carefully choosing her words.

"Whether or not it's true, in Aunt Patty's mind, everything is connected," Myrtis continued. "If Anton returns home like a good son, then Uncle Michael will stop running around, and he might even start making level-headed business decisions."

"But Patty seems happy enough dating the priest," I countered.

"Who?" Myrtis asked, clearly confused.

"Reverend Todd?" I reminded her.

"Oh, the priest, right," Myrtis said with an uncharacteristic smile, though it seemed to be one of mockery more than anything else.

"Does the reverend also live with Patty back in Swanson?" I dared to ask, though I tried to sound like I was interested only for the sake of gossip, not because I was trying to put disparate pieces together in order to stay one step ahead of this bizarre family.

"Todd stays in the pool house," Myrtis answered knowingly. "Uncle Michael doesn't seem to mind too much since he's found a way to work with him."

Work with him? I sensed that I was getting closer to some key piece of information, but then Bella changed the subject.

She cleared her throat. "Anyway, Charlotte's right. We shouldn't talk business this weekend."

I could tell I'd heard something that I shouldn't know, so I swallowed back further questions, even though I planned to keep an even closer eye on this crew. It was beginning to sound like they'd brought more than an uninvited guest this weekend, and that meant trouble.

"That's enough gossip too." Charlotte spoke with the authority of someone who very much felt she was one of them. "Myrtis forgets herself when she talks too much, don't you?"

We drove on in silence, the glow of the Christmas tree in the center of town coming into view. Such a festive atmosphere for a car full of family secrets.

Myrtis sat back in her seat, obeying Charlotte for whatever reason as Bella reached out a hand and turned up the music this time. We drove the last couple of minutes into town with Chris Martin's raspy voice crowing "A Rush of Blood to the Head."

THIRTEEN

I was relieved to park outside The Reel and step inside the theater to be reunited with the more stable side of this bachelorette party.

Lou, the grizzled owner, greeted us with an almost-smile when we stepped into his theater lobby decorated with greenery, lights, tinsel, and classic holiday movie posters. *It's a Wonderful Life*, *The Bishop's Wife*, and *White Christmas* were coming to life again this season. I'd never seen the theater this festive, and I was certain it was because Lou wanted to bring a bit of cheer to Lacy's bachelorette party, though he would never admit it.

Lacy threw an arm around the older man and pulled him close. He wasn't a family man, but he was considered an unofficial adopted uncle to most Aubergine residents under forty years old. He responded to Lacy's affection with a single pat on the back, which was basically the equivalent of picking her up and spinning her around.

"Thanks for staying open late for us," Lacy said, giving him a grin that seemed much more like herself. Though in our childhood Lou had shown late-night Friday films, he'd begun pushing them earlier and earlier as he aged. Now, at almost seventy-five, his last weekend showing was usually at 7 p.m.

"Anything for you," he said in his raspy register. "You practically kept me in business by bringing all of your starving classmates here each week."

I'd never thought of it that way, but Lacy had been our high school's unofficial social director. She'd planned, contacted, and coordinated, making sure each person in our class had a personal invite to the Friday night films after the home games.

I let the women know that snacks were on me, and Lacy grabbed a box of Junior Mints while Savilla and Jemma loaded up on peanut M&Ms and popcorn. When it came time for Bella and the cousins to order they hesitated, before landing on a bag of gummy bears to split between them.

As we made our way into the dark theater and took our seats, Lou went into the projection room and started the movie, skipping previews and commercials altogether. A quiet settled across our group, the only sounds the occasional rustling of a plastic bag or the shaking of a box of candy, and I began to breathe more easily. Maybe the invasion by the random cousins and Anton's ex-girlfriend would be something Lacy and I could laugh about sooner rather than later.

As Jude Law professed his love to Cameron Diaz halfway through the film, I was feeling good about having turned this weekend around—which should've been a flashing warning sign to me that something else was coming. We'd gone an entire hour and some odd minutes without incident.

It started with a noise coming from the back of the theater: a woman's voice calling for help. All seven of us spun around and Charlotte actually stood up from her aisle seat, but all we saw was a frowning Lou holding his bucket of popcorn. He lifted a hand to let us know he had it under control and then stepped into the lobby. I turned back around, watching Diaz's character try to cry, but the real-life woman's voice grew louder and, even more startlingly, a few seconds later, a baby began to wail.

"What in the—?" Lacy started.

"I'll go see what's happening," I said, catching Savilla's eye and motioning for her to come with me, then giving Charlotte a dagger-like look that told her to stay seated. Surprisingly, she obeyed.

The sound of the baby's cries grew louder. Almost as if pulled by a magnet, Savilla rushed forward, pushing the door wide open to find Valerie Hurt holding a red-faced and wriggling newborn. Valerie had been very pregnant two months ago at the class reunion, and this crying infant was apparently the end-product.

Savilla elbowed me, and I realized that I'd been grimacing at the sight before us. I couldn't help it. The child was making an incredibly high-pitched noise despite being so tiny, and Valerie looked unkempt—so unlike any other time I'd ever seen her. Always so prim and proper, tonight she had a kind of drowned-cat appearance, a bedraggled countenance, and a sunken face. Dear Lord, was this motherhood?

"Lacy invited me to the party," Valerie said, almost defensively, as she set eyes on me. I hadn't even had a chance to ask a question.

"Oh, yeah, I know," I hedged, vaguely recalling that Lacy had mentioned that we should invite Valerie to the bachelorette party since Will was a groomsman. In the busyness of the end of the semester, I had forgotten to extend the invitation, but Lacy had been in touch with Valerie anyway. Of course, that was before I realized that Will was somehow involved with the Swanson family.

"My sitter fell through, but I was at home, listening to him scream and worrying about..." Valerie hesitated. "Lord, I don't know, worrying about everything." She motioned with her chin to the baby in her arms as if she couldn't quite believe that he belonged to her. "So I thought I might as well come here." She glanced at Lou behind the counter and the candy in front of him with a mixture of vacancy and longing. "It was a stupid idea. You don't want to listen to my baby lose his mind for the next few hours."

Valerie tightened her arms around the baby and slowly started toward the door, her expression resigned—and also slightly distraught. For the first time, I noticed that she was wearing sweatpants with frayed edges at the bottom, and her shirt was stained with a murky green color that I didn't want to guess at.

On a recent phone call, Aunt DeeDee had mentioned that Will and Valerie had been struggling since the baby had arrived. Apparently he had been in NICU for ten days. "You know," she'd tisked, as she'd prepared them a casserole dinner, "with Will out of a job and Valerie quitting teaching, their health insurance isn't great, not to mention their bank account. I wish either of them had family who could help." At the time, I'd let the comment pass me by as part of the list of updates on Aubergine residents. I'd certainly had no idea things were this bleak for my former class-mate and her husband.

Lou raised his eyebrows as if I should know what to do, but I'd never spent time with a screaming infant—and on top of that, I'd never cared much for Valerie anyway. Even back in high school, she'd always seemed uppity and judgmental.

After a bit of pronounced head-jutting from Lou, I stepped forward. "No, stay," I said, not adding what I was really thinking: that this night couldn't get much worse—or weirder. What would adding a belligerent newborn and exhausted mother really do to our odd little band of women?

"Really?" Valerie put the baby on her shoulder and bounced him while he continued to wail.

"Really," I said, swallowing back my concern about including a rowdy infant in our night's festivities.

"I'd love that," Valerie exclaimed, upsetting the infant once again. She lowered her voice but continued, her words coming faster as she began to speak in a monotone hum that quieted the baby. "I told Will that he should be the one to stay home, but no, he always gets to go out without the baby and have a grand ol' time. He's off doing God knows what while I take care of everything at home. Do you know how much babies spit up?" Valerie's face contorted into a look of disgust, and she peered down at the baby as if not quite sure to whom he belonged. "Anyway, Will said he abso-lutely couldn't miss the bachelor party tonight, that if I wanted to be a stay-at-home mom, he had to pursue 'new opportunities.'" Valerie spat the last two words as if they were distasteful. "What kind of man doesn't want to sacrifice one evening so he can let his wife have a few hours to herself? Tell me, what kind of man?"

My mind snagged on her claim about Will's near-mandatory attendance at the bachelor party. Why would his absence impact Valerie's ability to be a stay-at-home mom unless he was indeed working some kind of job for the Swansons? Otherwise, he totally could've missed the party tonight—he was the third groomsmen, the one invited just so there would be an equal number to the bridesmaids. Anton barely knew the guy.

Questions surged through my mind, but I reminded myself that no one was under investigation here. No one had died. Nothing tragic had happened. And, after all, this didn't seem like the time to pry into Valerie's marriage, especially with the haggard look in her eyes—and the finally calm baby.

"You're welcome to join us," I said, trying to channel Lacy's brand of hospitality. "You and the... baby."

I nearly stumbled over the last word, not used to saying it. Like, ever. Bringing a kid to something like this was foreign to me, but also, when I talked about the young, I was always referring to animals. Puppies, kittens, calves, foals, hatchlings. I wasn't familiar with babies, but that was apparently about to change, I realized, as Valerie shifted the infant and the diaper bag from her arms to mine so quickly that I didn't have time to protest.

"Perfect," Valerie said, as she eyed the counter full of snacks. "Are these free?"

I nodded, surprised by the question, and she grabbed three packs of M&Ms and a bottle of soda from the counter, already opening one package and throwing a fistful of candy into her mouth. Finished, she cracked the soda and took a long swallow, before taking a deep breath, her tone authoritative as she gave me directives. "Bottle is in the bag. Just bring him in when you're ready."

And then Valerie was gone, leaving Lou, Savilla, and me to

stare at one another in bewilderment. This was not the Valerie any of us knew.

I only broke our gaze when the infant made a gurgling noise. I looked down at the bundle that weighed about as much as a full-grown chihuahua, which is not my favorite dog. The yippy bark climbs up my spine just like the baby's earlier cries.

"Is he asleep?" Savilla asked, peeking over my shoulder. Her expression was awe-filled.

"Nope," I answered.

The baby, whom I calculated must be about six weeks old based on when Aunt DeeDee had mentioned the birth, gazed up at us with wide eyes. Then his face began to crumple into a whimper, as if to say that I was not the person he would choose to hold him, which then made me afraid that he was about to let out a new round of wails.

I held him away from my body as a kind of offering to Lou, who picked up his popcorn bucket and shook his head.

"What? Don't you like kids?" I tried to say the question in a way that didn't show my own aversion.

"They're fine on a case-by-case basis," he grumbled, as he shoved a handful of popcorn into his mouth.

I thought that might be a pretty good summary of my own feelings, but I couldn't exactly leave the kid on the counter, tucked in among the bags of candy.

"He's probably just hungry," Savilla said, extending her hands. "Give him to me."

I hadn't even considered that as an option. Savilla had never seemed the baby type. If someone offered her a new pair of Manolo Blahniks or a piece from Harry Winston, sure. But a baby?

The infant had found his fist and was rapidly shaking his little head in sporadic jerks. I maneuvered the baby into Savilla's arms while I fumbled with the diaper bag, finally finding the bottle in a refrigerated compartment.

"You've got to warm it up," Savilla informed us, turning to Lou.

"Can you get a large cup of hot water? We'll drop the bottle in for two or three minutes."

He went behind the counter to do as bid, and Savilla put the baby on her shoulder, pacing with a bouncing march back and forth across the lobby.

"How do you know how to do that?" I asked.

"Babysitting," she said with a lifted shoulder, as if it wasn't a surprise that an heiress had spent time working for a few dollars an hour as a babysitter at one point in her life. She cooed down at the infant, her eyes crinkling at the edges as she rubbed her cheek against his fuzzy bald head. "Ollie isn't my first wailing baby. No, he isn't."

For the first time, I noticed a piece of tape with all capital letters written across the front of the diaper bag. I pointed it out to Savilla. "His name is Oliver."

"Oh, I know," Savilla said easily. "But he goes by Ollie. I visited him in the NICU and brought him a stuffed bunny with his name stitched along the ear. It's blue and fuzzy and so cuddlicious," she continued. Then, catching my bemused expression: "What? Valerie and I are friends—or, at least, friendly-ish."

I raised my eyebrows, surprised by the clarification. Honestly, the Valerie I'd known in high school didn't have many true friends. Frenemies, sure, but she was the kind of girl who pushed people away eventually.

"Valerie has been stressed and lonely, so I've invited her to The Rose for lunch a couple of times." Savilla sniffed the top of Ollie's head, grinning at him as if she'd won him as a prize. "I think she and Will are going through a rough patch too. He's constantly looking for work to pay the hospital bills, and Valerie feels"—she considered the best word—"adrift."

Lou brought the warmed bottle, and Savilla nestled the baby into the crook of her arm before plopping the formula into Ollie's eager mouth.

"Good luck," Lou said. "If you keep him quiet, you two can head back inside."

Lou sounded as if he was planning to keep an eye on us, even if it was just to make sure the baby didn't spit up in his theater.

We followed him into the dark space. The first thing I saw was Valerie Hurt in the back row, her frame slouched in the seat, her head tilted at an awkward angle.

She was fast asleep.

FOURTEEN

As the credits rolled and we tossed candy and popcorn boxes into the trash, I was still determined that this night would proceed as planned.

"Whose baby is that?" Jemma asked, narrowing her eyes, as if I'd been hiding a surprise—and unwanted—twist to the evening. The sugar and the length of the movie had sobered her up, and she was back to her usual critical demeanor.

"Valerie Hurt's," I said quietly, trying not to wake the baby, who'd finished his bottle and promptly fallen asleep on my chest while Savilla was in the restroom. "Remember? Valerie was at the reunion weekend." I mimed her pregnant belly.

"Ah, yes. The self-righteous whale."

I heard a snicker from the direction of the cousins, and I was fairly certain it was Charlotte who was getting a laugh at Valerie's expense.

"I just love babies," Savilla said, returning from the bathroom and reaching again for the bundle in my arms, which I was more than happy to release.

"I need to wake up Valerie before our next stop anyway." I moved to the back of the theater and touched the new mother on the shoulder, but she didn't budge. In fact, she didn't so much as flutter an eyelash.

"Valerie," I whispered, trying to be gentle. When she still didn't flinch, I said her name again and put a hand on her shoulder. Nothing. My heart beat faster in my rib cage, and for a second I wondered if she was breathing. I shouted this time as I called her name, emphasizing each syllable. "Va-le-rie!"

That time she shifted in the seat but didn't open her eyes. "No, thank you," she mumbled, before her head lolled against her shoulder again.

I tried one more time to wake Valerie, this time practically propping her up and holding one eyelid open, but her only response was in the form of two words: "So sleepy."

Apparently, the desperate need for rest in these early days of motherhood—in addition to the stress I assumed came from whatever shady business her husband was up to—could basically mimic the effects of a strong dose of Ambien. Since I didn't hear Ollie crying, I decided to leave her for as long as Lou would let her stay.

I made my way back to the front and told him as much. He shrugged and gave a curt nod, which was as much communication as I could expect from him. Then he told me he would put on *It's a Wonderful Life* and let Valerie sleep a couple more hours—as long as we would take the baby with us.

I considered, wondering if my old classmate might wake up terrified that we'd run away with her child, but then I realized that we would literally be two storefronts and one flight of stairs away from her at The Attic, one of the town's beloved boutiques and my aunt's most recent hobby. Surely it couldn't be called kidnapping if you're no more than a few yards away and you wish the mother was there?

"Deal," I told Lou as I checked my watch. "Valerie can call Savilla whenever she wakes. We won't be far."

"Sounds good," Lou said, starting toward the projection room, where he would put on the soothing tones of Jimmy Stewart's and Donna Reed's voices.

I kind of wished I could stay myself, but instead I turned to round up the ladies and pull out the second clue, handing it to Lacy, who cleared her throat and read aloud the next riddle.

You've always wanted
to glimmer and shine.
High above Main Street
you pick the jewels this time.

Lacy narrowed one eye, knowing immediately that our next destination was one of her all-time favorite spots downtown, partly because it was the only shop that ever carried the vintage-chic clothing she liked to wear, but also because Aunt DeeDee dropped off cookies each afternoon for the salespeople to give out to shoppers. In elementary school, Lacy would practically pull me into the store on our walk home; inside, there were usually a handful of other customers—and sweets. It had been a happening little place, especially for a town of our size.

"The Attic opened late for us?" Lacy asked, excitement in her words.

"I kind of know the new manager," I said, smiling as I referred to Aunt DeeDee. "She was excited to be asked."

We wrapped winter coats around ourselves and Savilla folded the sleeping baby against her chest as we braced for the brief but very chilly walk to the store.

When Bella muttered something about being shocked that this town even had a real store, Myrtis giggled while Charlotte side-eyed the baby. I'd noticed her doing the same to Valerie on our way out of the low-lit theater, and I wished I could read past the curious expression on Charlotte's face. Did she hate Valerie? Did she want to be her? Or was Charlotte merely in shock that a postpartum woman could sleep so soundly?

I couldn't think about it too long because Lacy put an arm through mine and leaned close.

"Thanks for being so great tonight," she said quietly. "You've

kept everything, including me, afloat even though we've had a few"
—she glanced behind her and lifted a chin toward the three women
—"a few surprises."

Lacy wasn't the kind of friend who needed defending or
protecting very often, so I felt pleased that she'd noticed me come
through for her this time.

"Happy to," I said, squeezing her gloved hand.

We climbed the stairs, gripping the cold metal railing, and as
we reached the stairwell, Aunt DeeDee was there to greet us with
a smile and an invitation to hurry to the warmth inside.

"Come in, come in, ladies!"

We scurried into the foyer of the boutique, which had been a
series of tiny apartments for the mining families in the late 1800s.
The conversion to a store had kept the exposed brick and the high
wooden beams, and Aunt DeeDee had added a simple festive flare
by stringing white lights across the room.

When we were all inside and standing in a half-circle, Aunt
DeeDee surveyed us, taking in the extra three attendees and the
baby one by one with a kind nod. Ever the gracious hostess, she
welcomed all of us, taking the hands of Bella, Charlotte, and
Myrtis and introducing herself to them each in turn. When she
reached Savilla and the baby, her words of welcome turned to
murmuring as she moved in for a closer look.

"And this must be Oliver," Aunt DeeDee cooed.

"Ollie," Savilla gently corrected, beaming as if the child were
her own. "Valerie and Will's baby."

"I got to visit with him in the church nursery a couple of weeks
ago." Aunt DeeDee rubbed the baby's back, but he didn't stir. "Precious boy."

"Valerie is meeting up with us later," I explained. "She fell
asleep during the movie." I decided not to mention that she'd
shown up late, looking bedraggled, before going practically
comatose.

"Which is totally fine because this little wonder is precious."

Savilla sighed, nuzzling against Oliver's bald head for at least the fifth time that night.

"He certainly is," Aunt DeeDee agreed, before putting her hands together and turning back to face everyone. "Well, welcome, everyone. I'll pour a few more glasses of prosecco, and we have plenty of designs ready for your perusal. All on the house, of course."

As Bella's eyes roamed the room, for the first time that evening she didn't act as if she was completely bored by this town. In fact, all three of the Texas ladies seemed intrigued, their eyes lighting up as they noticed the art hanging along the wall. Though they weren't for sale, Aunt DeeDee had hung them to enhance the store's ambiance.

Charlotte's hand waved toward the frames as she asked DeeDee, "Who painted these?"

Aunt DeeDee followed the gesture to the three Impressionist images of our majestic Blue Ridge Mountains outlined in mottled grays, purples, and ivories.

"These were painted by a resident at our Aubergine Art Collective years ago," Aunt DeeDee answered. "Her name was Anna Perry. She won our town's annual Rose Palace Pageant in 1926. Eventually, she moved here in the 1960s and became a full-fledged citizen of Aubergine for the last couple decades of her life." She smiled. "And she actually mentored me before I competed in the pageant."

"And won," I noted, proud of my aunt in ways I hadn't known to be before this past year.

"The Collective allows Aubergine businesses to rent them out for display," Aunt DeeDee clarified. "So the artwork can be admired rather than languishing in a store room."

"Hmmm," Bella mused, moving closer to the paintings to study the brushstrokes. "An Impressionist-style painting, though well past the official period."

"Post-Impressionist, but just barely," Charlotte remarked.

Too knowledgeable for a ranching family, I thought, before catching myself. Of course rural living didn't equate to stupidity or a lack of culture. I should have known that better than anyone.

Still, something about their interest nagged at me, though I couldn't have verbalized why. I continued to watch Bella absorb the painting, and something about this cozy space and the people milling about the room made me think of a weekend train trip Charlie and I had taken up to Boston from New York.

We'd visited the Isabella Stewart Gardner Museum, holding hands as we walked through the gallery displays, which felt more like rooms at an Italian villa than a museum. Afterward, I'd read all about the 1990 heist in which thirteen paintings had been stolen. There was still a $10 million-dollar reward to anyone who could provide substantial clues as to the whereabouts of the artwork.

I had no idea why such a thought had come to mind, except that there was something hungry in the looks of the three Texan women as they stood admiring the paintings—rather than the shiny jewelry only a few yards away.

"I must say that I'm impressed to find such quality pieces here." Charlotte looked around as if she couldn't believe where she was standing.

I caught Aunt DeeDee's eye and gave her a look that said I was annoyed by not only Charlotte's condescending tone but by the way she was distracting us from where our focus should be—on Lacy.

Aunt DeeDee gave the slightest shake of her head as if to tell me to be polite.

Though I wasn't willing to be nice, I was willing to engage them. "Have you ever heard of the Gardner heist? I believe Impressionist paintings were stolen from that museum."

Charlotte's eye caught mine for a split second before she looked back at the painting, as if she either couldn't tear her gaze away or she didn't want to meet mine.

"I have heard of it," Myrtis offered, stepping forward as if she was afraid of being left out of the conversation. "There have been at least nine other thefts of Impressionist works in recent years, all across the world. In fact, more than five hundred million dollars' worth of paintings were taken from Amsterdam in 1991, just a year after the Gardner heist. That time the thieves just took them off the wall in broad daylight." Myrtis simpered, as though pleased with her own recall. "Except they loaded them into a getaway car with a flat tire. They were caught within the hour."

Aunt DeeDee chuckled at the story. "Perhaps thieving is best left to those with more reliable vehicles."

Charlotte lifted an eyebrow as if she wasn't sure whether or not Aunt DeeDee was joking.

"The most recent was a Monet in 2012 from a museum in the Netherlands," Myrtis continued eagerly. "When the thieves were caught and questioned, one eventually admitted that his mother had burned it in their kitchen oven to get rid of the evidence."

Charlotte touched Myrtis's arm. "That's enough."

Her cousin's face immediately fell, and I noticed that Bella was keeping a watchful eye on both of the women.

"Well, I'm pretty sure we don't have many art heists in our little hamlet," Aunt DeeDee said with a soft laugh as she extended a hand toward the jewelry, obviously hoping the three women would take the cue and begin selecting items they'd like to take home with them.

"Oh no. I'm sure no one would want to steal something quite so"—Bella wrinkled her nose as if she found the paintings somehow distasteful—"colloquially charming." She reached out and patted my aunt's arm, and I had the sudden urge to grab Bella's petite frame and toss her across the room. She continued in a simpering tone. "Works like these are best left here, where they can be experienced by the local community."

The last two words were said with such contempt that Bella might as well have been calling us ignorant imbeciles. I thought of Patty Swanson's vague threat about Bella moving to Aubergine, and I was now certain that idea was total crap. There was no way Bella Rivera would deign to move into our community—not even for Anton, the apparent love of her life.

"And I'm sure we will continue to enjoy them for years to come," I said, trying to keep the vitriol from my tone. "Now, why don't we join the others and pick out one or two pieces of jewelry for each of you to take home?"

The women turned to the display, eyeing the shimmery jewelry set against their backdrop of velvet. I was pleased that none of the women crinkled their noses as they took in the pieces. In fact, if anything, they seemed to be impressed.

"Did you make this one?" Bella asked, fingering a pair of tear-drop-shaped earrings that sparkled as they caught the twinkling lights.

"I did," Aunt DeeDee said, pleased to turn to a different topic. "It's become a hobby of mine of late. Those are made of topaz, and the color would go great with your skin tone. Do you like them?"

Bella nodded appreciatively, and I thought I caught of glimpse of humanity in her eyes. Aunt DeeDee had a way of bringing out the best in even the worst of people.

"Well, like I said, everything is on the house tonight." Aunt DeeDee grinned before her eyes flitted to me. "Or maybe I should say that my niece has generously offered to pick up the final bill."

Bella eyed me, seeming surprised that a girl like me had any extra funds. Not that I wanted people to know I had money, particularly if they might treat me differently, but if that knowledge somehow kept Bella in check the rest of the weekend, that was fine by me.

I gave my best Aunt DeeDee smile. "Select anything you like."

FIFTEEN

After we finished cleaning out Aunt DeeDee's stash of costume jewelry, bagging about a thousand dollars' worth of accessories that she would bill to me, she kissed me on the cheek and squeezed Lacy's arm. "Where are you gals off to next?"

"Two quick stops. And she'll love them both."

I handed Lacy the next clue. She read it silently this time.

If these walls could talk
they'd have stories of us to tell.
But now they hold
love-lorn tomes for sale.

Lacy squinted at me, trying to decipher the clue.

"It's a place that we loved when we were kids but that's been converted into something else entirely," I hinted.

"Oh! The Old Soda Shop?" With the way Lacy's eyes lit, I knew she was getting a second wind. We'd visited there for every major occasion in our classmates' lives—birthdays, breakups, bat mitzvahs—to bag up peppermint sticks, saltwater taffy, and fireballs from the jars lining the counter.

"It closed a decade or so ago," Savilla clarified for the non-residents as she gently bounced Ollie, who was still asleep despite the squealing during the jewelry giveaways in The Attic. "Now it's a bookstore—Sugar & Spice Books."

"They have a spicy romance section to die for," Jemma added, before catching our surprised expressions. "What? I've been back and forth from The Rose a lot the past few months, and I like my books extra *caliente*."

I laughed as we walked down the stairs, single file and gripping the rail so as not to slide to our deaths. The temperature had fallen even lower, and as we entered the lamplit Sugar & Spice, we had to stomp the chill from our legs and feet.

I hadn't yet been to the bookstore, but Savilla had recommended it when I was brainstorming the schedule for the bachelorette party. It was perfect, especially since Lacy and I had both been avid readers since middle school, when Aunt DeeDee would drive us to the only indie bookstore in Richmond. Her choice had always veered to romance, while my faves back in the day had been horse-girl books. After we had a stack to buy, Lacy and I would sit in the self-help section, pulling the most ridiculous adult titles we could find from the shelves. We would cackle as we read the titles like *Your Orgasm & You*; *Grave-Robbing Your Inner Demons*; or *How to Set Your Marriage Aflame*.

Looking around the store now, I guessed that the self-help section was small if non-existent. The offerings seemed to be entirely fiction and separated by genre. Giant tags—Sweet, Salty, Sour—hung at the top of bookshelves, and all of the books faced cover out, making a rainbow of color against the blue-gray walls.

"Welcome," the owner—a forty-something woman with a lilting Southern accent—called from the back of the store. She'd agreed to give us a quick tour and then help us make spine poems, stacking books to write a message with the titles in honor of Lacy and Anton. "Come in, come in."

But before we could begin perusing the shelves, a noise came from outside. We all turned toward the floor-length window display of popular novels just in time to see Charlie rear back and punch another man, flattening him to the ground.

I felt my pulse begin to race and I was first to the door, flinging it open and screaming Charlie's name as the other man attempted to sit up, a hand on his jaw as if protecting it from another blow.

"Do not get up," Charlie yelled at the man.

I hurried over and took my boyfriend's arm. "What are you thinking?"

Charlie blinked several times as if he didn't know who I was at first. I moved closer, taking his hand more gently this time as I tried to shake him out of whatever insanity had overtaken him.

"Charlie?" I said. "Look at me."

He met my gaze as reality settled in, and for the first time I noticed that Charlotte had gone to the other man—who happened to be the priest, Todd Anderson. She was helping him to his feet, brushing the ice off of his coat, and shooting daggers at Charlie.

Charlotte was carrying the pink bag with the mini arsenal inside, and my throat tightened at the idea that she could pull a weapon from it if she so chose. "We'll get you inside and warm you up," she said, as Todd stood and then slanted sideways before sinking into the brick wall.

"Looks like your priest can't hold his liquor," I said.

"And the police presence around here is obviously confused as to their real job." Charlotte spat out the last sentence at Charlie, even though she didn't make eye contact with him, and I once again wondered how she knew that my boyfriend was the "police presence" around here.

Charlie's truck was still running in the middle of the road, the passenger door open, as if the priest had fled without stopping to even shut the door.

Charlie shook his head at the priest, a look of disgust on his face. I'd never seen this side of him. I didn't even know he was capable of this kind of violent behavior, especially with a near-perfect stranger.

"Both of you, come inside," I said, trying to sound authoritative as I opened the door to Sugar & Spice. Jemma's, Savilla's, and Lacy's eyes were wide as they watched the scene unfold from the doorway, while Myrtis and Bella stood on the other side of the store, as if they didn't want to get involved.

"Do you have some ice? For the priest's jaw?" I asked the owner of the store, whose name I'd completely forgotten.

The woman simply nodded and gestured for me and the sheriff to follow her to a tiny back room, where she opened a fridge and took out an ice pack that usually went inside kids' lunchboxes. It would have to do.

I grabbed a couple of napkins and wrapped them around the pack before handing it over to Charlotte, who placed it against Todd's jaw. Then I grabbed Charlie by the shirt, pulling him into what looked to be a back office. The owner tactfully closed the door behind us.

"This is not you," I started, not knowing how to say everything I wanted to say to Charlie. Maybe that he was supposed to be my mild-mannered, ever-steady, measured anchor. Maybe that I'd never seen him overreact. Maybe that he never got into his head so much that he did something unhinged. The unexpected, the nonsensical, the righteous anger—that was occasionally my territory, but not his.

"Todd was saying threatening things about Valerie and the baby," Charlie said, his tone weary as the adrenaline started to wear off. He sat in the office chair and spun it around to face me.

"Threatening?" I repeated after a few seconds, making sure I'd heard him correctly.

Charlie breathed out a long sigh and hung his head, letting it fall into his hands. "I mean... I think so."

I could tell that he too was struggling to wrap his mind around what had just happened. He took a steadying breath.

"We played poker, we drank, we had a good time. The evening was winding down when Todd said he was going to drive into town for a nightcap. I told him that since we're a dry county, nightcaps don't really exist in Aubergine, but he insisted, got really fidgety, then started acting almost manic." Charlie shrugged. "He'd been drinking alcohol, so when he took his keys and headed outside, I took them from him. He was insistent, talking about how he had 'things to do' in town. When he started walking down the lane in the freezing cold, I got in my truck and told him to get inside." Charlie sighed and looked up at me. "I was planning to either show him how dead our town is at night or drive him around until he passed out, then bring him back to The Rose to sleep it off—whichever came first."

Charlie paused as if to consider how to explain the next part of the story, his brows darkening as he replayed the last few minutes. "But then Todd started shouting about how he needed to go to the bank."

"The bank?" I repeated.

"Yes—and saying he was going to kill Will if he didn't come through."

"Come through with what?"

"He wouldn't say. Then he totally changed course and started saying all of these awful things about what he was going to do to Valerie and the baby if Will messed things up. I stopped the car and told him to shut his mouth, but instead he saw you all in the store window, flung open the door while I was still driving, and ran out of the car. I assumed he was coming to find Valerie, so that's when I went after him and did the only thing I knew would get him to stop."

"Punch him in the face?"

Charlie shook his hand as if he could still feel the force of it against Reverend Todd's face. He stared at me. "I've never punched anyone. Ever."

This sounded more like my boyfriend, the one who didn't act without thinking—unless someone was a danger to himself or others.

"Todd could press charges against me," Charlie thought aloud.

"For what?"

"Assault."

I let out a huff of air. "I'll be impressed if the man remembers tonight, and if he does, I don't think he'll want to admit that he was running around threatening a woman and her baby."

Charlie let his head sink back against the chair and closed his eyes, as if he was trying to think clearly. "How is this man a priest? And what on earth does Patty see in him?"

An idea came to me, and I pulled out my phone.

I thought back to my first conversation with the priest, and I remembered Todd Anderson saying that he'd met Patty Swanson at a place that started with an "S." As soon as he'd said the words, he'd acted strangely, almost as if he'd caught himself. Then, he'd said something about the place being a homeless shelter. Had he been lying?

"What is it?" Charlie asked.

"Shhh. Give me a second." I closed my eyes, trying to recall the specifics of what he'd said. What was the name of the place? I grabbed my phone and typed in "Swanson + Texas + homeless shelter." Nothing came up.

I tried the same combination with a variety of "S" names. Sammy's, Sinclair's, Smith's. Then it hit me. *Sully's.* That was the name. I typed it in, and the only result was a restaurant—or, more specifically I realized, as I clicked on the link, a honky-tonk bar with dinner and line dancing.

That meet-cute sounded more like the Patty–Todd romance that I'd seen this weekend.

I held up the phone. "This is where the *supposed* priest told me he met Patty Swanson."

Charlie took the device and scanned the contents of the website, raising his eyebrows at the video of guests two-stepping to twangy music. "It's not that priests can't have a good time, but... to meet here?"

"Right. It's strange, especially since he told me it was a homeless shelter. He made it sound like they were volunteering together."

"Which would be a more wholesome story for someone trying to pass themselves off as a holy man," Charlie finished for me.

I realized now that Todd had almost blown his cover in that first conversation. Sure, a priest could go to a bar. He could even line dance. But with everything else on Todd Anderson's rap sheet, I was now sure that he was anything but a priest.

Charlie was obviously thinking the same thing. "There's no way he's a clergyman with the way he's behaved. He must've done one of those online ordination things to legally marry people." Astonished, he shook his head. "I'm actually relieved."

I tried for a smile, kneeling down in front of Charlie and meeting those hazel pools of his eyes. "I think you're safe—this time."

Something nagged at Charlie, though. "But why lie? Why not just come as Patty Swanson's plus-one?"

I considered that question and recalled my unofficial training with sleazebags at The Rose these past few months. "Sometimes it's easier to hide behind a persona, I guess."

Charlie gave me a sad smile and leaned forward to put his forehead against mine. He closed his eyes. "I'm glad you're okay."

I tilted my head. "Why wouldn't I be?"

"I don't know. I just keep feeling like there's something else happening this weekend, something that we can't quite see."

I knew exactly what he meant, but I didn't want to believe that anything other than my best friend's celebration was underway. Still, as I looked into his eyes, I was certain that, for both of us, the nagging feeling was here to stay. Something indeed was afoot, and I was beginning to think that whatever it was—as Momma would say —stank to high heaven.

SIXTEEN

After the altercation, the browsing at Sugar & Spice Books was half-hearted at best, and we completely gave up on our own attempts at making cute spine poetry.

As Charlie had expected to happen, the priest had passed out drunk on a wingback chair. Not knowing what other option he had, Charlie had got him to his feet and practically carried him back to the truck, which had been running in the middle of Main Street this entire time.

As if she didn't trust the sheriff with the man, Charlotte sent Bella to accompany the priest back to the estate.

Once the two of them were inside the truck, Charlie came to me at the doorway and pulled me to him. I could tell that the last thing he wanted to do was drive Bella and Reverend Todd back to the estate.

"Stay safe, and I'll see you at The Rose," Charlie whispered before kissing me once, studying my face as if he was considering picking me up and driving far, far away.

I apologized to the owner of the bookstore and bought a $500-dollar gift card for her troubles, before starting toward our last stop at the Morning Brew, the coffee shop where Lacy and I had studied regularly during our last two years of high school. I wasn't sure we should try to go now, but I didn't have the energy to get everyone home without a strong cup of anything Gladys could whip up. *With preferably a few thimblefuls of liquor in our coffees.*

This time, I handed Lacy the crumpled paper with the clue from my pocket, and said simply, "We need coffee." I didn't even read it with her, so she read it softly to herself:

"Though a bit jittery by the end,
this place kept us afloat.
Papers, tests, finals—
caffeine our company while we wrote."

She knew immediately, and the remaining party walked two by two a block down the street to the café.

The Morning Brew had become something of a staple for tourists over the years, but to me and Lacy, it had been a place to study and write papers late into the night, interrupting one another with a bit of gossip or to commiserate over a tough teacher before returning to our books. The owner, Gladys Liplich, would tease us about being the coffee shop mascots because during our senior year, she would refill our cups and leave the pot at our table before shuttering the store for the night, and telling us to make sure to close the door tight behind us when we left.

Now, it was nearly 1 a.m. as we entered the shop, and Gladys stood inside the door, waving a sash reading "Bride to Be" at Lacy, who managed a smile for the fifty-something-year-old woman.

Gladys placed the sash over my friend's head before adding a crown with the same message. "You never competed at The Rose, but this weekend, you're the queen," Gladys teased, giving Lacy a hug before turning to the rest of our motley crew. "I've got decaf and caffeinated, so you can pick your pleasure. All on the house, of course."

Gladys's generosity—giving us free drinks and opening the shop way past her bedtime—wasn't a surprise, but it was a reminder of how much people in Aubergine loved Lacy—and me. I felt that familiar tug at my heartstrings to move back to the place I loved and was loved after I finished my vet program in New York; but I wouldn't let myself dwell on possibilities about my own future right now. Maybe after the wedding on Sunday.

Gladys clapped her hands. "Come in and get settled and I'll take your orders for either a pick-me-up, a sleepy-time tea, or a hangover helper."

Savilla headed to the restroom to change Ollie, and Charlotte and Myrtis sat at their own table. Lacy sank into one of the comfortable corner chairs, facing Jemma, who seemed at a loss for words. The accumulation of the unexpected guests and the scene with Charlie and the priest had apparently stunned her, and she was about to be even more surprised as Will Hurt rushed into the store, a look of terror in his eyes, Valerie on his heels.

"How could you leave him with strangers?" Will shouted, startling all of us, especially Charlotte, whose eyes were unblinkingly fixed on him.

Valerie seemed about to yell back at her husband, but when she scanned the café and didn't see her baby, she became frantic herself instead. Her eyes were wide as she stepped closer to me. "Where is he? Where's Ollie?"

"I told you not to let him out of your sight this weekend," Will said, his voice strained, as if someone had him by the throat.

He was angry, yes—but also afraid.

"Your baby is fine," I said, stepping forward. "Savilla is in the restroom, changing him."

Valerie's eyes darted toward the bathrooms and then her husband before she started in that direction, a stricken look of relief on her face.

As soon as she'd passed through the door, Charlotte was at Will's elbow, her hand on his arm.

Without looking at her, Will shook her away. "Not now. I need to see my son."

Charlotte gasped, startling both of them, before narrowing her gaze. Almost immediately, Will realized he'd made a mistake.

His face froze, seeming to sense that he shouldn't speak this way to her. "Charlotte, I didn't mean to—" he started, before she interrupted him.

"It's fine." The woman stood to her full height and lifted her chin. "I don't expect any show of gratitude, even after everything I've done for you."

Will swallowed hard, and I couldn't tell if he wanted to hide or fight. Either way, he was on edge.

Surely it wasn't just the late hour and the need for caffeine veiling the meaning of Charlotte's actual words—*everything I've done for you*. I ran back over them in my mind one more time—Charlotte had arranged something, something for which Will should show gratitude.

Nope, still didn't add up.

"After Todd left the party, I was just worried about Valerie and the baby," Will said, this time his hand on her arm and Charlotte shaking him off. "I couldn't get a hold of Valerie on her cell, and when I went by the house, they weren't there."

"She fell asleep at The Reel," I said, before I could think better of it.

Will stared at me as if he hadn't realized I'd been listening to their conversation. When he saw me, he suddenly shut his mouth and wouldn't speak. Thankfully, a moment later Valerie and the baby emerged, Ollie all smiles as his mother carried him, Savilla following close behind.

With a look of disdain at his wife, Will hurried over to Ollie and yanked the baby from Valerie's arms.

"Careful. He only ate a half-hour ago. He still hasn't burped much," Savilla said, sounding hurt and defensive, which was fair. She hadn't taken the child of her own accord. Valerie had thrust him into our hands.

"Watch his head," Valerie chided her husband, as if she didn't trust him to hold the baby.

"I know what I'm doing," Will spat back at her. His eyes had a wild look of terror in them as they darted from the baby to his wife to the door. It was almost as if he wasn't registering our presence at all as he continued their argument. "I told you how important tonight was. I told you to stay home and keep the doors locked and the alarm on."

That sounded unnecessarily extreme, especially in a town where crime never happened—okay, except for two recent murders at The Rose, but those were definitely anomalies.

"I'm sorry if I need a break from being a twenty-four-hour dairy cow!" Valerie, mascara smudged at the corners of her eyes as if she'd been crying, looked ready to pounce on her husband. The mascara was the only makeup she was wearing, and I could just imagine her earlier that evening, trying to rake the wand across her eyelashes with a restless baby in her other arm. "And I'm sorry if I'm intruding on your 'new gig'—whatever the hell that means. I just thought it might be nice to be around other grown-ups, instead of cooped up at home like the little obedient wife you always wanted."

Will's brow furrowed, and he shook his head. "You have no idea what you're talking about."

"Oh yeah? And whose fault is that?" Valerie pointed at Will. It was her turn now to appear oblivious to her audience. "You won't tell me anything. You just give commands. Open this account, move that over here, stay home with the baby."

"It's for your own good," Will hissed, obviously about to come undone.

He dared a glance at Charlotte, who merely eyed him, her arms crossed. Apparently, regardless of what was happening between them, Charlotte was not about to get involved in this marital spat.

Lacy's wide eyes found mine, and Savilla gripped my arm. Myrtis and Jemma appeared just as stunned. We could all see that these new parents were fragile, on edge, and about to burst into flames.

As Ollie started to fuss in Will's arms, Valerie took the child from her husband. "You don't even know how to properly hold him."

"We need to go," he said, voice quivering even as he lifted his chin and tried to push back his shoulders to reclaim some sort of dignity. He led Valerie out of the café, his eyes fixed straight ahead, as if on a death march.

When the door closed behind him, it was as if air had suddenly been let back into the room. I heard clinking behind the counter and saw Gladys's head pop up from the bottom of the glass case she'd been cleaning. She removed a earbud from her ear and raised an eyebrow.

"What did I miss?"

None of us answered. I wasn't quite sure how to explain the tension in the air or the way that Will had looked at Charlotte one last time before hurrying his wife and baby out of the store.

One thing I knew: Will Hurt was terrified.

SEVENTEEN

Charlie was waiting at the door to Lacy's and my guest suite when she and I arrived back at The Rose.

"Sorry," he said apologetically, as he looked at Lacy. "I need to talk to Dakota for a minute, and I thought it'd be better in person."

"It's fine by me," Lacy said, though she raised an eyebrow at him as she took the key from her purse and opened the door. "I'm going to fall into bed and sleep like the dead till at least noon. Just don't punch anybody else, especially not my fiancé, got it?"

Charlie gave a hesitant nod of his head as if he knew he deserved that kind of teasing.

Lacy closed the door behind her, and I turned to Charlie, my stomach flip-flopping at the sight of him. I was both relieved he was okay and still very concerned that he'd lost his cool enough to punch a priest this evening—although, perhaps that assessment wasn't fair. As he'd said, it did seem like it was the only option at the time. Unfortunately, whatever the Texan side of this wedding was up to was making me doubt everything—even Charlie.

"A half-hour ago Will stormed into the Morning Brew with Valerie and then slunk out with their baby," I said, starting mid-conversation after mulling over the scene all the way back to The Rose, Myrtis and Charlotte tucked in the back seat, practically refusing to say a word. "He seemed afraid, but it doesn't make any sense because..." I trailed off, not quite knowing how to explain Will's unjustified fear.

Charlie glanced up and down the hall as if to check no one could overhear us. "Maybe we should talk in my room."

Before I could agree, he grabbed my hand and pulled me close, as if he wanted to ensure I couldn't get away... or that someone couldn't get to me. I wasn't sure which.

Charlie led me down the hall and a flight of stairs, toward the wing of the house reserved for hotel guests who wanted more modern accommodations. When I tried to ask him why we were hurrying, he put a finger over his lips and motioned for me to keep quiet, as though someone might be listening around any corner.

I realized I'd been holding my breath when we finally reached his room and he shut the door behind us. "What's with all the secrecy?"

Charlie peered through the peephole in the door before scanning the room and the bathroom. He opened the closet doors and checked to ensure no one was on the balcony as I watched in astonishment.

"Are you okay?" I asked, frowning. Charlie didn't seem like any version of himself that I'd ever seen.

"Something strange happened when I got back home and lugged Todd to his room."

I sank to the edge of the bed, waiting for him to continue.

"There was another man there, one with a gun. I know because it was pointed at us as soon as I opened the door." Charlie's brow wrinkled as he continued letting the evening unfold in his mind.

My heart leapt into my throat. "Someone pulled a gun? On you?"

"It was aimed at Todd. I just happened to be there too."

"Who was it?"

"Anton's father." Charlie narrowed his eyes and stared into mine. "I jumped in and showed him my badge, and he backed off real fast, pulled out his license to carry and insisted this was all a misunderstanding. He said his wife gave him a key to the room, and he was just operating out of self-protection."

"Why would Patty give him a key to the priest's room?"

Charlie lifted a shoulder. "No idea, but since the man hadn't actually hurt anyone, there was nothing I could do. He actually left when I did. Said he was going to take the key back to Patty right away."

I bit my lip, trying to wrap my head around this addition. So, Charlie pummeling Reverend Todd to the icy ground of Main Street wasn't the only time the priest had been threatened tonight, although it sounded like he wouldn't remember Michael Swanson and his gun. Regardless, Todd didn't seem to get along well with others.

"I thought Anton's dad wasn't coming until tomorrow," I said, unable to voice all of my other questions.

Charlie shook his head ever so slightly. "Whenever he was supposed to arrive, he's definitely here now, and he was waiting."

"Maybe he's angry because the priest is dating his wife? Anton's parents are still married."

Even as I said the words, they didn't quite add up to the way Anton had explained his parents' split. According to him, the pair still lived in the same giant house, though in different wings. Presumably Anton's parents knew when the other was dating someone, bringing them home. Patty's very public displays of affection with the priest in the Winter Garden would be hard for anyone, much less an estranged husband, to miss.

"That's what I asked him after I scared him enough with my badge and he showed me his license. His name is Michael Swanson, but he told me that he goes by Big Mike." Charlie nearly laughed at the detail, but we were both too tired to appreciate any humor right now. "Mike apologized and said that he'd been concerned about an intruder."

"In Todd's room? Why?"

"No idea." Charlie hung his head as if he couldn't believe that whatever was happening was on his watch. A police job in

Aubergine was supposed to be easy, straightforward. Jaywalking was supposed to be the worst offense, but somehow The Rose had changed all of that in recent months.

He thought for a long moment and then stared into my eyes. "I know I told you at the bookstore that something strange is happening this weekend."

"To put it lightly," I added, before recalling what Myrtis and Bella had said in the car on the way into town tonight. "Actually, there was talk about some kind of business between the Texas cousins—and maybe Will Hurt. I tried asking questions, to get them to keep talking, but Charlotte cut them off. Basically told them to keep their mouths shut. She seems very interested in being part of their family, for better or worse."

"Business?" Charlie asked, leaning forward on his elbows. "What kind of business does someone conduct during a wedding?"

"Something they don't want other people to notice?"

Charlie nodded. "You're right. Something that gives them an alibi, that provides a distraction." He considered this then added, "Whether we like it or not, nothing illegal has happened yet."

I ran back over the night, fast-forwarding and stopping at specific moments when Anton's side of the family said or did something off. I saw us in the car on the way downtown, at The Reel, at The Attic. Suddenly, my mind froze on the image of Charlotte in my aunt's store, chatting with her about the art hanging on her walls and the details about the heists.

But surely they wouldn't be chatting casually about art theft if they were actually thieves themselves? Unless they weren't at all afraid of getting caught.

"You don't think they're doing something off the wall, like trafficking in stolen art, do you?"

Charlie tilted his head and studied his hands for a long moment. "If that was it, why would they bring their business to Aubergine? Do we even have anything worth stealing?"

I liked the way Charlie used the pronoun "we" when he talked about this town. It reminded me that he felt like a part of the community that I loved.

"We have the Aubergine Art Collective. Savilla and Aunt DeeDee display their pieces, so I suppose they could have put work all over town."

"Anything worth real money?"

"Great question," I said, pulling out my phone. "My aunt has three Anna Perry paintings hanging in her store. Perry was also a former pageant winner."

As I spoke, I googled the name, and he leaned close to see what I'd found. There was a Wikipedia page, a link for an exhibit at the Virginia Museum of Fine Arts, and a featured painting on an auction site. I clicked on the last one, my eyes widening at the figure her painting had earned. "Two hundred and fifty grand. Not bad."

"It's not as big as some of the million-dollar auctions you hear about, but that could be a good payout for a smaller operation," Charlie mused, before falling backward on the bed, lost in thought.

I noticed for the first time the purple rings under his eyes. We were both exhausted.

I lay back on the bed beside Charlie. "Whatever the Texas constituency is up to, after tonight, I'm convinced that it's shady."

"I just want you to be careful," Charlie said, moving a strand of hair behind my ear as we lay facing each other. "This weekend... it doesn't feel right."

His eyes were watering from the late hour, but despite his fatigue, I could see a longing to protect me, to keep me safe at all costs.

I tucked myself closer to him and let his arms stretch around me, pulling me into his chest. After a few seconds, I lifted my face and kissed him, setting off an invisible flame between us. I'd thought I was too tired to want him, but I was wrong. My body pulsed with sudden longing, and he responded immediately, running his hand down the length of my back as he kissed me with a hunger I hadn't expected.

Something about the danger and fear and uncertainty made us want to hold one another even closer tonight.

I pressed nearer, my body against his as he slid a hand down my thigh, tugging up my dress. Desire beat a steady thrum in my lower belly. Charlie inched downward as he continued to kiss my throat, my neck, my shoulders, my breasts... but just as longing roared within me, there was a heavy pounding at the door.

EIGHTEEN

I wanted to ignore the sound, but it was the middle of the night, a time when no one should be awake unless there was a definite reason.

Reluctantly, Charlie crawled from beside me and glanced at the door as if he hoped the intruder would simply go away.

The pounding came again, this time somehow even louder.

His jaw clenched, Charlie stood and pulled himself together as I readjusted the length of my dress. He went to the door, looking through the peephole again before sighing heavily and turning to me. "It's Michael," he said.

At my puzzled expression, Charlie reminded me, "Anton's father."

I didn't have long to process this fact as Charlie opened the door. Standing in the doorway was a giant of a man, with a long, gray beard.

Charlie stood to his full height with his jaw raised almost imperceptibly and looked the man squarely in the eye. I'd always thought of Charlie as tall and strong; in fact, the first time I met him, I remember joking in my mind about how well his last name—Strong—fitted. But this man, with his barrel build, made my broad-chested boyfriend appear fun-size.

Still, in a contest of these two pitted against one another, Charlie stood a fighting chance, mostly because he was at least three decades younger than the burly man in front of us.

Charlie checked over his shoulder at me, as if to assess that he was standing as much as possible between me and the towering figure. Because of this, I had to peer around my boyfriend to see a visible holster with a gun hanging from the older man's left hip. It must have been the one he'd pulled on Todd and Charlie earlier that night.

"Hey, Sheriff," the man said in a gruff voice. His words weren't slurred, which meant he was sober. "I asked the front desk for your room number. I'm glad you're still awake, although I'm sorry for interrupting your"—Michael cleared his throat and gestured toward me with a courteous nod of his head before finishing his sentence—"to interrupt your company."

If Charlie hadn't already given me the visual of this man waving a gun around while threatening a priest, I would've thought that Michael Swanson was a Texas gentleman—and his gun might've scared me far less than it actually did. But suspecting this man of heading up some kind of criminal ring rightly put me on edge.

Charlie was all business as he crossed his arms in front of his chest. "What do you need, Mr. Swanson?"

"I can't find my boy," the man said, getting straight to the point.

"You can't find Anton?" I repeated, the hairs on the back of my neck standing up.

The man nodded again.

What did he mean that he couldn't find Anton? Sure, The Rose was a sweeping estate, but by this time of night, Anton should have been sound asleep in his room. I said as much.

"I checked there, ma'am. He didn't answer his door or the phone in his room."

Flashbacks from this past summer of a missing man later found dead ran through my mind, but I pushed them away. The past did not repeat itself, not like that. Maybe Anton had gone to find Lacy.

Maybe he'd gone for a walk in the cold air, needing to clear his mind. Maybe he was actually still in his room and just didn't want to talk to his dad.

"I shouldn't be bothering you with something this small, you being the sheriff and all," Michael said. "But this isn't like my son. "

"What isn't like your son?" Charlie asked, seeming as unsure as I was about this man's reliability when it came to knowing his son.

The man gestured inside the room. "You mind if I come inside and explain?"

Charlie hesitated a moment. I gave him a slight nod to let him know that, except for the holster on his hip, I wasn't afraid of this guy. Still, Charlie kept his body edged between us as he allowed Anton's father to step across the threshold and toward the only chair in the room.

The man sat down hard but perched forward, his elbows on his knees as he explained the last time he'd seen his son.

"After I left Todd Anderson's room..." Mr. Swanson cleared his throat as if he had difficulty saying the young man's name, "well, I did find Anton in his room. We decided to have one more glass of brandy, man to man." Michael's gruff demeanor slipped and a confused scowl settled across his brow. "We were talking about some business issues—you know, back at the ranch."

"What kind of business issues?" Charlie asked, which was good thinking. Perhaps we could kill two birds with one stone: find out what Mr. Swanson really wanted from us, and what he'd gotten his family mixed up in.

The older man swallowed and stroked his beard for a few seconds. This was a calculating man, one who chose each word deliberately. That along with the fact that he'd come to the sheriff for help spoke volumes. Mr. Swanson was obviously used to being able to solve his own problems, but he also knew where to go when he was at a loss.

"I'll just say that we've had a bit of a hiccup moving some stuff."

"What kind of product?" I stepped forward, inserting myself into the conversation even as Charlie shot me a look.

Michael Swanson's gaze went to me, running down the length of my dress, though his gaze seemed more critical than admiring. He didn't want to tell us anything else, I could see.

"I only ask because Lacy said that your town is basically a massive cattle ranch," I clarified.

Charlie put a hand out as if to silence me. He didn't want me engaging in conversation with this man, but I was fairly certain that the elder Mr. Swanson wasn't the kind to pull a gun on a lady. On another man, sure, but not on me. Not tonight.

"We've been expanding," Michael said simply. "I was hoping Anton might be able to step in and help us move things along this weekend."

"Doesn't seem like the most opportune timing," I said innocently, tilting my head as if I was simply a confused little woman. "You know, with it being his wedding," I added, in case the man had forgotten why he was actually here this weekend. "In fact"—I lowered my voice, but my tone was steady—"your wife, Patty, also seems to have an ulterior motive for coming here this weekend. One that has nothing to do with Anton marrying Lacy."

Michael stared into my eyes. "I can't answer for my wife's behavior, and I don't care who Anton marries, as long as he comes back home to work when the ceremony ends."

The image of Anton dragging an angry Lacy across state lines came to mind, and I shot Mr. Swanson an angry look. "Anton and Lacy are starting a new life together, one that has nothing to do with the activity your family is involved in."

Charlie huffed out a quick breath as if someone had punched him in the gut.

Michael's eyes flickered to Charlie as if to ask why he wasn't keeping his woman quiet.

Charlie ignored the unasked question, saying instead, "I'm still not sure exactly what you need from me at this late hour, Mr. Swanson."

The man inhaled and studied the floor for a long moment. There were obviously many things he wasn't saying and he was measuring what to reveal.

"Listen, my son and I went back to the Billiards Room to talk business," Michael continued, glancing at me as if waiting for me to interrupt. I crossed my arms and let him keep talking. "A few minutes later he excused himself to go to the restroom. I waited for a couple minutes, then five, then ten, then a half-hour before realizing Anton wasn't coming back." Michael's eyebrows dipped slightly. "I didn't mean to run him off, so I called him, went to his room. Hell, I even went to find his mother again. I got an earful about how she hadn't seen him or that damn priest that she brought with her this weekend."

The vitriol in his tone as he said the last few words was enough to concern both me and Charlie if we hadn't been on guard already.

I mentally scanned The Rose, thinking of the place where Anton was most likely to go. Then I realized that when we'd arrived back at our guest suite, I hadn't gone inside. Instead, I'd followed Charlie back to his room. Of course, Anton had been in there, waiting for Lacy.

Not that I would say this out loud, but I was 99 per cent sure where Anton was right now; and I was equally certain that I wasn't about to tell his father where to find him.

NINETEEN

It took a few more minutes and a promise to look for Anton and call Mr. Swanson immediately if we found him, in order to get the older man to leave Charlie's room.

As soon as the door shut behind him and the sound of footsteps echoed down the hall, I turned to Charlie, who caught the expression on my face.

"What are you thinking?"

"Anton's fine. He's with Lacy, has to be." As I said the words, I started toward the door, certain of where I was headed next, although unsure of what I would say when I got there. Would I need to convince Anton that his family's business—likely criminal business—wasn't his responsibility? Would I need to reassure him that he could have a life separate from them? I hoped not. If Anton wasn't the kind of man who could see that truth for himself, then he didn't need to be marrying my friend.

"I'm coming with you," Charlie said. I could see that he didn't want me wandering the halls of The Rose alone at this hour.

A minute later, with the door locked, Charlie trailed behind me, glancing back and forth over his shoulder to make sure no one was following us as we made our way to the opposite wing of the estate and up a flight of stairs.

"Mr. Swanson didn't seem that dangerous. Grumpy, but not terrifying," I said, though I kept my words to a whisper.

"The worst criminals never do," Charlie answered.

I thought back to the ones I'd met over the past few months. They were everyday people, people who seemed reasonable and friendly enough before planning—or actually committing—murder. Thankfully, no one had died tonight, but plenty had gone wrong and plenty reeked of suspicion. Patty Swanson, the priest, Bella Rivera, and now Anton's father—all of them seemed capable of something nefarious, if not downright illegal.

When I reached the guest suite that Lacy and I were sharing, I knocked lightly, not wanting to just walk in on whatever might be going on inside. No one responded, so after trying one more time and getting nothing, Charlie motioned for me to use my key and then stepped in front of me so he could enter the room first.

We walked in to find the room empty and the windowed door to the balcony open. I wrapped my arms around myself and hurried toward the cold night air—just in time to see a gun pointed straight at me.

"Oh my God. What the hell are you doing?" I screamed as I stared down the short barrel of the pistol that Lacy held.

She lowered it immediately, muttering curses under her breath. "I thought... I was afraid you were someone else," Lacy said, obviously flustered as she practically shoved the gun into my hands and moved toward me, shivering in her silk pajamas.

"Like who?" I asked, as I passed the gun to Charlie. Within seconds, he'd disarmed the weapon. I suddenly understood the fear he'd felt when he'd entered Todd Anderson's room earlier this evening to find Mr. Swanson with a gun held high.

"Oh my goodness," Lacy said, moving toward the gas fireplace. "I don't know what I'm doing anymore." As she grabbed the remote from the mantel, I noticed that her hands were shaking.

I went and put an arm around her shoulders, pulling her close.

"It's like I need a *Bride's Guide to Happiness and Homicide* just to get through this weekend," Lacy said, her voice shaking.

Then, she stared at me. "A gun, Dakota. I was holding a *gun*. I've never done that before."

"It's okay, you're safe," I said softly, before pulling back and meeting her gaze. "But where in the world did you get a weapon?" I thought of Bella's pink bag of deadly tricks. Surely Lacy hadn't confiscated it from there?

Lacy huffed out a long breath and her shoulders shivered one more time as she moved closer to the fireplace, stretching her hands toward the warmth. "Anton gave it to me," she admitted quietly.

"What is it with his family and guns?" I asked, as Charlie closed the door to the balcony, keeping more chill from stealing into the room.

"Anton was here tonight when I got back."

I nodded, knowing I'd been right.

"He gave it to me then... just in case," Lacy continued. "I didn't want it, told him I'd never even fired a gun, but he said his dad had been blabbering on about something going down this weekend and he would feel better if I kept this in the room."

Anton must've come straight here from the Billiards Room, where he and his father had been "talking business." His first thought had been of Lacy. I was glad for that at least.

"Do you know where Anton went after he left you here?" I asked. "With a loaded gun," I added.

"I assumed he went back to his room." Lacy considered. "But actually, I have no idea. He said he only came here to make sure I was safe."

"Did Anton give you anything else?"

Lacy thought for a moment and then went to the end table between our queen beds and picked up a stack of pamphlets. "He left these. Said the last thing his dad needed was an invitation."

I came to her side, took one of the pamphlets from her hand, and turned on the nearest lamp.

Words showcasing the Virginia Museum of Fine Arts—the same museum I'd seen a link to moments earlier—were splayed across the front in tall, blockish font, each letter a different color. Inside was information on their permanent exhibits: a mixture of Native American, African American, and Asian, as well as modern and contemporary art. There were several pictures of the art as well, including one that looked very familiar. I held it close to my face, studying the image: a winter road with two travelers set against a dusky sky. I'd seen a similar one before—here at The Rose. I was sure.

I closed my eyes, mentally traveling the rooms that I'd been trying to get to know since discovering I was half-owner of the place.

"You all right?" Charlie asked.

I put up a finger and told him to hush for a minute. I went floor by floor, room by room. My eyes popped open. I knew where we needed to go.

"Come with me," I said, hurrying to the door with one of the pamphlets in my hand. "And Charlie, bring the gun."

Lacy's and Charlie's expressions were hesitant, but they'd both learned that when I was on a mission, I would not be thwarted.

We made our way past other guest rooms, down dark hallways, and down a flight of stairs to the Salon, where I'd found Bella earlier that evening. The lights were dimmed to a low yellow glow at this time of night, so when we entered, I told them to be careful around the overturned Christmas tree and the glass ornaments on the floor. Still, I heard the crunching of glass behind me as they followed me.

I headed straight toward Lacy's tulle and satin wedding dress, pulling the swath of fabric I'd found earlier that evening from my pocket.

"Help me move the dress," I told Lacy and Charlie: the train was too long for one person to do it properly on their own.

"Are you sure?" Lacy asked. "Aunt DeeDee's friend is fixing it tomorrow. We don't want to mess it up even more."

I nodded, even though I wasn't sure of anything at this late hour. Still, I was fairly confident the dress was covering something important on the wall.

With a bit of hefting and tugging, we transported the bridal apparel from hangers to couch without further damage. And as soon as the wall was visible, we saw the real crime that had been committed here: An ornate gold frame hung on the wall, empty.

Someone had stolen a piece of art from The Rose. My guess was that this someone was none other than Bella Rivera, and I'd unwittingly caught her in the act much earlier this evening.

I stepped forward, inspecting the frame and motioning for Charlie to shine a light on the back of the frame until we could see the heavy-duty nails on the wall. Sure enough, at the edges on the back of the frame was evidence that someone had hastily cut the fabric directly from it, leaving bits of canvas behind.

"But why would someone steal something from here?" Lacy asked, as the three of us stood staring at the empty frame.

"Two hundred and fifty thousand dollars," I murmured, trying to think of any other possible reason she would've taken it.

"Wait. What?"

I handed Lacy the pamphlet. "It looked a lot like the painting in this."

Lacy squinted at the description in the painting. "*Snow at Argenteuil* by Claude Monet," she read. "But surely The Rose didn't have a Monet."

"I highly doubt it, but we do have art by Anna Perry, winner of the second Rose Palace Pageant. Charlie and I looked her up, and her pieces are worth a decent amount."

"We could ask Savilla about the painting," Lacy suggested.

Charlie checked his watch. "Except that it's 4 a.m."

"Which is why I'm about to fall onto that fainting couch and sleep for days," Lacy said, as she fell back onto the settee.

I felt her pain. I was so tired that I could barely think straight.

As I was contemplating what to do next, Anton suddenly rushed into the room, looking over his shoulder as if someone might be hot on his trail.

When Lacy saw him, she burst into tears.

Her reaction jarred me. My friend, who rarely cried, was suddenly sobbing. In fact, I'd only seen her this way two other times in my life: once at Momma's funeral and once when her high school boyfriend had threatened to end his own life. Tonight was nowhere near that magnitude of emotion, but I supposed this entire weekend was now a loss of sorts.

Lacy had planned her wedding from the time we were six years old, asking her mother to buy her the summer bridal magazine at the grocery checkout each May. She would cut out veils and dresses, rearranging them and drawing herself wearing them. It was her first foray into fashion, and it fueled her love of planning, which had served her well as a grown-up. My heart sank as I realized how much Lacy was losing this weekend, despite my best attempts to help hold things together for her.

As Anton took his bride-to-be in his arms, Charlie darted to the door and looked both ways down the hall, his hand on the holster. When he saw that no one was following Anton, he turned to him. "Who were you running from?"

"I don't know, but someone was following me when I went back to check on Lacy. I think it was the priest," Anton answered.

Anton held Lacy close, letting her cry against him.

"I looked him up," I said. "I have no idea why your mother is saying Todd Anderson is a member of the clergy, as I'm positive he's not."

He hung his head for a moment, processing the information. "That makes sense. She wanted him here this weekend, and she needed to make him look legit. My mother would be embarrassed to bring a random man years younger than her to my wedding, but as a church-going lady, she would feel better about a man of the cloth. Plus, if he did the ceremony, we couldn't ignore him. It would guarantee he'd be part of the wedding in a big way." Anton raised his eyes to the ceiling, exhaled, and turned to Lacy. "After I left you, I went go find my mother, to make sure nothing shady was going down this weekend, and then Todd—not a priest—showed up to her room just as I was leaving. I'm afraid he overheard us. He didn't look happy, and I could swear that I heard footsteps following me down the hall. That's why I raced in here."

I could see that Anton was relieved to have found us inside the room.

"What did your mom say?" Lacy asked, swiping at any mascara under her eyes as she returned to what mattered even more than the priest stalking Anton. "*Is there something bad happening during our wedding weekend?*"

When Anton hesitated, Lacy pulled away, eyes narrowing at him. They were rimmed with sleeplessness and her cheeks appeared sunken in the lamp light. It had been a long night, and it didn't seem like it would get easier anytime soon.

"Anton," Lacy said, sniffing back further tears and composing herself as he looked at her, shame in his eyes. "I need to know what's happening. For me, it may..." she paused to consider her words before taking a deep breath and continuing, "it may affect what happens with us this weekend."

Anton met her plaintive gaze, concern etched in the lines of his face. "Okay, but first, you've got to believe that my family and their business have nothing to do with me. I swear. Getting away from them was a definite perk when I decided to move to Aubergine."

Lacy's eyebrows dipped into a concerned V. "I thought you moved here because you wanted to be with me."

"I did." Anton sighed heavily. "I'm just saying that leaving them behind was a good thing too."

Lacy swallowed back her frustration. "I hear you, but you still haven't answered my question. What is your family planning this weekend?"

When Anton still seemed reluctant to speak, Charlie stepped forward. "Anton, it would be really good if you could tell us what you know."

Anton closed his eyes for a few seconds before attempting to wipe away the fatigue. Then he lifted his head and met Lacy's eyes first.

"I told you when we met that my family have been cattle ranchers for a hundred years, and even before that they were cowboys and ranch hands. At least that's what I was raised to believe. What I suspected but didn't actually know much about until tonight was about the side business they've been running for years now."

As he said the words, I imagined the various members of his family and friends, including Bella Rivera, trading in their lassos for box cutters.

"It's not what you're thinking," Anton said, looking from Lacy to me to Charlie before reconsidering. "Or maybe it is?" He shook his head, his expression one of betrayal and confusion. "Oh God, it could actually be really, really bad."

"Why don't you sit down?" Charlie suggested, motioning toward the low couch and wingback chairs arranged for cultural conversations—not late-night confessions.

Still, this small act of decency, of normalcy even, seemed to give Anton some kind of courage to finally tell us what he knew.

"My family traffics in..." Anton paused as if he still didn't want to confess his family's sins.

As he took a deep breath, my mind tried to fill in the end of the sentence. *Guns? Drugs? People?* Then, it hit me: the pamphlets, Charlotte's conversation with Aunt DeeDee, Bella cutting out a painting and accidentally slashing Lacy's dress in the process.

"Your family traffics in art," I finished for Anton.

"That's right." Anton stared at me, surprised and a little relieved that he hadn't been forced to say it first.

Lacy inhaled a sharp breath at the confession, and she pointed to the empty frame on the far wall. "Your ex-girlfriend has already left her mark."

His eyes widened and Charlie stood and motioned for Anton to inspect the frame. Anton examined the edges where the thief had cut out the artwork. "Do you know what painting was hanging in here?"

"It was a snowscape of some kind," I answered, a bit embarrassed that I had no idea about the pieces in my own home. "Likely by an artist named Anna Perry."

"Was it an Impressionist piece?" Anton asked, as if he expected as much.

"I think so." I fished the pamphlet from my pocket and showed him the Monet painting inside. "It looked similar to this one."

"That's their specialty." Anton inhaled and let out a steadying breath. He was realizing something—or confirming something he'd already known—in real time, and he needed a second to think. He placed his elbows on his knees and his hands in the form of a prayer as he made eye contact with each of us again.

"Look, tonight my father cornered me after the bachelor party. He laid out a few details for me about my family's business in the hopes that I would join them."

"What happened to good, old-fashioned ranching?" Lacy asked, her voice raised.

"For my entire childhood, all they talked about was the price per head being down," Anton answered. I assumed by that he meant price per head of cattle, which made sense coming from a rural community. "My father had been looking for another stream of income for years, and somehow—I still don't know how—he stumbled into this line of work. He trains and hires people to take paintings by minor artists, ones that won't be missed for a while, ones that bring in a decent amount of money without raising worldwide alarms."

I noticed the way Anton was trying to cage his words, using specific descriptions—*stumbled* instead of "embraced", *takes* instead of "steals", and classifying the artists as *minor*—to make his family's crimes sound less terrible.

"And my mother..." Anton swallowed. "Apparently, she also does some light art forgery of these minor artists."

"I thought your parents didn't get along?" I asked, recalling our earlier conversation.

He lifted a shoulder. "Marriage is complicated."

It certainly was.

"My dad seems to think this business will help make up for him cheating on her a few years ago." Anton let out a deep breath. "Anyway, stealing less important paintings allows us—or them—to stay under the radar of the FBI and other large agencies." He caught Charlie's eye before looking away quickly. "But because they move so many pieces so quickly, it's... well, it's become rather lucrative. They've even discussed"—Anton hesitated again—"expanding their operations outside the U.S."

"Are you involved in this on any level?" Charlie asked. He too had obviously noticed the way Anton was couching his words.

"No, I swear that I'm not a part of this." Anton looked Charlie directly in the eye, his gaze pleading. "When I left Swanson, I knew that my father was building a special storage facility for art, and I knew that they were having a lot of closed-door family meetings that I avoided. Big shipments were coming in from around the country, and suddenly my father had plenty of money to modernize the ranch, to renovate our home—to see other women. I knew something wasn't right, but it was easier to ignore it all, to run away. Maybe I was in denial..." Anton shook his head at his self-imposed ignorance. Then, he looked straight at Lacy. "I admit that I should've taken a closer look at what they were doing. I should've raised a red flag, but I swear I didn't know the extent of their"—he struggled against the next word—"crimes. My father told me an hour ago that he wants me to come home and join him. He said that he's been waiting to ask me until he has everything in place." Anton swallowed hard. "Apparently, they've brought in ten million in the past two years and think they can double that in the next two."

Again, Lacy looked wounded, and I understood why. Though Anton may not have known the ins and outs of the business, he'd known something was awry. He should've shared that much at least.

"I'm sorry," he said, reaching out his hand and covering hers. "I was never planning to join them, so I didn't think it mattered for us." He blinked and it suddenly sounded as if he might cry. "And I'm certainly not joining them now. Obviously. God, I'm even outing them in front of a sheriff."

For the first time I noticed that Anton's expression was more than desperate: He was torn about doing the right thing when it meant betraying his family; he was also concerned that Lacy believe him at all costs.

Anton held her hand tightly. "Being with you is not an escape plan, but it has allowed me to imagine a life completely separate from my family. While I've been gone—maybe even before I left—they carved out this destiny for me, one that I do not want to fit inside."

Charlie cleared his throat, interrupting the moment between Lacy and Anton. "I'd like to get an official statement from you." His tone of voice had shifted, his words direct and his gaze steady as he turned to me. "I assume you'll be pressing charges about the stolen painting, and I'll need to bring in the woman you found in here."

Lacy's eye caught mine. There was no way I could press charges against anyone—particularly Anton's family—during her wedding.

"I'll need to discuss it with Savilla," I said, buying myself time.

Charlie narrowed his gaze as he studied me. He didn't like my response, but it was all he was getting for now.

"It's just..." I let the sentence linger as I considered Lacy above all. "Can't all of this wait until after the wedding?"

"It's much easier to deal with people when they are still here in town," Charlie answered, in a tone that seemed to question whether I'd actually lost my mind.

Anton's head swiveled between the two of us as he kept his hand on Lacy's. "Look, I know I've told you a lot about my family tonight, but I do think you need to wait on pressing any charges."

Charlie lifted his chin. "Why?"

It was a simple question—and a fair one. After all, Anton had just revealed years of crimes his family had been committing. He'd offered no proof, except for the missing painting in this very room, but presumably finding that proof wouldn't be hard to do.

"Because something else is going down this weekend, and I'm afraid it's worse than theft." Anton bit his lip before speaking again. "I'm afraid it's murder."

TWENTY

The three of us sat stunned for a long moment.

"Murder?" I finally repeated. Then the questions came fast. "Who? When? How? Why?"

Anton shook his head. "I don't know the details, but my mother... she said that she thinks someone on the inside is working against us— God, I swear, I mean against *them*—this weekend." He ran a hand through his hair, visibly upset. "She said that one of the primary buyers on the black market sent her some kind of warning about a person in our family's organization offering a piece at a discount to work directly with them, said something about taking down the Swansons from the inside this weekend. The buyer didn't like the idea, thought something sounded fishy, so he contacted my mother."

I tried to wrap my mind around this claim. Someone inside the Swansons' art heist business was trying to break off, to do their own thing, to take money for themselves.

Anton continued to grip Lacy's hand as he spoke. *Buyer, black market, warning, taking down*—these were not the words I'd expected to hear this weekend.

"If we're dealing with the black market, does that we are in danger?" I asked.

Anton simply stared at me before swallowing hard and answering, "I assume anyone who gets in the way of the person who wants to sell the painting could be considered a problem." He took a deep breath and tried to collect his thoughts.

"Do you know exactly who here this weekend is involved in your family's business?" Charlie asked.

Anton lifted his shoulder. "They haven't given me names, but I would suspect all of them."

"I think I can narrow it down," I said, beginning to list people on my fingers. "We know Bella Rivera took a painting from this very room, and we strongly suspect that the priest isn't actually a priest. He also somehow knows Will Hurt. Anton's mother and father are the ringleaders, but Charlotte Swanson seems to have some kind of heavy sway and she seems to know Will too—not to mention that Myrtis loves to gossip about the vagaries of the family business." I lifted my hands. "That's at least seven people who are likely involved."

"Sounds like you know my family better than I ever have." Anton stared at me, dumbfounded. "Speaking of which... I forgot about this." He pulled out his phone, opened his camera, and passed it to Charlie.

Looking over his shoulder, I could see photos of a series of scrawled messages on torn paper, all in the same handwriting.

Take the Perry during the festivities, but watch your back.

Keep an eye on the sheriff. He'll be around.

The gun is in your bag. Wait until the right time.

I'll give the cue during the ceremony.

When you hear from me, pull the trigger.

"Who wrote these?" I asked.

"Mother found them in her boyfriend's... ugh, I hate using that word," Anton said, interrupting himself before regaining his footing. "They were in Todd Anderson's things. She found them when she was in his room waiting for him to finish getting ready."

I took the phone and studied the images myself.

"The Mob, the mafia, all of them at one time or another have been involved in art theft," Charlie told us. "Sometimes it's one major piece—they get in, they get out. Other times, it's like an entire arm of their crime ring. Because of the supplies, planning, and coordination necessary for this kind of theft—and later, the sale of such pieces—you often need connections that run deep. Organized crime syndicates can provide those." He paused. "Not that I think anyone here's mobbed up," he added quickly. "Just saying—it takes serious resources."

I handed Anton his phone. "Is your family part of the Mob?"

"I don't think so, but then they are full of surprises this weekend." Anton hung his head, ashamed.

It was as if the wedding festivities had been a kind of pressure cooker for the Swanson family, and the situation had just happened to bring out the very worst in them. It was probably a stretch, but it almost felt like someone on the inside was moving between criminal worlds—between the Swansons' small-town, under-the-radar thieving, and the big boys who were considerably more dangerous.

"Can you text me the images of those notes?" Charlie asked. "And thank you for coming to me with all of this."

"I didn't have much choice." Anton sighed. "Not that I wouldn't have anyway, but now that I've brought all of this mess here, I just want to make sure Lacy—and everyone else—is safe."

I caught Charlie's eye. "You can't move forward with questioning until we know more, right? It could interfere with possibly catching the bigger criminal—whoever is sending these notes, and directing everything behind the scenes."

"It could also put people in unnecessary danger," Charlie said, as he checked his watch. "We've got another thirty-four hours or so until the ceremony, which isn't much time for us to investigate, but it will be enough time to contact the FBI and get them out here."

"No. Please," Anton said, his eyes plaintive.

"We're talking about a sophisticated crime ring," Charlie said. "I can't just overlook that."

Anton beat a rapid staccato against his leg and bit his lip as he thought. "Give us that thirty-four hours. Then you can have them swarm the headquarters back in Texas, and I'll tell the FBI everything I know. They won't find much evidence at The Rose anyway."

"Impossible," Charlie responded, his voice firm. "Someone appears to be planning a shoot-out at your wedding. We need to act now."

"Just wait," Anton said, putting out a hand as he began to pace, putting pieces together. "If you move in now, we will be letting a violent member of my very own family slink away into the shadows."

I caught on to Anton's logic. He made a good point.

"If we wait until the ceremony," Anton added, "then we'll have a controlled environment where we can catch the killer in the act."

I paused, studying Anton and then Charlie, who was listening carefully. "Anton's right. If we move in too early, the real murderer will likely escape."

Charlie considered the idea. "I'm still making a call, but yeah, I can direct them to Swanson instead of here."

Anton gave a curt nod as his jaw clenched. I couldn't tell if he was trying to protect himself, his family, or Lacy. Probably all of the above.

"So what do we do here in the meantime?" Lacy asked, clearly horrified by the idea of doing nothing.

"Act normally," Charlie answered.

"If that's even possible," I clarified. After all, we weren't professionals at catching criminals—and I'd have preferred that neither my friend nor I were a sitting duck.

"We all need to sleep in order to think straight," Charlie said. "Why don't you three go back to your rooms, try to rest, and let me consult with the professionals about next steps? I have a feeling that not much else will happen until the actual day of the wedding."

It was early Saturday morning now. Even if we managed to get in five or six hours of sleep, we'd be waking around noon. Surely by then, Charlie would have some answers. Maybe we would figure out how Will Hurt was involved in this mess. Maybe we would find out who'd been sending notes to the priest—and what exactly this person wanted him to do.

As to that, I really hoped it was only stealing a piece of art, and not murdering in cold blood.

It was a long walk back to our rooms, and when Lacy and I arrived at the door to our guest suite, Charlie entered first, hand on his holster while he scoured the space, ensuring that no one was inside. Once he was certain the room was clear, he planted a kiss on my forehead and gave me a look that said he would do every-thing possible to make this all go away as soon as possible.

I knew he wouldn't sleep and that thought was comforting, even as I was concerned for him.

Anton considered staying behind with us, but Charlie reminded him that we needed to operate as normally as possible.

"That's the safest way to behave right now," Charlie reminded us.

"As if none of this is happening?" Lacy asked, for clarification.

"Unfortunately, yes." Charlie met her eyes. "The less you know, the safer you are. Any criminal activity usually stays among criminals—unless bystanders get in the way."

Lacy obviously didn't like the answer, but she trusted Charlie. I did too.

The two men left us alone. Almost immediately, we crawled under the comforters in our separate beds, facing each other, our expressions mirrors of fear and uncertainty.

"My wedding wasn't supposed to go like this," Lacy whispered into the room, low-lit by the rising sunbeams streaming through the windows.

"I know," I whispered back.

As the moon completely faded from the sky and the sun rose on the horizon, we fell into oblivion for a few blessed hours.

TWENTY-ONE

I slept like the dead and, when I woke, I was surprised to find that Saturday was non-eventful, after all of the chaos and confusion from last night.

I even managed an afternoon horse ride to the backside of the property, which looked much as it had this past summer except for the shedding trees and the lack of wildflowers around the gate. As I clicked and shifted my weight to signal that we would be trotting around the perimeter of the original homestead, I allowed myself to think about anything other than the wedding, and immediately my mind turned to the decision I had to make about where I would live in just a few months. San Diego, Aubergine, or elsewhere.

Moving to the West Coast would allow me to work with a greater variety of animals, including those being cared for at the famous San Diego Zoo. I would learn complicated procedures, and I would become one of the few vets in the country with these specialties. Even after San Diego, I would be called all over the country, getting the opportunity to travel. It was not an opportunity to be shrugged off.

On the other hand, thanks to my newly acquired status as heiress, I had enough money—and, according to Savilla, a built-in location in the Carriage House at The Rose—to set up a practice in these mountains I loved.

I gazed up at those high peaks, cutting into the gray sky. The morning fog that created the blue tinges for which these mountains were named had already melted away, and in the bleak start of a snowless winter, the leaves were more rust-red and murky brown after a long autumn of color. The thin branches on the periphery of my vision appeared ready to snap with the slightest tug. Even still, this place felt like it belonged to me, like I could tuck the panorama in the recesses of my mind, returning here from anywhere in an instant.

I spotted two Carolina chickadees, their black-and-white faces distinct against the evergreen. One tiptoed to the edge of the branch and angled itself to hang upside down as it went after its meal. The pair reminded me of my genetic connection to a creature with the courage to step onto the stage of life and take a chance. Savilla, the sister I never knew I wanted, had become a fixture of my day, and now just thinking about her lugging Baby Ollie around from venue to venue made me smile. A year ago, I would've never guessed that she would be part of my consideration for returning home.

The light was already fading, and I patted my horse's neck before tugging on the reins to send us back in the direction of The Rose—which was weirdly taking on the designation of "home" in my mind.

I went to the rehearsal dinner, where, despite the revelations of last night, I sensed that temperaments and behaviors might be calming. Sure, Anton's family would eventually need to account for their misdeeds, but perhaps the rest of the weekend would pass uneventfully.

. . .

I had tried to keep a positive state of mind throughout the evening, which was part of the reason it was so jarring to stand in the holly bushes, staring down at the body of Todd Anderson. Based on the notes we'd read in the Salon last night, Todd was supposed to be the one committing murder—not that anyone wanted that either. Still, he wasn't supposed to be a victim, and my boyfriend wasn't supposed to be a suspect.

I stared at Charlie wide-eyed as I held up the thin strip of paper with the words *blame Charlie* scribbled on them. "What does this note mean?"

The top edge was torn along its length, as if it had been ripped out of a jotter.

The top edge was torn along its length as if it had been ripped out. I recognized the handwriting from the short missives we'd seen last night on Anton's phone.

Charlie put up both hands. "I have no idea. I'd never even met the priest before this weekend."

I knew he was telling the truth. None of us knew the man, except for those who'd traveled from Swanson, Texas, to Aubergine, Virginia, for the wedding of the century.

I tried a different tack, blinking against the water at the corners of my eyes that was on the verge of freezing. "Any ideas about who might've been sneaking onto the property?"

"I didn't find anyone or any sign of breaking and entering."

I studied him for a few seconds longer. This was Charlie, my Charlie, as I'd come to think of him in the past month as our relationship had shifted.

Though I couldn't quite pinpoint the exact moment things had changed between us, I was pretty sure it had something to do with Thanksgiving Day, when he'd spent the entire afternoon in the kitchen with Aunt DeeDee, slicing and boiling and mashing pota-toes to make his mother's recipe for garlic ranch twice-baked pota-toes. Then, he'd asked my aunt to teach him how to mix and roll out the perfect pie crust. Savilla and I had been in and out of the kitchen, running to the store to pick up an ingredient they'd forgotten, hurrying to take out the overflowing trash can, and being on standby to wash mixing bowls they would need for the next recipe.

I could tell that Aunt DeeDee was loving the day as much as Charlie, whose kitchen prowess wasn't exactly a surprise—he'd effortlessly fixed many a dinner for us when he'd traveled back and forth for visits—and definitely something I appreciated about him.

In the past, I'd invited guys home to meet Aunt DeeDee and Momma, but always informally and never for a special occasion. It had felt like second nature to extend the Thanksgiving dinner invite to Charlie though, especially since his parents were basking in their retirement years and traveling for the holiday.

As the four of us had sat around the table that evening, laughing and enjoying the food, I'd looked over at my boyfriend and suddenly realized how much Momma would've liked him, would've appreciated the way he blended so easily into our family, like a jigsaw puzzle piece that fit just right. That night, I'd had the feeling that I would be happy spending the rest of my holidays sitting across the table from Charlie Strong.

Now, on this cold winter night with a dead man at my feet and my sheriff boyfriend the most obvious suspect, I forced myself to take the lead, steeling myself for the reality that Charlie might be taken off the case at any moment.

I went into go-mode, dividing up duties. I sent Savilla inside to find a sheet to cover the body from further snowfall, and I told Charlie to call Deputy Wright to the scene while I phoned for an ambulance—a strange task when I knew that the person was already dead.

"911, what's your emergency?"

"Um, I found a body," I said into the phone.

The responder didn't miss a beat. "What's your location?"

"The Rose Palace, front of the house." I didn't have to explain. In a map search, the estate came up right away as both a business and a residence; besides, anyone within a hundred miles knew about our house.

"A team is on the way," the responder said, her voice steady. "Is the person conscious?"

"No," I breathed into the phone.

"Male or female?"

"A man," I clarified, before beginning to ramble. "He is—or was—supposed to officiate my friend's wedding. I was picking up a case of wine for the rehearsal dinner and found him in the bushes. He was shot and then he fell or—"

I almost said "was pushed", though I knew that couldn't be the case because Charlie was the only one who'd for sure been in the room with him. Charlie didn't push him. That was impossible.

I held the note in my hand, the one that said those terrible two words: *blame Charlie*. But blame him for what? Charlie was the one who solved crimes, not committed them. I also knew that I didn't need to explain all of this to the emergency responder, but I couldn't help myself. The words were pouring out like a rushing stream.

"My boyfriend is here at the house. He's the sheriff, and he heard the man in his room and went inside, but please don't think that he had anything to do with..." My mind trailed off, not quite knowing where to go from there. It wasn't like the responder was going to arrest the local sheriff.

"What's your name?" the woman on the other end of the line asked me, trying to bring me back to some semblance of rational thinking.

"Dakota," I answered. "Dakota Green."

"All right, Dakota. I'm going to stay on the call with you until the ambulance arrives. Don't go anywhere, okay?"

Tears sprang to my eyes and the back of my throat clenched. I nodded, unable to speak.

"Are you still with me?"

I coughed back a cry. "I'm here."

"Good. You're doing a great job." The responder paused for a beat as if listening to the other end of a conversation. "The ambulance is about seven minutes away. You just stay near the body, but don't touch anything, okay?"

I didn't have the energy to explain that I'd already put my hands on Todd's throat to check the pulse, and I'd already rifled through his pockets. I supposed that the investigators would see as much, but at least I would have an explanation. Kind of.

Minutes passed, and I remained on the phone, occasionally letting the woman know I was still there and I wasn't further disturbing what was likely a crime scene.

Charlie had already hung up with Deputy Wright and was sitting on the stone steps, wearing an expression of disbelief at the situation in which he'd found himself. He didn't have to tell me that he knew how this looked. No one else had been in Todd's room when Charlie burst inside earlier and there was a note blaming Charlie for God knew what, both of which made my boyfriend appear guilty. Unless we found evidence of another person nearby or the actual gun that had seemingly killed the man with one shot, this didn't look good for Charlie.

"Is Jill on her way?" I asked, referring to his deputy, the second-in-command.

Charlie nodded but couldn't speak. Thankfully, he didn't have to because just then the medics arrived, immediately springing into action. They prepared to resuscitate, but as soon as they lifted the sheet Savilla had lain over the man, they knew it was too late. Still, the head medic and his team assessed the body for several minutes, examining the pupils, recording the skin color, and eventually determining that Reverend Todd Anderson was indeed dead. He estimated the time of death as very recent, perhaps a half-hour to an hour ago, which matched my arrival on the scene, as well as Charlie's account. It took all of ten minutes, and we looked on, wishing they could do something to revive the man.

"How did you find him?" the head medic finally asked Savilla, once they'd finished. She motioned for me to answer.

"I was going into the house when I spotted something in the bushes," I said. "It took me a second to realize it was... a body."

"He was shot and then fell from the balcony," Charlie said, pointing to Todd's room. The railing was still intact. "I was in his room... after."

The medic looked up and nodded once. "Law enforcement will be up there soon, I'm sure." His eyes flitted back to Charlie, who was well known around these parts. The man seemed confused as to why Charlie wasn't already on the case, but he didn't ask any further questions.

When Jill arrived, she brushed past me, immediately pulling Charlie aside to question him.

I wanted to listen, but I knew it was more important that I reach out to Lacy to let her know what was happening—as gently as possible. I considered calling her directly but then thought of an alternative. I could let Aunt DeeDee know, and she could relay the news in person at the end of the rehearsal dinner, before everyone headed back to The Rose. This weekend had been anxiety-inducing enough for Lacy. She didn't need a call out of the blue saying that we wouldn't be returning with the wine because of a dead man.

The phone rang three times before Aunt DeeDee picked up on the other end. "Dakota, you okay?" Her voice was filled with worry, almost as if she had a sense of foreboding.

"I'm fine, or, maybe, I don't know," I said haltingly. The clatter of cups and plates and voices at the rehearsal dinner was coming over the line. "Can you go somewhere quiet for a second? I need to tell you something."

"Sure." A few moments later and the background noise had quieted as Aunt DeeDee came back on the line. "What's going on?"

I gave her a quick rundown of events: the dead priest, Charlie knocking down the door to his room, and a possible intruder at The Rose who was still yet to be found.

"Oh my Lord," Aunt DeeDee said. I could almost see her clutching her pearls. "And all of this with Lacy's wedding tomorrow."

She didn't have to remind me. The last twenty-four hours had been fraught, tainted particularly by the Texan side of the family. I hated that the commonality between everything was Anton, and I hated even more that a dead body was the end result. At this point, all I wanted for Lacy was whatever she wanted—to flee, to marry Anton in front of a justice of the peace, to pull the covers over her head and stay in bed until next New Year's.

"I know," I said to Aunt DeeDee now. "I'm calling you because I don't want Lacy to hear it second-hand, and I wanted someone that she trusts to be there with her when she gets the news. This will derail her entire wedding, so she needs to hear that, one way or another, it will be okay."

"I got you, doll." Aunt DeeDee inhaled as if steeling herself. "I can pull her and Anton aside privately and let them know what's happened."

I smiled despite the situation. Aunt DeeDee would be a calm and steady presence if nothing else. "Thanks."

"No problem, sweetheart." I thought she was going to hang up but then she said one last thing. "You just make sure to look after you—and your man."

"Charlie?" I asked.

"Unless you're two-timing him, that's the one. I saw him skedaddle out of the dinner about the time you ran off to the bathroom to have a good cry, and he seemed to have something heavy on his mind."

Aunt DeeDee's words of wisdom could seem at times clairvoyant—and she had been the one to suggest a fake séance to solve a murder a couple of months ago—but as far as I knew, she didn't actually have special powers.

I shook my head in wonder. Aunt DeeDee always noticed more than she let on.

"Sometimes even our best intentions come back to bite us in the rear end," Aunt DeeDee finished, the words cryptic enough for me to wonder if she was actually having the same concerns about Charlie's method of investigating as me—namely, that it could put him behind bars. "I'd best go relay the news to the intended. Talk soon, darlin'."

"Talk soon," I said, as the line went dead.

TWENTY-TWO

As another squad car pulled up, I made my way inside, hoping to catch my breath, but when I stepped into the vestibule, the deputy was scribbling frantically in her notebook as she questioned Charlie. I was concerned by the defeated expression on his face.

I started toward them, but as I approached, Deputy Jill Wright's eyes darted from Charlie to me. Two months ago, she'd shown signs of romantic interest in him, and while I'd been able to learn to trust Charlie enough not to let it bother me, I hadn't seen her in person since then—and I certainly hadn't expected her to be interrogating him, which was definitely happening here.

"Dakota arrived after Todd Anderson fell," Charlie said, angling his body as if I wasn't welcome in the conversation. He was always protecting me.

I burst in anyway, speaking with feigned confidence. "I was the first to examine the body."

Deputy Wright frowned at me and then added something to her notebook. Charlie had trained her well.

"Dakota had nothing to do with his death," Charlie insisted, as if this were up for debate.

"Of course I didn't," I said, confused. "But neither did you."

Jill took a deep breath as her eyes darted over the pages of notes she'd already made. "Charlie was the only one present when the man fell from the balcony, correct?"

"Well, yes, as far as I know, but he was searching the property for an intruder," I said, trying to keep my voice even. "He received a call from the security company—"

"It wasn't the security company," Jill said, interrupting me. "I just called and checked in with the system that monitors The Rose. They weren't the ones who contacted Charlie."

"Then who did?" And, I wondered, why would Charlie believe them? He was savvy and smart, experienced from his time as a law-enforcer. He wouldn't leave the rehearsal dinner to wander around The Rose close to nine at night without good reason.

"We don't know," Jill answered. "The number is untraceable so far—just ends with a disconnection notice."

"A prepaid phone." Charlie shook his head, eyebrows drawn close together. "I was stupid, distracted by the party."

"Had you been drinking?" Jill asked.

"That shouldn't matter," I countered. "He wasn't on duty."

Jill stared at me. "If he was drinking, then protocol would dictate that he forward any security issues to the station."

"I had one glass of wine." Charlie sighed. "But you're right. I should've done what I was trained to do: ask for credentials and call it into the station, especially since the call was to my personal phone. It was really stupid of me."

"One glass of wine?" I scoffed. "One drink did not interfere with your judgment."

All three of us knew that was true, but the lingering question between us was why Charlie hadn't followed directives. Had it been intentional? I couldn't believe that, so what else might've distracted him?

My eyes darted between Jill and Charlie, her in uniform and him in plain clothes.

"This doesn't look good," she told him. "You forced your way into his room, and your fingerprints are all over the crime scene."

"And he was staring down at me when I found the body," I added, feeling more and more defeated with every breath. I tried to regain my logical footing. "Even so, that makes Charlie a witness, not a suspect." The deputy didn't seem to agree with me, so I tried another direction. "There have to be security cameras; they'll show you that Charlie had nothing to do with any of this."

"There are no cameras," Jill said, more familiar with the ins and outs of this estate's security than me. "Savilla said that she hasn't had them installed indoors for privacy reasons, although she may change her mind after this."

I should've already known that. I was sure Savilla had sent it in one of her many updates about the goings-on at our family home, but I'd been so focused on finishing up my last semester and applying for that fellowship.

"You should be using your energy to figure out who called Charlie, not questioning him like he's some kind of criminal," I protested, turning to him as if I could show an example of the kind of work the deputy should be doing. "What did the security person sound like? What did they say?"

"It was a light voice. Soft. And they spoke quickly."

"A woman's voice?"

"I think so. It was hard to hear in the restaurant, and by the time I made my way outside, they'd hung up."

Charlie held up his phone for me to see his call log.

The time stamp matched with his account, and the caller was listed as Athena Alarms. I took out my phone and kept my eyes on Charlie's screen as I searched for the name of the company. Athena Alarms was indeed real and appeared to serve wealthy homes and profitable businesses "across the greater Richmond area." But then I noticed the phone number at the bottom under "Contact Us."

"It's one number different," I said. "See, there's a seven at the end of the actual phone number and a four at the end of the number that called you." I clicked on the "About Us" page and scanned the contents as well. "And it's Athena *Alarums* on the real company's website. I guess they wanted to sound old-timey."

"Someone found a real alarm company and pretended to be them… just to get me out to The Rose? But why?"

"Maybe they knew someone was after Todd? And they were hoping you could help?" I suggested before reconsidering. "Or maybe they were the killer and it gave them some kind of thrill to be so close to getting caught?"

"Are we done here, Matlock?" Jill asked, her tone wry.

I glanced at Charlie, and though I couldn't read his mind, I did have a strong suspicion based on his raised eyebrows that he was thinking along the same lines.

"Look, it gives me no pleasure to do this," Jill said.

I didn't believe her.

Charlie dropped into a nearby chair and rubbed his hands over his face. I couldn't help but notice how handsome he was in his button-down and khakis. When he'd met me at the rehearsal three hours ago, he'd smelled like citrus and cedar and he'd been so relaxed in that off-duty way of his. Now, his expression was tense and his hair a mess from nervously combing his fingers through it one too many times.

He caught my eye and he must've seen the worry in my face because he took my hand. "It'll be all right, Dakota. Jill is just doing her job."

He might have thought it would be all right, but I didn't have the same confidence. I didn't just need him to help get me through this weekend. I needed him—not Jill Wright—to help solve this case.

"Once Jill can determine that I didn't leave the dinner to come here and kill someone—and once the tech guy can confirm the caller—that should help." Charlie tried for a half-smile. "Besides, they can only keep me in temporary custody for up to forty-eight hours. I know the law."

"I'll say it again," Jill cut in. "I don't like doing any of this." She looked to the ground for a couple beats and pushed her shoulders back as if gathering her courage. "Will you let me question you without being arrested?" Jill looked hopefully at him, and I could imagine how hard this must be for both of them.

Charlie let out a long breath and nodded. Then, he stood, motioning for Jill to lead the way back outside to the waiting cop car. He knew what had to happen, so no handcuffs were necessary.

"Wait." I trailed behind them, my mind spinning fruitlessly with ways to keep him here with me.

As we walked outside, the medics were loading the body into the ambulance. I'd overheard them discussing the official time of Todd's death, so I assumed that the coroner had been notified. It all felt so final that it gave me pause once again.

Reverend Todd had not been a good man, certainly not a priest who should guide anyone's spiritual life, but he had been a person who didn't deserve to be murdered. My thoughts swarmed as I hurried to Charlie. He was nearing the police car, and the deputy looked to the sky as if she couldn't quite believe she was about to put her boss and former police partner in the back seat.

In a moment of surprising kindness, Jill took a step back to give us a minute. I didn't like her better for it, in part because I knew she was listening to us, but I would have taken any opportunity to get close to Charlie right then.

"What do I do?" I whispered as I leaned in, confused and probably still a bit in shock.

"Wait, watch, puzzle it out," Charlie said, brushing hair off my face. "The truth will come to light—and in forty-eight hours I'll be back at your side."

That wasn't good enough for me, and we both knew it.

He examined me with tenderness. "Please be careful. Don't do anything that could get you hurt."

I knew that he didn't want me involved in something that could be dangerous. It was too late though. I was involved. I was the maid of honor at a wedding weekend where a man was now dead. I was the girlfriend of the man who was willingly turning himself in for questioning. I was the half-heiress to the Rose Palace estate where the death had occurred. I was in it, for better or worse.

"Waiting isn't my forte. I'll figure this out." I planted a quick kiss on Charlie's lips. As I moved closer, his hand reached out and touched mine. He slid something into my palm before closing my fingers tightly around the object.

"Dakota, be careful who you trust," he said, before turning to Jill. "I'm ready."

I swiped at the tear slipping down my cheek, trying to stay strong and trying to distract myself from the thing that was biting into my skin. "We'll have you out in time for the wedding," I told Charlie, as if it was still on. "You gotta be my plus-one."

Charlie attempted a smile as he ducked his head and climbed into the back of the car.

I waved at him and then turned around and counted to thirty as the car drove around the bend in the driveway. Only then did I allow myself to slip my hand into my pocket and feel the object's edges.

I knew what it was immediately, but I had no idea where it had come from or why Charlie would be entrusting it to me.

My super-ethical, follow-the-rules-no-matter-what sheriff boyfriend had slipped me a key.

TWENTY-THREE

I stood outside, shivering in the snow and clenching the key that Charlie had slipped into my hand. I needed to find out what it actually opened, and the only place I could think to start was Todd's room, if I could get inside.

As I climbed the stairs to the fourth floor, I tried to still my rapidly beating heart, giving myself time to think through a good excuse to gain access to the space. Thankfully, I recognized the officer standing guard at the door. It was Keith Becker, a guy who had graduated a couple of years after me and joined the force straight out of high school.

"Hey, Keith," I said, trying to make my voice sound casual even though it was late, a man was dead, and my boyfriend had been taken into temporary custody. "The deputy asked me to take a look up here, to see if I noticed anything that seemed out of the ordinary." I swallowed hard. "I won't touch anything," I lied.

To his credit, Keith narrowed his eyes, unwilling to believe me just because I said so. Still, I had been involved in solving two recent investigations, which had given me clout in our town.

"You can call Jill, if you like," I said before quickly adding, "but she's probably busy since she's, you know, not here."

Oh Lord. I sounded ridiculous, and I suddenly wondered if

word had already gotten out that Charlie had been taken into the station.

"Just a second," Keith said, lifting his two-way radio to his ear before speaking to the person at the other end. "Deputy, Dakota Green is here. Says you want to take a look inside the guest room."

In the five seconds that he was silent, I thought about taking off at a sprint. I shouldn't have done this, shouldn't have snuck up here with the key in hand, shouldn't have lied. But then he put the radio on broadcast, and Deputy Jill Wright's voice came across loud and clear.

"You there, Dakota?"

I glanced at Keith uncertainly but leaned toward the receiver. "Yes... ma'am."

"All right. Officer Becker, let her in. She was the one who found the body, and she's been involved in the details of the wedding this weekend. Let her see if anything seems out of the ordinary," Jill said, startling me as much as the officer. "Dakota, you've got five minutes. But don't touch anything."

I rolled back my shoulders and tried to fix my face to make it look like I'd known this would be the deputy's response all along.

Keith moved out of the way so I could step across the threshold, taking in the place where the deceased, known as Reverend Todd Anderson, had been staying for the past twenty-four hours. Except, I noticed immediately, the bed was made, each corner tucked tightly—just like the staff did every time I stayed here—and the towels were still folded into the shape of swans and sitting squarely on his pillows, as they would be only upon arrival.

Unless he'd been expertly trained on bed-making just after his arrival, I was fairly certain that Todd hadn't actually slept here, which I supposed made sense, what with his close relationship to Anton's mother. I cringed at the idea of the two of them together and was glad that I didn't have time to dwell on that image.

Five minutes. The clock was ticking, and the officer was in the doorway, though thankfully with his back to me.

I had no idea what I was looking for—maybe a lockbox? Or a

safe? I started in the closet, where there were a couple of suits and one pair of men's dress shoes, the same ones that he'd fussed over in the Winter Garden when I'd broken a potted plant and dirt had sprayed on the suede. *He won't be needing those anymore*, I mused, before berating myself for the callous thought.

I went to the bathroom. On the counter was a grooming kit but nothing else. Inside were nail clippers, an electric shaver, and a toothbrush as well as a couple of expensive items—aftershave and cologne.

I didn't see any kind of strong box or safe that might require a small key like the one in my pocket, so I changed course, stepping back into the main room. Maybe I was looking for a journal—or maybe the key went to a traveling trunk of some kind. I searched under the bed and came up empty, so I scanned tabletops and dresser drawers for clues that might tell me something about the man who'd died.

On top of the dresser was a first aid kit that was already open. I read the contents on the outside and looked inside to see what might be missing. The ice pack was the only thing that no longer seemed to be in place, which made sense given that bruise from Charlie's knuckles last night. I shivered at the incident, which would've fallen under the category of minor assault—but which made all of this seem so much worse now. A fight that was a precursor to murder, perhaps.

I went to the bedside table, pulling my sleeves over my hands to avoid getting fingerprints on the handles of drawers. The only thing in the bedside table was a Bible, and I knew that Savilla hadn't placed it there.

"I don't want anyone who stays at The Rose to think we're trying to indoctrinize them," Savilla had told me. By that, I'd assumed she meant "indoctrinate" and "evangelize".

I picked up the Bible, and since I couldn't use my fingertips, I held it binding side up and shook it until two pieces of paper fell out. I bent to the floor, angling my body so my shadow didn't keep me from being able to read the writing.

The first page was a script for a wedding, starting with, "Dearly Beloved, we are gathered here today in the sight of God and man to witness the union..." Spotting something, I looked more closely at the top of the page. It had been printed from a website that used words in bold font across the top: **Become an Ordained Minister & Perform Weddings TODAY!** Two small electronic signatures were scrawled across the bottom: Todd Anderson's as the applicant and Patty Swanson's as the witness.

Charlie had been right in his assessment of this man's priesthood, and here was confirmation of what we'd both strongly suspected: Todd Anderson had planned to perform the ceremony with a quickie, online license, and Patty Swanson had known all about it. I was kind of relieved to have the proof because with his circumspect behavior this weekend, that was the only explanation that made sense.

No one questions an officiant's presence, so it was the perfect cover for what Todd was planning. Patty must've known her boyfriend wasn't really a priest, but this disguise would've worked in her best interests too—dating a minister could help silence gossip about their age difference. I could see Todd easily convincing Patty to go along with the idea—even if she didn't know all the reasons why he wanted to act like a priest this weekend.

I picked up the license with the nails of my forefinger and thumb and dropped it back into the Bible. Two things had fallen out of the book, so I looked around for the second sheet, turning on the light on my phone and shining it under the bed. A few seconds later I spotted a slender piece of paper with torn edges.

I wriggled my body to reach it, and as I read the contents, I instinctively reached for the slip of paper that I'd found in Todd Anderson's coat pocket. I held that scrap against this new find. Both slips of paper were part of the same thin page, the torn edges matching exactly, and now I could see the entirety of the short note.

I mumbled the words as I read them aloud: "Meet Big Mike with product, after ceremony on Sunday—if it goes wrong, blame

Charlie." The last two words had been scribbled at the bottom, almost as an afterthought.

My eyes narrowed as I read the message again, but I didn't have long to think about it because the voice of the officer standing guard outside the door rumbled through the room.

"Everything all right in here?" Keith called, putting his head through the doorway and spotting me on the ground.

I startled and sat upright. "Fine. I just dropped my, um, my earring... It fell out."

Keith frowned at me. "The others are about to be here to sweep for prints. Hope you didn't touch anything."

"I didn't." I stood, tucking the slips of paper in my back pocket as I attempted to lie easily. "Not much here, and I was super careful."

"Yeah, I don't think he was actually sleeping in here," Keith said, raising one eyebrow as if this piece of information, rather than the man's death, was the hot gossip. I supposed it was in Aubergine, where any indiscretion was either kept underground or, if it happened to make it out into the open, was analyzed at length over early coffee at the Morning Brew. It was one of the things I both loved and hated about my town.

I could only imagine what might happen if I told Keith that Charlie had slipped me a mysterious small key, and that in my back pocket were scraps from a note about a meet-up with Big Mike while Todd was supposed to be officiating a wedding—and instructing the reader to *blame Charlie* for something he surely didn't do.

TWENTY-FOUR

Charlie is in jail. Charlie is in jail. Charlie is in jail.

These words echoed in my mind, looping and tumbling over one another as I sat in my suite, staring down at the key in my hand. He'd given it to me because he'd thought it would somehow either help the investigation or clear his name—or both. I just had to figure out what it opened.

As I fell back on the bed and stared at the ceiling, imagining a variety of locks, Lacy threw open the door and rushed inside, straight in from the rehearsal dinner.

"Why weren't you answering your phone?" she demanded with a mixture of fear and anger, though I had no idea why she would be directing that at me.

I reached for my phone in my back pocket and held it up so she could see the "Do Not Disturb" light. "I turned off the ringer because we were supposed to be celebrating you and Anton tonight." I ran my finger and thumb across my eyes, trying to make them focus. "Are you angry with me?"

"Of course not, but I was scared to death." Lacy gripped her chest before heaving out a deep breath and sinking to the edge of the bed beside me. Now that she was here with me she seemed to be running out of steam quickly. "Tell me everything."

I didn't want to tell her everything. I wanted to shield her from all that had gone wrong. She must've sensed my hesitation.

"Dakota Green, this is my wedding, and I need to know what's happening."

I took a deep breath, meeting her eye. She was a strong woman, and she was right. She deserved the truth.

As gently as I could, I caught Lacy up on the events of the night, everything between leaving with Savilla to pick up more wine, to Charlie's key, to searching the fake priest's room.

Lacy stared wordlessly at me for thirty seconds as she processed the information before finally saying, "We made an announcement at the rehearsal dinner right after DeeDee told us. They were in shock, Patty most of all, but Anton's father was there to comfort her. But now, with Todd, with Charlie, with everything... the wedding is officially off."

I jolted, studying her face, which didn't appear nearly as devastated as I would expect after an announcement like that.

"I don't mean that Anton and I won't get married," Lacy continued, her voice low and steady, as if she'd been pulling her thoughts together for some time. "But maybe we don't know each other as well as we should. Maybe we should've taken our time and let our families get to know each other. Regardless, we obviously can't have a wedding after the chaos of this weekend." Her eyes widened as if she was realizing the magnitude of her own words. "A man—the man who was supposed to marry us—is dead, and out front, the bushes have caution tape around them."

I took Lacy's hand, sighing deeply. "I know it's awful, but if it's any consolation, I'm getting the feeling Todd Anderson was up to no good anyway." I didn't mention the *blame Charlie* note that I'd found. It was too much to unpack when Lacy was already dealing with the weight of a collapsed wedding. Instead, I put both hands on her shoulders, making her face me so I could read her expression as well as hear her response. "Tell me the truth: Do you want to marry Anton?"

Lacy let out a long breath and blinked back tears. "I mean,

after everything this weekend…" Her face contorted into a mixture of sorrow and worry. "I still do. His family, this man's death, it isn't his fault. Ultimately they have nothing to do with what Anton and I have, right?"

Lacy looked at me with such expectation, and it pained me that I couldn't answer that question for her and we both knew it. The best I could do was squeeze her hand.

"I know Anton." Lacy inhaled and exhaled, closing her eyes as she thought. "I do. He's the one for me."

I considered Lacy's words. The chaos had come to Anton and Lacy, but it wasn't their fault. That's why she deserved her wedding, even if happily-ever-afters were mostly make-believe.

"Okay, then," I said, my tone adamant. "The wedding will go on."

Lacy's face scrunched and she looked into my eyes. "That's impossible. There's no way we can fix everything that stands in the way of us getting married this weekend. What about the priest? Not to mention Anton's awful family."

"We can't fix his family, but I'll ask Aunt DeeDee to contact her church to find another minister. We'll tell everyone that the wedding ceremony *will* be at 3 p.m. tomorrow, regardless. We can move through this. I won't let the universe—or whoever is dismantling this weekend—stand in your way." I jutted my chin, more determined with every word. "And maybe just as importantly, I have a feeling that keeping everyone here might help us figure out who killed Todd Anderson."

Lacy blinked several times, letting my words sink in. Her expression appeared almost grateful at my willingness to take control and call the shots. "Is it wrong that at this point I just kind of want to get the wedding over with? And it's not because I don't want to marry Anton." She paused, considered. "I think it's more like I am ready to start our lives together, and I don't want to put it off for whatever nonsense his family might try down the road."

"That totally makes sense," I said, pulling her in for a tight hug, more resolved than ever that she would marry Anton tomorrow afternoon, come hell or high water.

Lacy shivered, and then tried to gather herself, her spine straightening. "Do you have any idea who might've killed Todd? Because people are saying..." She hesitated as she studied me.

"What are people saying?"

"People are saying that Charlie was involved."

I narrowed my eyes. "Never."

"Right. I mean, I wouldn't believe for a second that he had anything to do with killing a man, but..." Lacy raised an eyebrow and spoke more gently. "Charlie *is* behind bars."

"I know," I said. "But he didn't shoot him or push him over the balcony—or have anything else to do with Todd's death. Why would he?"

Lacy bit her lip, as if considering whether or not to say more.

"Spit it out," I said, sounding like Momma when I was little and didn't want to tell her the truth about who'd eaten the last cookie.

"I know that Charlie wouldn't *mean* to hurt anyone." Lacy's words were hesitant, making me wonder if she believed them. "It's just... we saw them fighting outside the bookstore, right?"

Sure, I'd seen them fighting. I ran back over the events sequentially in my mind. We'd just left The Attic, goody bags in hand, and all of the women—even Bella and the cousins—were actually in a decent mood. Shortly after entering Sugar & Spice Books, we heard men's voices, and the next thing I knew Charlie was throwing a punch and Todd was splayed on the ground. I'd stared at my boyfriend, who looked back through the window with an expression of utter frustration, and the reality of what I'd just seen did not compute.

"I know his behavior was out of the norm," I said, thinking about the conversation I'd tried to have with him after the fact. Charlie had been vague, but that was from confusion, nothing more. "But Charlie had his reasons, and maybe this can help."

Lacy took the key from me, setting it in her palm and examining it under the light of a nearby lamp. "It has engraved numbers." She squinted as she read them. "Four-three-six-eight."

"What do you think it opens?" I asked, hoping she had some idea.

"Likely a lockbox, and unless it's for a personal safe, the only place with lockboxes in Aubergine would be the bank," Lacy said, a gleam in her eye. Even though this weekend had been derailed, she was willing to help me figure this out, I could tell.

I remembered what Charlie had told me last night, right after he'd punched Todd: "Todd started shouting about how he needed to go to the bank." The idea that this key would open something at the bank made more and more sense. Whatever was inside that lockbox was something Todd wanted.

I took the key from her and ran my fingers across it. For the first time I felt, even though I hadn't first been able to see it, some kind of imprint or engraving. I flipped it over, and on the other side of the key, opposite to the numbers, was a tiny, almost invisible logo imprinted onto the brass. I moved close to a lamp and held it underneath to see a laurel wreath and the letters "ANB."

"Aubergine National Bank," I said, pointing out the logo as confirmation.

"Didn't the Finches found that bank, like, a hundred years ago?" Lacy asked.

"At least a hundred and fifty." I nodded, not quite following her thought process.

"Which means you're probably a shareholder now."

I narrowed my gaze. I'd read through the list of assets that Mr. Froble's law office had sent me as one of the heiresses to the Finch estate. The document had been extensive, running for three entire pages in tiny font, and I certainly hadn't memorized them all. I did know that the Finch estate consisted of the palace, pageant funds— which were mostly depleted—a ton of stock holdings, and investments in about two dozen businesses, most of which were no longer operational. Had there been a line item for the local bank?

"It's getting close to midnight," I said, glancing at the clock. Lacy met my gaze. "Probably the best time to break in."

TWENTY-FIVE

Everyone knows everyone in Aubergine, and our lives are entangled with other citizens' lives in ways that we never imagined possible, which was why my newly acquired status as a wealthy member of the citizenry was the very thing that now allowed me access—or at least an alibi—to peruse the lockboxes at Aubergine National Bank well after closing time.

Lacy and I drove downtown in record time and parked in the only alley in Aubergine. It was between the Morning Brew and the bank, and when I glanced above us, I saw the outdoor stairway leading to Charlie's apartment. I was glad that Charlie had boarded Kitty for the weekend, because otherwise his Great Dane's nose would have appeared between the blinds and he would have started barking his head off for me to come upstairs and pet him already.

"Are you sure we should be doing this?" I asked Lacy, hesitating as we sat in the car outside the back entrance of the bank. Even though it was past midnight, there always seemed to be eyes on Main Street. It was how Momma always knew if Lacy and I had stopped by the soda counter at the drug store after school, rather than going straight home—someone would always mention having seen us there.

"If anyone asks, just say you're checking on, I don't know... your assets? And I'm along for the ride." Lacy spoke with a confidence that I hadn't heard from her all weekend.

I gave her a look that said, *Welcome back.*

"Look, everyone here knows us," Lacy continued, sounding more convincing the longer she spoke. "Our parents definitely leaned into the whole 'it takes a village' mindset. Mr. Coppell probably wouldn't even press charges if he caught us rummaging around inside the main safe."

The Coppell family managed the bank, and I'd known Mr. C since the day Aunt DeeDee had brought me up here at five years old to open a kid's bank account with the twenty dollars I'd received in birthday money. Back then I would've never dreamed of being one of the owners.

I pushed back my shoulders and tried to convince myself that I wasn't doing anything too illegal. Besides it was for a good cause, namely figuring out why Bella had stolen a piece of art from The Rose and who the heck had killed a fake priest—and how the two might be linked.

"You're right," I said to Lacy as I narrowed my eyes at the brick building. "If worst comes to worst, I'll claim my rights as an official Finch descendant and say I was doing an inspection." The more I talked, the more certain I became that we could do this. We could get in and get out without going to jail ourselves.

"Got it." Lacy smirked. "When it comes to breaking the law, you're willing to be a Finch."

I gave her a half-grin and motioned for us to get out of the car as silently as possible.

To avoid immediately alerting anyone who might be watching from window blinds in the lofts above the shops, we decided to sneak in the back entrance. Getting inside the only bank in town should've been more difficult but, years ago, as part of Aubergine High School's course curriculum, I'd chosen to take a locksmithing elective just to try something different and earn an easy credit. In that class, we'd learned how to use a bump key to open almost any lock, and I'd kept one on my key ring for such a time as this. Just for a refresher though, I pulled out my phone and searched up a YouTube video to guide me through each step. I turned down the volume as low as I could while still hearing the instructions.

"What are you doing?" Lacy asked.

"Breaking in," I said, surprising myself at how easily the words rolled off my tongue. "I'm sure these locks haven't been updated in decades."

Lacy stared at me as I slid the symmetrical key into the lock and gently hit it with a hammer that I kept in the car for underwater emergencies. "That was almost too easy."

So far no alarms had sounded, unless they were silent ones, and the bank seemed as sleepy as it did on most weekdays. A town of our size didn't exactly have big deals being made or huge loans being negotiated. It was more the kind of place where parents deposited their checks in the hope that they would someday earn enough to treat their kids to a trip to Disney World.

"This way," Lacy said, motioning for me to head to the right. "My mom has kept a lockbox here for a long time."

"Why?"

"Jewelry passed down through the generations. Dad said we should get a safe at the house, but I think she secretly likes the formality of coming here and having the banker open it for her." Lacy laughed softly. "When I was little, she would bring me with her to pick up a necklace or a pair of earrings before our annual Christmas party. We always walked to the very back and they would go through this elaborate display of safety protocols before pulling out her drawer."

It was dark inside, so we carefully navigated the space, passing the cash counter and the computers where the tellers worked. To our right was the entrance to the safe, which might or might not be filled with actual dollar bills. The last time I'd seen inside had been on the third-grade field trip when the day had culminated in us counting coins. Even back then, I hadn't been impressed with the short stacks of bills.

Within a minute or two, Lacy and I had reached a wall that was essentially floor-to- ceiling rows of metal drawers. I checked the number on the key Charlie had given me against the labels, and it only took me a few seconds to find the one that matched.

Breathing deeply to steel myself, I stepped forward, inserted the small key, and turned it to the right. The lock clicked, and the door opened.

The drawer only contained one item: a wide cylinder container.

"I know this container," I said softly. "Bella had it tucked under her arm last night after she slashed your wedding dress."

"Open it," Lacy replied, her voice resolute and tinged with anger. Thinking about Anton's ex cutting up her dress was a sore topic, which was totally fair.

I glanced around, looking for a paper towel, a handkerchief, gloves. I'd already made the mistake of putting my fingerprints on the drawer, but I didn't want to make things worse by rubbing them all over this container.

A few feet away I spotted a pair of white gloves, which must've been used for handling delicate items. I silently thanked whoever had left them there as I slipped them on and opened the lid at one end of the container, sliding out a rolled-up canvas.

Lacy cleared off a space on top of the counter and I pulled her sleeves over her hands. She held one end of the canvas while I stretched it out, to reveal a painting in the Impressionist style.

The primary subject was of two horses pulling a sleigh through a snowy landscape, and it appeared as if the subjects were heading toward a sprawling house in the distance. In the corner was a faded signature, but I could only make out the last name: *Perry*.

"This must be the one that Bella cut out of the frame at The Rose."

Lacy peered over my shoulder and shone a flashlight on the canvas, making the colors pop. "It's surprisingly good."

"And detailed," I said, inching closer to the depiction of the animals pulling the sleigh. "Those are American Cream Draft horses."

Lacy bent forward to examine it more closely. "They're pretty. Kind of the color of champagne."

"It's a rare breed," I said, as my finger hovered above them. "They're descended from a mare in Iowa about a hundred years ago. She was called Old Granny."

Lacy laughed at the name.

"When we were kids, there was a woman who boarded two of them at the stables here," I recalled. I'd been impressed by the horses and had asked the owner if I could muck out the stalls just so I could more closely examine them. They'd been strong and beautiful, not to mention as sweet as golden retrievers.

Lacy seemed to vaguely recall the detail. "And the stables are right next to a retreat center for artists, right? I remember visitors coming and going. Some of them were dressed like hippies."

"The Aubergine Art Collective," I confirmed. "When we were growing up, Aunt DeeDee volunteered there, making meals and entertaining visitors in the evening. She said they brought much-needed culture to Aubergine with them."

"You think this piece of art was painted there?" Lacy said, but her perplexed look told me she had no idea where I was going with this.

"I think there's a good chance." I pointed to the painting again, this time motioning toward the building in the distance. "What does that look like to you?"

"Not sure." Lacy squinted. "The house is so tiny, and cuts off at the edges."

"But it looks like the backside of the property out at The Rose, right?" I'd really only spent substantial time out there during the beauty pageant when I was trying to figure out who might be involved in Mr. Finch's murder, but I'd also seen it on my ride earlier that afternoon, so the look of the place was fresh in my mind. The house was readily recognizable, particularly since it was the spot where the original Finch homestead had been, while The

Rose was being built, more than a hundred years ago. "This piece could've been painted right here in Aubergine—a kind of snapshot of our little town."

I examined the image for any kind of dating, lifting the edges to peer at the back. "Look, here it says '27. Perry painted it the year after she won the pageant."

Lacy studied the canvas a moment longer while I tried to piece together why Bella Rivera would have this painting, and what it might mean for Todd Anderson's death.

"The painting must be expensive," Lacy mused. "Otherwise, why keep it in a lockbox?"

"And why would Charlie have risked his standing in the police department by slipping me the key, rather than just handing it over to the station?" I pondered. "That man would not hide something from his own department unless he thought it was absolutely necessary."

"He gave you the key because he trusts you," Lacy suggested.

"I'm sure he wouldn't want the entire department stumbling into the bank publicly before the wedding. That would basically announce to the murderer that we're onto them."

I told Lacy about the two halves of the torn note that I'd found: *Meet Big Mike with product, after ceremony on Sunday—if it goes wrong, blame Charlie.*

"So, someone was planning to blame Charlie if an exchange went wrong during my wedding?" Lacy asked, trying to make sense of it.

"Sounds like it, and if Todd was the 'someone,' then the 'someone' is now very dead." I clenched my jaw, still frustrated that my boyfriend was inadvertently involved in all of this. "I have no idea what Todd's death means for the planned exchange, but I imagine that other people were working closely with him."

I thought about what Anton had told us about the other notes his mother had found. Todd Anderson had been working with the Swansons, but he also appeared to be the man on the inside working against them. The only other individuals involved in the family business who were also outsiders included Bella Rivera and Will Hurt.

If I'd had to guess which one needed money more than the other, I would put my money on Will, a man who had lost his job, a husband whose wife had quit teaching, a father whose baby had received expensive NICU treatment for several days, and a man who had seemed very on edge during the festivities of Friday night. All of that added up to some kind of desperation.

"I guess we should—" I had started to say that we should keep a close eye on Will, but before I could finish, I froze at the sound of a creaking door.

Lacy shrieked before throwing a hand over her mouth and shutting off the light on her phone. Instinctively, the two of us hit the floor, trembling.

TWENTY-SIX

The two of us remained crouched at the back of Aubergine National Bank with a stolen Anna Perry painting between us as footsteps headed our way. It was still dark inside the bank, but we could see a small circle of light coming toward us with each step. I swallowed hard and prayed that this person didn't have a gun pointed in our direction.

"Hello? Anyone here?" a woman's voice called, the words tentative. There were steps on the tiled floor as she slowly made her way through the lobby before opening another door and letting herself into the back of the bank. "You're not in trouble. I just want to talk to you."

Suddenly, I recognized the voice. It was Charlie's deputy, Jill Wright. Her footsteps moved closer, but she was slow and methodical as she ran her flashlight across each piece of furniture and underneath each desk.

"It's okay. You're not in trouble." She paused. "Yet." The deputy's words echoed against the steel cabinets and tables, the cold laminate flooring, and the blank walls. "Charlie told me that you might be here."

I frowned at Lacy, who looked uncertainly back at me. I didn't like Charlie tattling at all. He was supposed to be hiding things from his deputy, not from me.

As soon as I had the thought, I realized that Jill might be lying. I blinked into the darkness, no longer knowing who or what to believe.

Deputy Wright obviously had a key to get inside, so she must've gotten permission from the manager to be here. She didn't flip on any lights, which likely meant that she didn't want to draw the attention of prying eyes in the lofts above Main Street to the goings-on inside the bank at this late hour. Jill was also moving slowly, indicating she likely wasn't scared or frantic about what she might find. I wasn't much of a danger, after all.

"You set off the alarm," Jill said as she circled the cabinets, moving steadily into our orbit.

We must've triggered a silent one. I cursed under my breath.

"When we got the call, Charlie said I should come alone," Jill continued. "He said that it would be fine, that it's just you and me, Dakota. Don't make him into a liar."

Lacy's fingers gripped my arm, and my heart pounded hard in my chest. We could stay hunkered on the ground and hope that the deputy's light wouldn't fall on us, which was a shot in the dark, or I could reveal myself of my own accord and hope for a good-faith response; hope that Jill would appreciate the fact that I'd been honest by giving myself up. My head said to stay down, but my gut said that I should take a chance, that if Charlie had trusted Jill as his partner for so many years before bringing her to Aubergine as his second-in-command, then maybe I should give her a chance too.

In a split-second decision, I chose to stand and confront whatever the consequences would be for breaking and entering a bank. I could only hope that Deputy Wright was telling the truth and that she hadn't brought anyone else with her.

"I'm back here," I called, as Lacy tried to pull me back down—we both knew that crouching in front of a lockbox while holding a stolen painting wasn't a good look for either of us. "We're back here."

Jill shone her light on me. I blinked against the brightness.

"We? Who's with you?" she asked, but even in the darkness, I could see her shoulders relax as the beam of her flashlight wandered to where Lacy was hunkered. Her relief told me that she must've been less sure than she'd sounded when combing the bank for us.

"Thank God, ladies." Jill huffed out a long puff of air and bent forward, her elbows on her knees as she put a hand over her heart and tried to calm herself. "I was scared out of my mind that it was one of those Swanson goons. I had no idea what I'd actually do, and Charlie told me not to bring backup."

The confession and the vulnerability in Jill's voice made me want to trust the deputy even though that did not sound like advice Charlie would ever give. Still, I also would've never expected him to slip me a key before being escorted to jail. He was changing his tactics as he grew into this job. I supposed that, unwittingly, so was I.

"Charlie didn't want any of the other officers getting involved," Deputy Wright said, answering my unasked question. "Said that they might do something reckless, because they don't understand what's really happening here."

I wondered if she understood what was really happening. I wasn't sure I did.

"Has he contacted the FBI?" I asked, trying to get a feel for what she knew.

"They're already on their way to Swanson, getting their search warrants in place." Jill lifted her head and met my eyes as she said the words, letting me know she was in the loop and daring me to trust her. "What did you find with the key Charlie slipped you?"

I raised my eyebrows, realizing that he must've decided to trust her with this too—and deciding that at this point I had no other choice than to do the same. I still couldn't help but grip the key more tightly in my palm.

Jill sensed my hesitation. "It's okay. I swear that Charlie sent me."

"I actually want to believe you," I said, my voice gruff with fatigue and emotion.

"As long as there isn't a herd of officers standing outside ready to arrest us," Lacy continued, standing to her full height, "we can work together."

Jill balanced her flashlight face-up on a nearby desk. Then she placed her hands on her hips and tilted her perfectly symmetrical head as she looked from one of us to the other.

"Look, Charlie didn't have a chance to tell me much of anything without another officer around or without us being recorded, but in the few minutes we had while I was getting him from the squad car into the station, he did tell me that he had found a key that he passed along to you and that when I got a security call from the bank, I should go alone and you would be here."

"Why didn't he just give you the key?" I asked, my ego a bit bruised at not being the only one with inside intel.

"Charlie said he didn't want me to have to answer to any higher-ups. In other words, you can't lose your job over this."

Jill inhaled deeply and rubbed at her forehead as if she couldn't believe she was here with us, like this. "So, can you please—for the love of all things holy—tell me what is going on here?"

I glanced at Lacy and she lifted a shoulder. *Time to dive in.*

"Charlie was right," I started. "Before you drove him back to the station, he gave me a key. We figured out that it must be to a lockbox, so we came here." I unfurled the canvas that I'd been holding close and unrolled it onto the long steel table. "This painting, which was stolen from the Salon at The Rose, was inside. I can only imagine that Charlie took the key from Todd's room right after the man... fell."

"You mean right after he was shot," Jill clarified. "The coroner confirmed that it was a single bullet right through the heart, almost like a sniper had fired the pistol. They found it lodged in his sternum."

Just as Charlie had suspected. The air left my lungs like I'd been punched. I'd known that Todd had been shot, but this confirmed beyond a shadow of a doubt that we were dealing with a murder.

But, I realized, it also meant that Charlie was in the clear. I turned to Jill. "Charlie was outside of Todd Anderson's room right before he was shot, which meant he couldn't have been the one to kill him."

"Unless Charlie went inside Todd's room, they had a confrontation, Charlie pulled a gun on him, and shot him as Todd was standing on the balcony."

I shook my head. "That's ridiculous."

The deputy nodded. "I agree, but Charlie actually suggested the scenario."

I tilted my head, studying her as if to determine whose side she was on.

"Not because that's what happened. But because he's thinking like an investigator, which is smart," Jill clarified. "Charlie also said that he didn't hear a gunshot before the man fell, which means someone was likely using a silencer."

I studied the floor for a beat. "And I can only guess that Charlie's not involving the other officers because he thinks they'll either mess it up or that one of them may be in on it."

The deputy flinched at the last few words as if I'd physically slapped her.

I narrowed my eyes, trying to read her but coming up short. "Wait. What's wrong?"

Jill bit her lip, obviously considering whether or not to tell me, before relenting. "There is one person that I've been monitoring, but I have no idea how he would be involved in something to do with a man from the backwoods of Nowhere, Texas."

"Who do you suspect?" I asked, my voice growing louder with urgency.

"Not suspect, exactly. Like I said, I've just been keeping an eye on one of our volunteers. He only comes in on the weekends, so honestly, I don't think he'd even have intel for something like this." As she spoke, Jill tapped a restless staccato against the tabletop and frowned as her mind moved quickly.

"Who is it?" I practically demanded. I needed to know if her thinking was paralleling mine.

Jill studied me for a beat before relenting. "It's Will Hurt."

As soon as she said the name, another piece of the puzzle fell into place. Valerie's husband was indeed involved in all of this, though I wasn't sure how deep.

"Will comes in for a volunteer shift twice a month, but once I found him snooping around files that he had no business accessing," Jill continued. "And another time Charlie said that he went on a ride-along with an officer. Not a big deal except Will didn't sign in or out—or get permission from one of us. It was almost like he wanted to observe under the radar."

"I assume the department ran a background check on Will before he started working there?" I asked, thinking about a way we might be able to figure out how far back Will went with Todd Anderson.

"That was before I transferred here, but sure, that's standard."

"Can I see it?"

The deputy's eyebrows tilted down as if she was trying to determine if this was privileged information. Then, she raised her shoulders as if to say she had nothing to lose at this point.

"Sure." Jill sighed, pulling out her phone. "We've gotten this far, so why not?"

As Deputy Wright said the words, I realized that she must have been going against all kinds of protocol to listen to Charlie and to trust me, especially after I literally broke into the local bank. Even as Charlie was trying to protect her job, she was taking risks. It made me appreciate her more as she made a few clicks and pulled up the information.

"Doesn't look like much of anything," Jill said, scanning it before handing me the electronic report. "Two speeding tickets, but even those are years apart."

I ran my eyes over the information, which was indeed sparse, but it did have a list of four addresses, the most recent of which was in Aubergine.

"Are these the places Will has lived?"

Jill glanced at the list. "Yep."

The other three locations were in Cambridge, Massachusetts, which surprised me since Will didn't have a Northern accent—but then it hit me. Even though Will didn't have a tell-tale Bostonian dropping of the "R" sounds on "car" or "scarf," I knew someone this weekend who did have that heavy sound.

Todd Anderson.

"Can you run a similar report on the man who died?" I asked. "On Todd Anderson?"

Lacy seemed to catch my train of thought. "Will and Todd may have known each other before this weekend."

"Maybe," I muttered, but in my gut, I could feel that I was right. "Maybe they were working together to move the art. If Todd was the man on the inside of the Swansons' illegal business, then maybe Will was working for him."

There were a lot of uncertainties in my statement, but I knew from past experience that all of these maybes could eventually add up to something. We just had to keep looking, keep dropping details into place, even if they sometimes didn't exactly match at the edges. Eventually, we would have a complete picture.

"I can only pull up reports that are already in the system on my phone," Jill said. "I can't generate new ones to see where Todd Anderson lived, unless I'm logged in at the station."

"Let's go, then." I motioned to the back way out of the bank.

"You gotta put the painting back," Lacy said.

"I think we should bring it with us," I said, looking to the deputy for permission. I couldn't exactly take it out of the bank without her say-so. "If this is one of the pieces that the Swansons were trying to move, and if Todd was the insider betraying them, then it feels important to keep it as evidence."

Jill hesitated, though I could tell she wanted to agree with me.

"Unless this lockbox is in the name of Todd Anderson, then we need to notify the owner that we are confiscating it. Who's renting this lockbox?"

"I'm not sure." I glanced around and spotted her heavy-duty flashlight. I gestured toward it. "May I?"

The deputy handed it over.

"There's sure to be a hard copy of a registry somewhere around here," I said. "Aubergine's bank hasn't quite made it into the twenty-first century."

"Very true," Lacy said, likely thinking about the fact that they still didn't have direct deposit or online banking options.

I shone the flashlight on the rows of ledgers and notebooks on a tall bookshelf along the opposite wall, pulling out covers that had a variety of dates listed.

Lacy joined me with the light from her phone. "What exactly should I be looking for?"

"Anything that seems like it might tell us who owns which lockbox."

We scoured the shelves for a few minutes before Jill spoke up from behind us. "Something like this?"

I turned to see that she'd picked a lock on a lower cabinet and pulled out a giant, cloth-bound book. Across the front was written the words, "Safety Registry."

"Looks promising."

"What was the lockbox number?" Jill asked, as she opened the book to the center.

"Four-three-six-eight," I said, having memorized it by now.

Jill flipped through several pages until she reached a recent entry. "Looks like it was secured a few weeks ago."

I followed her fingertip down the row, reading aloud. "Opened November 1 by…" I let out a gasp as I read the signature. "But why would…?" My words trailed off again as I tried to wrap my mind around what I was reading.

The signature indicated the renter of the lockbox was Valerie Hurt.

If the deputy was suspecting Will Hurt of some kind of snooping around the station and if his wife indeed knew the contents of this lockbox, the Hurts were in a world of trouble.

TWENTY-SEVEN

My mind tried to wrap itself around this new detail. Valerie, the woman who'd dropped off her baby, fallen soundly asleep in the theater, and then burst into the Morning Brew with Will to retrieve her child as if we'd kidnapped him, was the same one who'd presumably opened this lockbox and stored a painting that didn't belong to her. In addition, Todd Anderson had the key to her lockbox in his room.

"Wait, what's this other date?" Lacy asked, squinting at the numbers in the registry book.

"It looks like the date that the lockbox rental agreement ends."

"And it's in two days? The day after my wedding."

"Which means this box was opened November 1 and will expire on December 29." I bit my lip, considering the two dates as I asked Lacy, "When exactly did you announce your wedding?"

"We sent out a digital save-the-date on the morning of..." Lacy puffed out a long breath and closed her eyes as the realization hit her.

"What?" the deputy asked, obviously confused.

"Lacy sent out the save-the-date on October 31," I said.

Lacy nodded. "That's right."

"So Valerie rented this lockbox the next day," I said.

"Or Will rented it and put her name on it."

"This looks like her signature, though." I'd seen that handwriting in every yearbook every year since middle school. "Either way, this lockbox was reserved for a very specific purpose."

"To hold a stolen painting during the weekend of my wedding," Lacy finished for me.

I thought for a moment, tried to envision the painting hanging in the Salon at The Rose. I remembered something that Savilla had told me. She said she'd borrowed winter landscape paintings from the town's art collective specifically for this weekend, and if I knew my sister, she would have called and selected the pieces for display as soon as Lacy had told her she'd want to be married at our estate. Savilla went all-in for any kind of festivity.

I snapped my fingers as the details of the timing snapped into place. The painting had to have recently been transported to The Rose in preparation for the wedding this weekend. Unfortunately, my new home—with its lack of tight security—would be a much easier place from which to steal a painting.

"The early arrival of the Swanson family—and the uninvited ex—had to have something to do with the timing of stealing the artwork. They wanted to take the painting while it wasn't under lock and key at the Collective—and before everyone else descended on the estate."

Jill was following my logic. "It's got to be much easier to steal a piece of art from the wall of an unsecured room rather than an actual storage facility."

I nodded absently, considering Valerie's possible involvement, as well as Jill's demand that we communicate the fact that we were confiscating the contents of the lockbox.

"Obviously we can't let Valerie know that we have this painting," I said. "Whether or not Valerie is actually involved, she would tell Will, which would likely mess up any chance of figuring out who murdered Todd, not to mention who is actually trying to sell this painting. That said, here's what I'm going to do—without the permission of law enforcement." I shot a look at Jill. "I'll take the painting with me and keep it close so no one else gets their hands on it."

I could tell that Jill was about to interrupt me to protest.

"It'll be fine," I tried to reassure her. "And if it's not, I'll take the fall."

Jill's cheeks were pink and she seemed anxious about the entire situation while also realizing we had no good options here.

"Fine. Just keep it close," Jill said. "We're not calling it stealing or even confiscating. You've just"—she seemed to be searching for the words—"temporarily borrowed the artwork for investigative purposes."

Despite my initial hesitancy to like this woman, I did appreciate Jill's ability to work around the law.

I grabbed the cylinder in which the painting had been stored and gently pushing it back inside.

"I'll go to the station and run background checks on Todd Anderson... and maybe Valerie, too," Jill said.

"We'll try to check in with you at the station before we need to get ready for the ceremony."

Despite the hesitancy in her expression, Jill nodded.

"First thing in the morning, Lacy and I will go to the Aubergine Art Collective and see what we can find out about the painting—exactly what it's worth, who has owned it, where else it's been displayed, if anyone has been inquiring about this specific one." As I spoke, I shut the lockbox and handed her the key for safekeeping.

I ordered the things we knew for sure in my mind once again:

1. Bella Rivera cut the Perry painting out of the frame at The Rose.
2. This same painting somehow made its way to a lockbox in Valerie Hurt's name.
3. Will Hurt was likely working with Todd Anderson to sell this painting on the black market.
4. The Swansons had an art theft operation at play.

5. Most significantly, a man was dead.

I let out a shuddering sigh as Lacy and I made our way back into the cold night and to the frigid car, thinking as I went.

If we could figure out why this painting was important and how long Will had been working with Todd, then maybe we would better understand the Swansons' sudden interest in our little town —and we would be that much closer to finding Todd's killer... or at least I hoped we would.

TWENTY-EIGHT

I only slept about four hours because Lacy set our alarm for shortly after sunrise. When I opened my eyes, she was already sitting in the wingback chair, dressed, and looking fresh as she tapped her foot restlessly.

"It's my wedding day," she said, the words tinged with fear rather than the excitement she deserved to be feeling, but for the first time that weekend, she seemed more like the friend I'd always known, a woman determined to take names and get shit done.

"It's your wedding day," I repeated back to her, forcing a smile as I struggled to open my eyes against the morning sun already glaring off the mounds of snow that had fallen overnight. "How long have you been awake?"

"Long enough to shower and get ready." Lacy pulled the covers off of me, and I rolled out of bed. "Your turn."

"I can be ready in ten," I managed as I ran the hottest shower known to man before washing my hair super-fast, toweling off, throwing on my comfiest jeans, and brushing my teeth.

I grabbed the cylinder with the rolled-up canvas of the painting, hefted it over my shoulder, and started out the door, thinking about how Bella Rivera had done this very thing when she'd stolen it on Friday night.

Bella, in her desperation to be one of the Swansons, must've thought she was working for the wealthy family the entire time. At some point though she'd handed the painting off to Todd, who was acting as a kind of double agent in this entire scheme and must've had it deposited in the lockbox at the bank for safe keeping. Unfortunately for Todd, whatever his plans might've been, they'd obviously gone very, very wrong.

As we turned the corner of the hall, I stopped and faced Lacy, taking a long look at her before we continued on. "How are you feeling about today?"

"I couldn't sleep much last night, so I thought a lot." Lacy's words were resolute as she met my eyes. "Anton isn't his family, and they aren't him. That much I know. So, if we get married today or next week or next year, I don't really care. But to answer your question, I'm ready for today, whatever it looks like."

"I know how you've dreamed of your wedding," I said, as we made our way down the hall.

"But today isn't our life together," Lacy said, almost as if reminding herself. "You've been trying to take care of me all weekend, and I realized before I fell asleep that I want to return the favor. Yes, I want my wedding to be amazing, but I don't want the man you love behind bars while I'm walking down the aisle. Charlie doesn't deserve that and neither do you."

"But this is your day," I said. "You're not supposed to be worrying about me."

Lacy huffed out a long breath. "We've always shown up for each other, and I'm showing up for you now. Whatever you need from me today, you have it."

I swallowed hard. I knew Lacy meant those words with everything inside her, just as I'd meant to protect her this weekend.

We grabbed a couple of cups of coffee from the lobby of The Rose on our way out the door, thankful no one was yet roaming the halls. Within a half hour, we were sitting outside the front door of the Aubergine Art Collective, an old homestead that had once been the location of a flour mill, complete with a stone base and slatted wooden beams rising up three floors. Nearby was the mill with a giant wooden wheel that was still in the frozen water.

The Art Collective was on about five acres of property west of downtown, and the Finches had appointed various managers of the nonprofit over the past century. The current director was Mr. Weathers, a fifty-something-year-old man, half of the couple who ran this place, though as far as I knew, the Finch money was still actually keeping this place afloat.

Mr. Weathers answered the door after almost a full minute of us knocking. He was bleary-eyed and wearing a robe, and I could see striped pajamas peeking from above his toes. His bare feet must've been cold against the wood floors because as soon as he put on his glasses and spotted his slippers nearby, he scurried away from the door and slipped into them.

"My, my, my," Mr. Weathers said, his Virginia accent thick as the honey that Mr. Finch used to harvest. "How can I help you ladies? Is everything all right?" He had the slightest lisp, which made him that much more charming, and though I knew I'd spoken with him at some point while living in Aubergine, I'd forgotten this detail about him. "We don't have any guests—and we aren't exactly open to visitors... at present." He eyed me. "But wait, aren't you Dakota Green—or Finch?"

The man's cheeks flushed and he blinked several times, nervous as if I'd come to ask him to give a personal accounting of the funds provided by my family. I wondered if the worried look in his eye was something that I would need to get used to as I became ever more ingrained in the Finch family.

"I'm so sorry to wake you up on this holiday morning," I said, in what I hoped was a calming tone. "We just needed to ask you a few questions about the paintings stored here."

Mr. Weathers nodded slowly and his shoulders relaxed as he looked past me to Lacy— before checking a nonexistent watch on his wrist. "Aren't you supposed to be getting married today?"

"I hope so," Lacy replied, in a chipper tone. I wondered

suddenly if this man had been invited—and if he hadn't, whether or not he might be offended. One never knew in a small town.

I didn't want Lacy to think about that right now, so I decided to try to find a way to succinctly explain why we were here before we froze to death on this man's doorstep.

"Mr. Weathers," I started, "I know that us showing up like this is"—I searched for the best word—"unorthodox."

The man raised an inquisitive eyebrow at me but didn't interrupt.

"But we have very good reason to believe that a painting once stored here was recently stolen from The Rose, where Lacy is supposed to hold her wedding today."

Mr. Weathers narrowed his gaze as he opened the door a bit wider. He was at least intrigued.

"Normally, something like a theft from the estate could wait until after Lacy's wedding, but last night..." I paused, trying to keep my thoughts from jumping around. I needed to streamline the situation, not only for Mr. Weathers but also for myself. How exactly to accomplish this goal was suddenly eluding me.

"Last night, a man involved in the theft was killed," Lacy said, stepping forward and finishing the statement for me. "And now my wedding hangs in the balance. I'd really like to find the thief and the murderer—if they are indeed different people—before my wedding this afternoon."

Mr. Weathers' eyes widened and his jaw fell open, and I was grateful for Lacy's ability to make everything so concise.

"Well, why didn't you say so? A theft, a murder, and a wedding, all in one? Come out from the cold and get inside." Mr. Weathers waved us into the foyer, which was toasty. "Anything you need, I'm here to help."

"Thank you," I breathed, relieved that we might be about to find some kind of answer. "If you point us in the right direction for finding out more about the paintings you keep here, we'll be happy to leave you alone."

"Nonsense," Mr. Weathers said with a wave of his hand, as he led us through the house and down a set of stairs to a locked archive room, complete with temperature control and rows of movable shelves. "I'm happy to help however I'm able. Nothing this exciting ever happens around these parts."

Except for the murders of Mr. Finch this past summer and a former classmate in October, I thought, although I supposed that both of those happened out at The Rose, which felt like a separate sphere from Aubergine itself—a bit like the Vatican inside Rome, but on a much less political or ecumenical scale.

Mr. Weathers pressed a button and the rows of shelves began to mechanically shift, the hum of the automatic levers and pulleys sounding as he moved the collection to the first shelf.

I was impressed, and I could tell that Mr. Weathers felt proud of his management. I could also tell that he wasn't planning to leave us down here alone with his goods.

"Which paintings are you interested in?" the man asked, standing at attention to do our bidding.

"We need information on works by an artist named Anna Perry. She won the pageant in its second year." I hesitated to show him the stolen painting in the cylindric container on my shoulder, but after a quick nod from Lacy, I decided that we had no choice but to trust him with the full picture, pun intended.

I spotted a table empty of everything except a microscope, a pair of white gloves, and a magnifying glass. It took me only a few seconds to stretch out the canvas, but as I reached for a heavy stapler to hold down the edges of the painting, Mr. Weathers hurried forward, tutting. He grabbed a frame that could temporarily stretch the canvas without damaging it, but before he did anything else, he put on the white gloves and gently nudged me aside.

As Mr. Weathers worked, I jabbered on. "After winning the second pageant, Perry painted landscapes here, at the Collective." I pointed to a specific spot on the now unrolled painting, hovering over the building in the background. "I think this is a depiction of the Finches' original house on the back property of The Rose."

To his credit, the man didn't slap my hand away even as my fingers inched too close to the work.

Mr. Weathers thought for a moment as he looked from the painting to his shelves. "With the Impressionist elements combined with the subtle use of geometrical patterns and bright colors, it has all the hallmarks of being painted in the early twentieth century—even if I didn't know the artist. The style of the Impressionists had mostly fizzled out by the 1930s, and after the Great Depression it was Modernism this, Modernism that. Experimentation was valued over muted colors and subtlety."

I knew none of this, but I was certainly glad that I'd found Mr. Weathers. I pointed out the demarcation of the year—'27—on the back edge.

"Lovely," Mr. Weathers said, beaming. "Confirmation already. Though it is a rather late Impressionist piece, it appears that this artist was rather young and inexperienced, perhaps just trying to mimic artists she'd seen on display at some museum or another."

"She must've improved over the years because one of her pieces sold at auction for two hundred and fifty grand," I said, recalling what I'd found online two nights ago.

Mr. Weathers took this in. "It is funny how that works. A piece is worth what someone will pay for it, and one that sells well can boost the rest of the artist's collection." He tapped a finger against the table. "It makes sense that she would come here the year after winning the pageant, especially after admiring our town during the summer. Who wouldn't want to return to see it in all its snow-laden beauty?"

Mr. Weathers smiled down at the piece of art like a father doting on his child. I could tell in that moment that he had a love not only for the art but also for Aubergine.

"Let's see what else she might've painted around these parts," he said, a gleam in his eye as he got to do what I imagined was one of his favorite things: researching the archives.

He flipped on his computer, navigated to a software program I didn't recognize, and searched for the name "Perry" within a six-decade date range from the 1920s to the 1980s. As the names of paintings popped onto the screen, he leaned back so Lacy and I could take a look.

I quickly counted thirteen paintings, one of which was named *American Cream & The Original Rose*. "This must be the painting we have here. That breed of horse is unmistakable."

Mr. Weathers smiled as he ran a finger along the screen. "You can see here the details of when and where it went out on loan."

We read the words for the American Cream painting.

Location: The Salon at the Rose Palace
Requested: Nov 1
Delivered: Dec 1
Duration: Three months

I scanned the list and noticed that four other pieces had red check marks next to them, indicating they were also out on loan.

"May I?" I asked, before clicking on them. One was currently located in Lacy's bridal suite, and three were at my aunt's store, The Attic.

"And these other paintings?" Lacy asked, motioning to the artwork without checkmarks. "Are the rest of the paintings stored here?"

"Depends. If we have the means to store them safely, then yes, but there are some we have to send out to more state-of-the-art facilities." Mr. Weathers pushed his glasses up on his nose and squinted at the screen. "But at least six of the paintings are..." His eyes roamed down the screen. "Oh good, they're here in our very own archives."

Mr. Weathers stood up and went back to the mechanical shelves, pressing buttons as the contents moved up and down and around. After a full minute of whirring, he walked into where the shelves had parted for him and began pulling giant folders and boxes aside.

As he searched for the paintings my phone rang, and I stepped to the back of the room. It was Aunt DeeDee. Hopefully she was just checking in. I answered, expecting to hear her ever-chipper voice on the other end, but instead her tone was stoic, as if she was holding back emotion.

I tried to swallow back the fear that she was in danger. "What's wrong?"

"I'm fine," Aunt DeeDee said. "Everything's fine. Well, not everything. Something happened, something strange..."

My aunt had a bad habit of beating around the bush, and I wanted to leap across the phone lines and shake her by the shoulders. "Tell me what's going on," I said, trying not to overreact.

"It's just... I came up to the store to pick up a necklace I'd planned to wear today, but..." Aunt DeeDee let out a long breath. "I think I have—or maybe the town has—been robbed."

Oh Lord. "What's missing? Your jewelry?"

"No. It's my paintings, the ones on loan from the Collective. The ones that Anton's cousin was admiring."

"Charlotte?" I asked.

"That's the one."

I could almost see my aunt biting her lip as she tried to reconcile the information in front of her with the people she'd met during the bachelorette party. She always wanted to believe the best in others, but this time, she couldn't.

"Anyway, the art she liked—it's gone. Cut right out of the frames."

Unfortunately, this made total sense with how Bella had stolen the American Cream painting—cutting it out of the frame.

"Do you see any kind of evidence the thief may have left behind?"

"Only one thing," Aunt DeeDee said slowly. "A silk button."

"Like the ones from Lacy's dress?"

"I think so. It was sitting here on my desk, so I couldn't miss it."

My heart beat rapidly and I clenched my jaw. Bella Rivera was a terrible person, leaving behind a token of her own jealousy and animosity toward my best friend.

"It's got to be Anton's ex," I managed, nearly shivering with anger. "She wanted us to know it was her without being able to prove it. That takes some nerve."

"Sure does."

My eyes flitted to Mr. Weathers, whom I barely knew. That said, I knew enough to realize that the loss of the paintings would be devastating to him.

"I'll let the police know," I told Aunt DeeDee, unable to explain in this moment how closely this was fitting into recent events. "In the meantime—"

But before I could finish my statement, I heard a sharp cry from Mr. Weathers, and when I spun around to find out what had happened to him, he was back in the room, holding empty boxes and looking devastated.

"Every Perry piece is"—Mr. Weathers hiccupped another small cry—"is gone."

TWENTY-NINE

I had neither the time nor the energy to comfort Mr. Weathers, keeper of Aubergine's art, but Lacy made an attempt, settling him into his desk chair and running upstairs to get him a glass of water that he wouldn't allow her to actually bring into the storage space.

"That's okay. I need to come up and drink my coffee anyway," Mr. Weathers muttered as he stared at the empty containers around him, but his heart wasn't in it. He'd gone from happily content to absolutely miserable in the past hour, as he'd realized he'd failed to do his job of protecting the art under his care.

"How could this happen?" Mr. Weathers' face fell as he turned to me with wide eyes. "Will I lose my post here?" He asked the question as if I was in charge. Which, in a way, maybe I was.

"You've done an excellent job," I tried to reassure him. "These are just... extraordinary circumstances." I leaned against the edge of a shelf as I thought out aloud. "We've lost one painting from The Rose, three from Aunt DeeDee's store, and six from storage. Anna Perry's work is in high demand."

"That means ten pieces have disappeared since..."

"We don't know when the ones in storage went missing, but at least four since Friday night. Whoever is taking them has been making quick work of it."

Mr. Weathers shook his head in disbelief. "I take inventory twice a year. We were about to do our second one on December 30, but it's been nearly six months since I would've inspected Ms. Perry's paintings at this facility."

"But you saw the three that went to my aunt's store when they were loaned out, didn't you? And two to the Rose?" I asked, trying to think about what this might mean.

Mr. Weathers nodded slowly, catching my drift as he went back to his computer and checked the dates for the loans to my aunt's shop. He seemed relieved to have something to do with his hands.

"We allow any business establishment in Aubergine to showcase the work. It's part of our cultural duty." Mr. Weathers ran a finger across the computer screen. "DeeDee Green had them delivered back in early October. I'm sure I would've checked on each of the Perry pieces at that time unless..." His voice trailed off as he considered. Then, his face appeared stricken. "...unless I had been too distracted by the other loans. Oh dear, that must've been it."

I gave him a compassionate nod. I didn't need Mr. Weathers feeling guilty for a theft that ultimately wasn't his fault. "Has anyone else had access to the paintings in the archives?"

Mr. Weathers bit his lip and then lifted a finger. "The volunteers. Let me check the sign-in sheet." He grabbed a clipboard hanging on the wall next to the door and handed it to me. "It's not very formal, but don't let that fool you. We do train everyone on proper techniques for preservation before we clear them to work closely with the art. I train them myself."

My eyes scanned the sheet, row by row of names I either recognized vaguely or not at all, but then I got halfway down the page and knew that I'd found what I was looking for.

There, signed and dated, was the name "Valerie Hurt".

"This woman, this one right here," I said, pointing at the same signature that I'd read on the lockbox early this morning. "Is she here often?"

"Valerie? Ah yes, one of our best volunteers."

I closed my eyes and let the information sink in. I'd never been a particular fan of the woman, but she did have a baby, which meant she had a big responsibility that she wouldn't be able to meet if she had to do jail time. I took a deep breath, trying not to jump to conclusions as I checked the date she'd last been here.

"She was last here on November 2."

"Shortly before the birth of Ollie," the man said, smiling.

I didn't dare say what I was thinking, primarily because I hated to be the one to burst his image of this woman—or his false belief in the security of this storage facility.

"Do you have other sign-in sheets like this?"

Mr. Weathers shook his head. "I throw them away."

This man was meticulous about his storage and the information about where his paintings were going. Why wouldn't he be as particular about who was milling about the archives and when?

Seeming to catch on to my train of thought, Mr. Weathers answered before I asked the question. "I'm a tidy person, as you can see. Sheet after sheet of volunteers would be unnecessary clutter. I know my volunteers, train them myself, and trust them implicitly." He crossed his arms as if that was all he needed to say about such things. "Valerie Hurt is not an art thief, as you seem to be suggesting. She's volunteered with me for five years now, and I've never known her to be anything but kind and upstanding."

Upstanding, I could see. Kind, however, surprised me a bit. Valerie had always struck me as a bit high and mighty, but maybe I was inserting my childhood view of her onto a grown woman, which wasn't really fair.

"Is it possible that Valerie's husband, Will, might have had access to the storage at any point?" I asked, stretching for another possibility that might clear Valerie's name.

Mr. Weathers' face screwed up and he snapped his fingers. "Funny you should ask, actually. Mr. Hurt applied to be a volunteer in the archives, but I rejected—or, shall I say, redirected—his application, which Valerie seemed to completely understand."

Both of those details felt relevant

"What do you mean by 'redirected'?" Lacy asked. "And when was that?"

"Oh, just a few months ago. I told him I could use him elsewhere in our work."

"And on what grounds did you reject his offer to help out in the archives?" I asked.

Mr. Weathers blinked at me several times as if he shouldn't have to explain such things. "Well, dear, he's not from around here."

I almost laughed at the statement, one I hadn't heard recently—and certainly one I didn't expect to hear from Mr. Weathers. I was certain he'd experienced enough judgment over the years to keep from participating in it himself.

Mr. Weathers waved a hand. "I don't mean my decision as any kind of disparagement of Mr. Hurt's character. He told me he'd lived in and around Boston growing up, but I'm not prejudiced against outsiders. No, it was also a matter of nepotism. I don't allow spouses or partners to work together—I had a couple in the past that couldn't seem to keep their hands off of one another in the archives, and I've always thought that it might be too tempting to lift a piece together." Mr. Weathers lifted his chin as if his thinking were completely logical. "So, instead, I eliminate any temptation. I told Will Hurt that he could help move pieces to locations around town if he didn't mind the heavy lifting. He seemed more than willing."

My eyes widened. Of course, Will had been willing, particularly if he'd somehow gotten involved with Todd Anderson and black market art dealers. Between Will's wife's work in the archives and his work moving paintings, he would have a pulse on the location of almost every piece in the archives. Useful information if he happened to need to make a bit of extra money.

My thoughts reminded me that Deputy Wright was supposed to be looking up any background information she could find on Todd or Valerie. I could only hope that the strings in our tapestry might finally be pulled together to create a complete image. We might even find our murderer.

THIRTY

As soon as Lacy and I were back in the car, I called the station, but the deputy wasn't there. Jill lived a couple of towns over, but I didn't know her address. Anyway, she wasn't the person I really wanted to see. I put the car in drive and headed toward the station, ordering victims and suspects in my mind as I went.

Todd had been a smart go-between, but now he was unfortunately a very dead one.

Bella Rivera had obviously been involved in stealing at least one Anna Perry painting from The Rose—and possibly others from Aunt DeeDee's shop—but I still believed she was working with the Swansons and had assumed Todd was doing the same.

Will must've stolen the other six paintings from the Aubergine Art Collective archives.

If I was reading the clues correctly, then Todd had been the handler, betraying the Swansons right under their noses. He'd kept the most valuable Perry painting for himself in a lockbox downtown, with the help of his old buddy Will Hurt, and possibly Valerie.

Finally, some kind of handoff was supposed to happen with Big Mike during the wedding ceremony this afternoon, but we couldn't let it.

And in not letting it, would this flush out the murderer?

It was time to stitch every detail together.

Lacy and I reached the concrete building that was the police station, the only real eyesore in town, in record time.

"You go inside," Lacy said, knowing why we were here. "I'll keep the car running."

Because there was so little crime in Aubergine—until recent months—the station was just an open-air office plan with three small cells along the far wall.

As soon as I walked in, I spotted Charlie through the bars of one of the cells, and our eyes met.

He was wearing the same button-down shirt he'd been wearing at the rehearsal dinner, and even from here I could see the stubble that ran along his pronounced jaw. My heart beat faster when I saw him sitting there, unable to do anything to help this case along —but I knew that I could fix that by talking to him here and now.

I started toward Charlie, a new determination taking shape. One way or another, I would get him out of here today.

"Ma'am, you can't go back there," an officer at the front called. It was Officer Keith Becker, the same one who'd let me inside Todd's room at the deputy's command last night.

"I'll be quick," I said, not making eye contact.

"Ma'am, I need to ask you to—"

"No, Keith, I need to ask you to back off." I spun around and stared him down, hoping that my voice would stay even and that I could sound more confident than I felt in that moment. "I know how Charlie runs this department, and I have the right to talk to him, to see what he needs, to find out at what point he wants me to get in touch with his lawyer."

At the mention of a lawyer, the officer appeared suddenly flustered. He lifted a finger and fumbled around in the stack of papers on his desk.

"Yes, Ms. Green, I understand, and... actually, I was just going to ask you to look at something that the deputy left here for you," Keith said, nearly cowering as he handed over the papers.

I took the sheets from the man and scanned the contents: one a background previously run on Will Hurt, and the other two new documents on Todd Anderson and Valerie Hurt, which Jill had requested. Valerie's was almost entirely blank with only two Aubergine addresses. On the men's documents, there were no crimes or previous offenses listed, but one address on each page was circled and next to it was written, "Episcopal Boys' Home."

I checked the dates of residence. For Will, the dates were from 2009 to 2012, and for Todd, they were even longer, 2003 to 2014. An overlap of only a few years, but certainly formative adolescent ones.

Todd and Will had definitely known one another before this weekend.

I checked the most recent residences on each page. Will Hurt had lived in Aubergine ever since he'd got engaged to Valerie a few years ago. In that same time, Todd had lived in Swanson, moving from apartment to apartment until about six months ago when his residence was listed as a house. I pulled out my phone and googled the address. Sure enough, it was the Swansons' house.

I could suddenly see how it had played out.

Todd had started dating Patty Swanson sometime in the year she was separated from her husband. Todd had obviously gotten close enough for Patty to reveal her family's real money-making business. When Todd had heard that Patty's son lived in Aubergine, it was the perfect opportunity to get his hands on some easy art and invite his old friend to come in on the job to make some extra cash. When the wedding was announced, it was all the better: a perfect distraction for their heists. They'd be back in Swanson before anyone was the wiser.

"Have you seen this?" I asked Charlie, who was now leaning against the bars.

Charlie didn't answer and instead motioned with his chin toward Officer Keith. He didn't want to talk in front of him, so I would need a reason to see my boyfriend. Alone.

I cleared my throat and narrowed my eyes at the young officer. "I'm going to need to speak with the sheriff on some urgent business in the interrogation room."

Keith looked confused. "Interrogation room? You mean the break room?"

I cleared my throat. I should've known there wasn't anything as official as an interrogation room. "Yes, that. Exactly."

Keith glanced from me to the sheriff and back again, conflicted. After a moment though, he straightened his spine. "I'm sorry, Ms. Green, but I can't let you do that."

I frowned at Keith and dared a glance at Charlie, as if to ask if he believed this guy.

A smile was playing about Charlie's lips. He was proud of the officer. He'd trained him well.

"Fine, then," I said, huffing out a breath as I addressed Keith again. "Where is Deputy Wright this morning? We were supposed to get some intel and then"—I searched for a word that sounded official—"and then reconvene."

"After the deputy ran this report for you, she decided to drive out to Richmond, to the state's cyber investigation headquarters," Keith answered, his voice steady. "She's hoping she can trace the fake security call that came in to the sheriff last night, right before Todd Anderson's death."

I was impressed at the deputy's proactivity, especially on a Sunday morning.

"She has an old friend on the inside who agreed to meet her," Charlie clarified.

Keith's gaze went to his boss and the younger man stood taller, almost as if at attention.

"Relax, Keith," Charlie said, with a half-grin. "I know you're just doing your job by keeping me locked up. I won't hold it against you, and hopefully whatever Jill finds out this morning will get me out of here a lot sooner."

I moved toward Charlie's cell, and this time Keith didn't stop either of us. In fact, I noticed that the younger officer politely turned away.

"So, you're just waiting?" I asked Charlie, lowering my voice.

"Waiting, yes, but not sure exactly for what. It's a long shot that the team can even trace a prepaid phone this quickly," Charlie said, rubbing one hand across his brow. They'd lowered the lights back here, and I noticed a pillow and blanket, but last night could not have been a comfortable night of rest.

"Any evidence tying you to the crime is circumstantial at best," I said. "Surely they can release you."

"If they figure out who made that fake security phone call to me, then it could send everything in the right direction. Otherwise, I'm in here for a full forty-eight hours, and I don't want any special treatment."

I didn't want to argue with Charlie, to tell him that being involved in the investigation from behind bars was a kind of special treatment, but then again, he'd let Aunt DeeDee participate as much as she could when he'd brought her in a few months ago. She just hadn't known nearly as much about how the law worked. I swallowed a sudden lump in my throat against the reality that in less than six months, two people I loved deeply had been in the very same place.

"I'm fine," Charlie said, trying to reassure me, even though he didn't know quite what I was thinking. "Lacy's going forward with the ceremony?"

I nodded, leaning my head against the bars. "I want you there with me, not just to figure out who is behind all of this."

Charlie kissed the top of my head. "I know."

An alarm beeped on my phone, one I'd set weeks ago when I'd added the hair and makeup appointment to my calendar. I was supposed to be sipping mimosas in the Salon while someone prepped me, Savilla, Jemma, and Lacy for our stroll down the aisle of the Primrose Ballroom.

"You need to go?" Charlie asked.

I lifted a shoulder, not wanting to leave him.

"You need to go," he said, not a question this time. "I'll be fine, I swear. I've got good company with Keith, and I'll be out soon, either way." He gave me a half-smile and spoke in a fake disgruntled voice. "I know my rights." Charlie kissed my head again and nudged me away from the cell. "Go. Lacy needs you."

Unfortunately, she wasn't the only one.

THIRTY-ONE

Savilla stopped by to check on Lacy and me just as we got back to our suite, and though she didn't come right out and ask the question, I could tell she wanted to know if the wedding would go on as scheduled.

"The wedding is as planned," I said firmly, and when my sister appeared confused by my tone, Lacy tried to intervene.

"Even though a man was murdered?" Savilla asked, stricken. "And even though Charlie is behind bars?"

Both of those were great questions, ones that I was pretty confident everyone here this weekend would be asking.

"Deputy Wright is on it, and her team believes it's an isolated incident. Someone had beef with Todd, and they did their worst. Keeping everyone here will buy her time to look into the suspects' backgrounds."

When I finished speaking, I realized that in my nervousness I'd been talking very quickly. Part of those nerves came from hiding so much from my sister, but at least the second half of my statement was true. The wedding was happening in part to solve a murder, but Savilla didn't seem convinced. She started to protest, but Lacy interrupted her.

"And, um, I'm dying to marry Anton, which is, um, a very poor choice of words, I realize, but it's just..." Lacy trailed off, looking to me to take over.

"It's what Todd Anderson would've wanted. He was very excited about being in this ceremony." That was likely true too, I realized, though Todd had probably been much more excited about filching an expensive painting than anything else.

I hated lying to Savilla, and I swore in that moment that when all of this was said and done, I would fill her in on every detail.

Savilla took my words in stride, sensing that I wasn't telling her the full story but also willing to trust me.

"Of course, you want your big day to be as soon as possible, and I'm sure you're right. Reverend Todd would want you two to be joined in holy marriagimony just like you planned." Savilla gave both of us a generous smile. "Everything will be perfect and I'll see you in the Salon in a few."

While we prepped and preened in the hours leading up to the ceremony, I heard nothing from Charlie or Jill. The Swanson family was strangely absent as well, no longer causing a fuss over who would marry Anton or bursting into the room with their loud personalities.

I kept checking my phone as the makeup artist and hair dresser worked their wonders, turning me into the maid of honor that I was always meant to be.

Aunt DeeDee popped in and out, zipping us up and pouring us more drinks, and Savilla and Jemma kept the conversation lively, making me glad that I hadn't let my sister in on this mystery at least. One of us needed to be oblivious enough to not be freaking out. I only hoped that mine and Lacy's nerves would be attributed to the large guest list rather than to fear of whoever had killed Todd.

I still hadn't heard a peep from Deputy Wright as I stood in the Salon in full makeup and an updo, ready to make my way down to the ballroom with the rest of the party.

Lacy's mother was helping her get into her dress, now fully repaired, and two photographers were milling about, snapping candids and buzzing in and out of view.

"You know you don't have to do this," Lacy's mother had told her. "It's been... quite a weekend. We can reschedule, perhaps try a destination wedding next summer."

Lacy hadn't told her parents about the stolen art or our side investigations, but they knew a man was dead and that was enough.

"I want to marry Anton," Lacy had answered, which was true.

I stood next to Savilla, who stood next to Jemma, in front of a long mirror, waiting to see Lacy in her full glory.

"Maybe it will be your turn soon?" Savilla said, interrupting my thoughts.

"For...?" I asked, genuinely unsure what she meant. *For thieving? For murdering?*

"For nuptials!" Savilla finished. "For maritated bliss!"

Although I guessed she meant "marital" and "consummated", the word sounded more like some kind of marination, a prospect that wasn't nearly as inviting. But I wasn't going to argue with her this afternoon.

"What about you?" I said to Savilla. "You really seemed to enjoy holding Ollie for hours during the bachelorette party."

"I have no romantic prospectives, but I'd love to be a doting auntie," Savilla answered, raising her eyebrows.

"Ooooh... me too," Aunt DeeDee said, coming into the room and immediately getting in on the conversation. "Can't you just see a little Dakota–Charlie combo running around these halls?"

I could not see it, but I didn't want to burst their bubble. "Maybe someday, but first we need to make sure he's out of jail. Visiting him at the penitentiary for two hours each Saturday might put a damper on our future plans."

Jemma laughed. She'd been mostly unfazed and unafraid by the events of the weekend, which was how she operated most of the time. I still remembered wandering through the tunnel under the estate during the pageant, with her attempting to keep me from freaking out.

"I never want kids," Jemma said, as she wrinkled her nose in distaste. "They poop and sleep. Then, they walk and poop and sleep. Then, they complain and walk and poop and sleep. Kids aren't like wine. They don't improve with age."

Savilla swatted playfully at her, and she put an arm over each of our shoulders, looking at our reflections in the glass. Momma would've been proud to see us like this, even if it was in the middle of a criminal investigation.

"Bridal party, ready?" called a member of staff who was applying to be the Rose Palace's full-time wedding coordinator. Savilla had told her that directing this ceremony could be part of her trial run.

"Ready."

I turned as Lacy stepped forward in her full regalia for the first time, swaths of fabric fitted around her perfect figure, tulle and satin shrouding her as if she were a gift to be unwrapped.

"You look like a dream," Savilla said with a sigh.

"Perfection," Aunt DeeDee declared.

"You look like the prettiest meringue ever," I said, making Lacy and the others laugh. I took her hand in mine and squeezed. "Really, though, you are so beautiful."

"Ditto," Lacy said, and I knew that she meant it in all the ways. "I'm sorry Charlie's not here."

"Me too, but it's okay. Like you said, today's just a blip on the rest of our lives."

"A blip," Lacy agreed, stroking the back of my hand with her thumb.

"Time to line up," the coordinator shouted, just as Deputy Wright burst into the room, startling all of us.

"We have it!" Jill called loudly enough for the other side of the house to hear. She was waving something in her hands, and Charlie was right behind her, looking just like I'd seen him a few hours earlier, but now free from behind those bars.

My heart raced as Charlie hurried toward me, pulled me to him, and lifted me off the ground in a tight hug. He smelled a bit musty, but in that moment I didn't care.

"What do you have?" I asked, finding my words.

"The prepaid phone registration," Jill answered.

"Who owns the phone?" Lacy asked.

"We don't have a full name, but we do have an initial," Jill answered. "Does M. Swanson mean anything to you?"

"It could be Michael Swanson, but Charlie said the person on the other end of the line was a woman, so it's more likely M as in Myrtis," I suggested. "She seems very in-the-know. If she didn't make the call herself, I could see her picking up a phone for someone."

Jill turned to Charlie. "Any idea how she got your number?"

He lifted a shoulder. "A quick search of the station's website would do it."

Jill's eyes were astounded. "Really? Is mine there too?"

"No, only the sheriff's. It's such a small community that it's been common practice ever since the station put up a website back in 2000."

"Probably needs to change now," I said, a bit saddened by the reality that Aubergine wasn't as safe as I'd once imagined. Apparently, trouble came to us even if we weren't looking for it.

"First things first." Charlie nodded slowly. "Dakota, we need you to do the heavy lifting. We can't exactly walk into the ceremony looking like this." He motioned to the deputy in her full uniform before pointing at himself. "And I'm supposed to be in jail. We'd be sure to spook the criminals."

"Wait." Lacy inserted herself into the conversation. "Are you planning to call this person during the ceremony?"

"That's the idea," Charlie admitted, though I could tell it pained him to interrupt her ceremony, especially after everything else this weekend. "Dakota will be our lookout from the front, and we'll be watching from the back to see if anyone checks their pockets or their bags when it buzzes."

"And if they threw out the phone already?" I asked, catching the confused expressions of Savilla, Jemma, and Aunt DeeDee, but also not having time to explain right then.

"They could've tossed the phone, yes," Jill said, "but my guess is that they haven't, especially since they don't have all of the paintings in hand yet." I knew this was true because I still had the Perry piece I'd taken from the lockbox hidden in my room.

Jill continued: "And the phone is obviously key in all the planning for this weekend."

"You think they'll only toss the phone after all this is done and dusted," I said, my mind racing. Charlie had received a call about security at The Rose during the rehearsal dinner; Todd was then shot and fell from his fourth-floor balcony at The Rose; there had been a note appearing to blame Charlie in the man's pocket...

Yes, everything about the murder started with that first call to Charlie.

As I thought about the phone, my eye fell on something pink peeking out from beneath the low couch, close to where I'd found the bag on Friday night when Bella had been in here slashing Lacy's dress and presumably stealing the painting.

It was the same pink bag.

I glanced at Lacy and then at the others gathered there. "Has anyone else been in here today? Besides us?"

Savilla shook her head. "Definitely not. This room is off limits to regular guests."

That didn't stop Bella on Friday night, I thought, but didn't say. "Then whose is this?"

Savilla's eyes widened and she tilted her head. "That's a Birkin bag," she said. "They're handmade by Hermès and worth twenty to thirty grand, easy. I noticed Bella carrying it on Friday night. Maybe she stopped by?"

No one answered Savilla's question as I opened it, remembering the weapons that had been inside two nights earlier. I saw that the pricey bag still contained the same items. I removed the box cutter, one that had likely cut canvases out of frames. I pushed open the blade and could still see the fragments of the thick fabric.

"There's also pepper spray, this short round telescope thing..." Jill wordlessly handed me gloves, and I removed the objects from the bag one at a time.

Charlie's eyes widened as he shot a look at the deputy. "That's a silencer."

That caught my attention. "Could it have been used when Todd Anderson was shot?"

"It's likely." The deputy turned back to me. "You mentioned that Bella was carrying this bag. Do you know for sure that it's hers?"

"It's a Birkin," Savilla clarified again, obviously not grasping quite what mattered in this moment.

The deputy shook her head slightly. "Do you know for sure to whom this Birkin belongs?"

"I thought it belonged to Bella," I said, trying to remember when I'd first seen her carrying it. Something vague she'd said crept into the edges of my mind. "But," I continued slowly, "Bella did say something strange when I found her here on Friday night: even as she asked me to give her the bag, she said it wasn't hers."

"Have you seen anyone else with it this weekend?" Charlie asked.

My eyes lit up. I had seen someone else with it.

At the Morning Brew in the late hours of the bachelorette party, Charlotte had slung it across her shoulder and patted it affectionately, almost as if she had her own baby inside. And then I suddenly saw the image of her when I'd first met her before the bachelorette party on Friday night.

She'd taken yellow-tinted glasses from her hair and placed them in the bag.

This bag was hers, and those glasses weren't for reading or for driving or for keeping the sun out of her eyes; in fact, those glasses wouldn't even be comfortable in the daytime. They were for night-time, for the minute that she needed to see clearly in the dark to take deadly aim.

"It has to belong to Char—" As I started to say the cousin's name, it was as if a light bulb went off in my head. Her name could've been turned so easily into a nickname by family and friends.

I let out a soft gasp as understanding dawned and I muttered, "Blame Charlie." I was stunned as I turned to Charlie. "That note wasn't talking about you at all."

Charlie studied me, trying to follow my reasoning.

"Big Mike is a nickname, so is Charlie, which means Charlie has to be..." I bit my lip, running the details through my mind at lightning speed to ensure they made sense. It did. It had to. "Charlie is Charlotte Swanson."

Jill looked at me puzzled, so Charlie explained the notes. "That could be it," she mused when he finished.

I started to hand the bag to Jill, but as I did so, I noticed that it was still heavy, with some kind of weight moving in the bottom of it. I reached my hand inside, but nothing was there. Still, I was sure this bag wasn't empty.

I flipped open the box cutter and reached inside to cut open the fabric in the bottom.

"Don't," Savilla said, with a gasp and an outstretched hand.

I gave her a gentle smile. "This is evidence, Savilla. Not just a pricey bag."

"It's not just a bag," Savilla said, "and it's a work of art."

"But not worth a man's life," Jill said, taking the bag from me and quickly cutting into the bottom. Her eyes widened as she reached inside and pulled out a gun.

Charlie studied it, knowing in an instant the make and model. "This has to be the gun that killed Todd Anderson."

THIRTY-TWO

The Primrose Ballroom had been transformed into its own winter wonderland, but an indoor one. The chandeliers still hung from above, but they were turned off, the lighting replaced by old-fashioned incandescent bulbs that let off a soft glow as if moonlight had been bottled up for this very occasion. Wisteria hung from white trellises suspended from the ceiling, and a plush white carpet now extended down an aisle created by the seating, and across the front of the room, where Anton waited with Joe Larson and Will Hurt—who seemed just as antsy as the last time I'd seen him.

The ballroom was filled with about four hundred guests, about half of whom had driven the fifteen minutes or so from Aubergine proper. Others had either checked into The Rose last night or were staying in the nearest big towns.

In the front row were Anton's parents—Patty and Michael. I hadn't gotten a good look at Michael since his conversation with me and Charlie on Friday night. According to the note I'd found, Todd was supposed to make a delivery to the man during this very ceremony, which certainly cast the groom's father in a whole new light. What had the Swansons planned? Some kind of art handoff during the ceremony?

The married couple sat side by side as if they belonged

together. As I watched them, Michael put an arm around his estranged wife, who seemed to be more than willing to accept his affection in this time of grief over her much younger, much deader boyfriend. Relationships were certainly complicated.

"Can I see the feed?" I asked Deputy Wright, who'd had just enough time for her team to set up four black-and-white cameras around the periphery of the room. One was at the front, focused on the groom's side.

Jill passed me the iPad streaming the camera feeds, and I let my eyes roam over the images, searching for anything out of place as well as the people that we were watching closely.

"Those are Anton's parents, and that's Charlotte Swanson," I said, pointing to the far left of the third row. "Right next to..."

I was about to say right next to her cousin, Myrtis, but then I noticed that they were sitting several feet apart, with something between them.

"What is that?" I asked, trying to enlarge the feed unsuccessfully.

Charlie took the screen and froze the image momentarily so he could zoom in. "Looks like a really large briefcase."

I almost wondered aloud what kind of person would bring a briefcase to a wedding, but then I knew. That must be the carrying case for the art. I told Jill and Charlie as much.

"But why would they be carrying it around in broad daylight?" I asked.

"Because no one expects an art heist at a wedding," Jill answered, her tone flat without being mean.

The art itself was long gone. Today's ceremony wasn't about stealing—it was about passing the goods on to their buyer while everyone else toasted the happy couple.

I supposed that was true. "Okay, so can't you go in there, open up the case, and bust them?"

I studied Jill and Charlie, trying to understand why they weren't moving in already. I was pretty sure at this point they wouldn't wait just to spare Lacy's wedding.

"It's too soon. We just don't know what's in that case," Charlie answered. "It could be empty, for all we know. And anyway, we don't want to take someone down on theft charges if they're actually a murderer. We want them to pay the full penalty for their full crime. So we need to see how this will play out. I just thank God Lacy was okay for us to do this."

As soon as I'd realized that the real "Charlie" in "blame Charlie" was actually Charlotte Swanson, I'd wanted her taken into custody. She didn't deserve the chance to get away—and I was a bit irritated with myself for taking so long to see her key role in this whole fiasco.

I'd been assuming that Charlotte was *just* a cousin, someone with a bit of sway but not much more than Bella Rivera or Myrtis Swanson. But Charlotte had been the one who'd silenced Myrtis in the car on the way to the bachelorette party. She'd been the one who'd chatted knowledgably with Aunt DeeDee about art. She'd been the one that Will was afraid of. She'd been the one to pull something like night-vision glasses from her hair and tuck them inside her bag of weapons, and I was certain, even though we were waiting to get her fingerprints, that she was the one who'd had someone make a security call to the sheriff while she'd waited in the trees of the estate, ready to pull the trigger. Perhaps she'd planned to kill both Todd and Charlie, though I couldn't dwell on such a thought. It was too heavy to consider.

Instead, Charlie and Jill had decided to keep a very close watch on her.

When I'd asked Lacy and her mother if they recalled Charlotte or Myrtis stepping out of the rehearsal dinner, they couldn't remember, which was fair considering that there were fifty people there. They hadn't even realized that Charlie or I had gone.

"You know what to do?" Charlie asked, all business now.

I repeated the plan back to him. "You'll make a call to the prepaid phone during the candle lighting, and I'll keep an eye on the groom's side to see if anyone reaches for a phone."

"It's not definitive proof by a long shot, but it could confirm our other suspicions," Charlie said.

"We just need to know we're moving in the right direction," Jill added, before moving on to the next step of the plan. "The Birkin bag is stationed behind the altar at the front."

The American Cream painting had been expertly rolled and was sticking out of the top. I nodded, knowing what to do with them when the time came. "Now we hope for the best-case scenario."

"Exactly," Charlie said.

As a string quartet off to the side of the platform began to play, Charlie gave me a kiss and a light pat on the back while Jill offered a quick nod as if to remind me that I could do this. Then, the two of them went into the permanent sound booth at the back corner of the room, trying to make themselves scarce until the right moment.

"Time to line up," I told everyone as the bridal party descended from the Salon. A minute later I was getting into my place at the back of the line while the groomsmen stood on the stage next to Anton. With Charlie out, we were down a groomsman at the front, but the balance wouldn't be too off.

After we were in place, I caught Lacy's eye. She gave me a quick wink, reminding me that all of this was fine—or, at least, understandable.

"I get to have a wedding, and a stakeout, all in the same thirty minutes," Lacy had said when we'd outlined the plan. I appreciated her efforts to hide any disappointment she might be feeling. "If you get a chance, tell Mr. Weathers I said thank you for coming —and for his help."

"Will do."

The ceremony proceeded beautifully from the flower girls to the wedding march. I walked down the aisle, holding a bouquet of white roses laced with baby's breath, trying to keep my eyes fixed straight ahead even though I knew there was a murderer in our midst. Despite what I knew was about to go down, my eyes welled as I watched Lacy come down the aisle on her father's arm. He was beaming proudly, even though he'd also been apprised of the changes to the day.

The music faded, and the opening benediction was given by an actual priest from Aunt DeeDee's congregation, a woman who'd been willing to come and officiate last minute. It almost felt like a normal wedding for the first few minutes as 1 Corinthians 13 was read by one of Lacy's college friends, and a cello played as a soloist sang a soft version of the Beatles' "All You Need Is Love." I sniffed back the tears as Anton and Lacy said their vows and exchanged rings. I could read the love in Lacy's eyes and the adoration in Anton's. This was a truly beautiful union, even in these fraught circumstances.

When it came time for the wedded couple to light a single candle together, I took a deep breath, knowing that things were about to change.

My eyes roamed from the happy couple to the front rows of Anton's side of the family, knowing Charlie would be calling the prepaid phone. I hoped to see one of them flinch as if they'd been surprised by the call, but no one moved, except for an older gentleman who was snoring and suddenly woke himself up.

My eyes flicked to the back of the room, where I could just make out Charlie shaking his head in the sound booth.

The call was a no-go, which necessitated the next part of the plan.

While Lacy and Anton stood at the unity candle, I handed my bouquet to Savilla and stepped forward, gently taking the Birkin bag from behind the altar, where we'd had the wedding coordinator place it. Whether because of the bag or because I was doing something unconventional, I felt every eye shift to me.

Mr. Weathers stepped out of his seat on the bride's side at the end of a row, carrying a canvas stretcher and an empty frame in his arms. He'd happily agreed to get in on the action, if for no other reason than to contribute to restoring his beloved paintings to their rightful place.

I removed *American Cream & The Original Rose* from the

Birkin bag and began to unroll it, sensing the hum of nervous energy in the room from those who had no idea what was happening—and particularly from the groom's side, as they peered forward to see what in the world I was doing, especially with a piece of art their family had stolen.

"The bride's and groom's families have asked for a special symbol to commemorate the joining of their two families," I said into a microphone near the altar.

Anton's parents stared at me, while Lacy's parents looked across the aisle and gave a polite nod as if this had all been discussed and agreed upon beforehand.

"In addition to the unity candle which the couple has just lit, Lacy and Anton will be signing their names in the center of this artwork, a late-Impressionist work originally painted in Aubergine, the very community where they plan to live and raise their family."

Based on the frowns on Michael's and Patty's faces, I realized that I might be driving home the point of where they would live a bit too hard.

"But first, the happy couple would like to invite their parents forward to sign their names on each side of the painting. After the ceremony, this piece will be available to be signed by all of you at the reception, testament to the masterpiece that will be the Abbott–Swanson home. Mr. Weathers, our curator at the Aubergine Art Collective, has kindly agreed to frame the painting to hang in their home."

I was having a hard time keeping my voice from quivering as I said the words, and I only hoped that what we were doing—seemingly defacing an expensive painting—would work. After all, this painting had been the thing that someone—likely Charlotte Swanson—was willing to kill a man over in order to keep him from stealing from her family's business.

Lacy's parents stepped forward first. I managed a smile even though my cheeks felt so tense that they might freeze that way forever. I handed Lacy's father and mother a marker pen, letting them sign on a piece of wax paper that I'd slipped over a section of the painting. Lacy's mom winked at me conspiratorially before turning toward the groom's side and extending the marker in the direction of Patty Swanson.

Rigidly, Patty stood first, then Michael. I could see their minds churning with the question of whether or not they were willing to deface a prized piece of art in front of the rest of their family—and, indeed, in front of whoever was really in charge here.

"Wait," I heard a voice call from the third row, right next to Charlotte Swanson. It was Cousin Myrtis. She shot up and seemed eager to speak, but then was at a complete loss of what to say next.

All eyes turned to her, and the force of them must've felt heavy enough to sit her right back down. Myrtis's outcry was helpful—at least we knew she understood the value of the painting and cared enough to say something to keep us from ruining it—but this simple action was far from enough to convict anyone of anything.

Patty moved forward, marker in hand. Her eyes went from me to the painting and back again before turning to her husband, a plaintive look in her eyes.

"We can't... can we?" she asked her husband.

Michael glanced over his shoulder, but I couldn't see who or what he was looking at. He obviously didn't get any kind of sign because he turned back around, still uncertain.

"Where... where... where do I sign?" Patty Swanson asked, her voice more subdued than I'd ever heard it before.

"Sign anywhere you like, the bigger the better," I nearly shouted, hoping against hope that someone would stop this. We had no alternative plan to catch the murderer otherwise.

That's when I remembered a piece of advice I'd gotten during my very first investigation: People kill for love or money. I'd assumed that this time the only love involved was between Anton and Lacy on the day of their wedding, but perhaps I'd missed something.

In a split second, the world froze around me almost like a painting, allowing me to focus on the specific subjects: those here who loved one another.

I looked at Patty and Michael Swanson, who were staring at each other, bewildered but lovingly so, as they wondered at how to handle the defacement of this valuable painting.

I eyed Bella Rivera, her gaze fixed on Anton even as he stood next to his bride, gazing into Lacy's bright eyes.

I saw Valerie on the bride's side, staring into the face of Baby Ollie.

And then I saw Charlotte Swanson, her eyes boring into Will Hurt. The truth hit me all at once: Charlotte Swanson was in love with Will. That's why she'd whispered to him in the Carriage House. That's why she'd been asking about Valerie and the baby. That's why Will had been so eager to get away from Charlotte at the Morning Brew. Charlotte wanted Will: I was sure of it. But my hunches didn't matter, and there was only one way to prove it.

Before anyone else could move an inch, I reached into the Birkin bag and pulled out the only other object it still contained: the box cutter.

I slid out the blade and held it aloft as I looked directly at Will, who'd been watching all of this, wide-eyed, from his place as a groomsman at the front of the stage.

"Will Hurt," I called, loud enough to be heard in the back, "I need you to tell me what you know. Otherwise, I'll destroy this painting."

A series of gasps came from around the room, likely because I was holding an object that could be perceived as a weapon for all to see.

I waited for Will to answer, but suddenly his face contorted into a grimace. For a millisecond, it seemed as if he might charge at me, but his expression wasn't one of anger. It was one of pain. Will gripped his arm, moving from forearm to shoulder and then to his chest, just as his knees gave way and he fell to the floor.

Will Hurt appeared to be having a heart attack.

"Will, Will, are you okay?" a woman's voice screamed. I looked around to see Valerie Hurt, frantic, as she knelt before him with their baby in her arms.

That's when I heard another voice, one that was authoritative and in control. Charlotte Swanson pointed at Myrtis. "Call 911. Now," she said, hurrying down the aisle toward Will.

Charlotte knelt beside Will, pushing away Valerie's hand before she rolled him onto his back and hovered over him.

"Will, listen to me. It's Charlotte. The ambulance is on its way." Charlotte studied him and then looked at the Birkin bag at my feet. Her expression told me she hadn't been expecting to see it again so soon. She turned to Valerie. "There's aspirin in the pocket inside that bag. Give it to me."

Valerie, eyes wide in shock, turned to do the woman's bidding, motioning for me to hand her the bag. Though this hadn't been part of the plan, I obliged, passing it along.

Charlotte took the Birkin from Valerie and paused for a moment as if she realized something was missing. She glanced at me for a brief second and shook her head before reaching inside and pulling out a bottle of aspirin, opening the bottle, and shoving a pill into Will's mouth.

Less than a minute later, Will's eyes were open as he stared up at the two women, both watching him with mirrored longing in their eyes.

"What happened?" he asked, looking to Valerie and gripping his chest as if he feared the pain might return.

"I think you had a heart attack," Valerie said, holding Ollie close even as he began to fuss. "This... this woman... she gave you aspirin, but the ambulance is on its way."

Charlotte's jaw tightened at the mention of herself as "this woman" and then her expression morphed from concern to suspicion, her eyes studying Will's uncreased brow, his sudden lack of pain, the way his hand caressed his wife's palm.

Charlotte looked from Will to the bag she was holding, to Michael and Patty Swanson. And, finally, to me. "You did this, didn't you?"

I stared straight back at her. "Guilty as charged."

THIRTY-THREE

Once we had the weapon that had likely killed Todd Anderson—and only needed the fingerprints to prove it—I'd suggested that we involve Will and Valerie Hurt.

We told Michael and Patty Swanson the most basic details, starting with the fact that their art storage facility at their Texas ranch was about to be raided, and they were happy to oblige as part of a guaranteed plea deal that would keep them from the most severe punishment.

Bella admitted to planting the Birkin bag where we would find the gun. She'd gotten cold feet after Todd was killed and she'd had a change of heart. Basically, she wanted Charlotte to be caught.

Valerie would be free and clear because she didn't actually know anything other than the fact that her husband had asked her to store something important at the bank as part of a business opportunity. Her only crime was that she hadn't looked more closely at what her husband had been doing and, thankfully for Ollie, that would not put her behind bars.

The medics never arrived because Charlie had called them off as soon as Myrtis had called them in, but Charlotte was on her feet, obviously unwilling to go down without a fight.

As for the mysterious buyer of the Perry painting, we would

never know their identity because the exchange that Todd had underhandedly orchestrated would no longer happen. Still, it made me wonder where he or she might've been as this bizarre wedding ceremony unfolded.

"If you'll come with us," Charlie called, as he started down the aisle, "we need to take you down to the station to ask you a few questions and get some fingerprints."

"Take your hands off of me," Charlotte said, attempting to shake off his hands.

"Ma'am, this will be much easier if you go quietly," Charlie responded in his smoothest sheriff voice.

"You have nothing to connect me to—" Charlotte started, but I cut her off.

"You've been giving orders to orchestrate an art heist right under our noses. You've been carrying around a bag of weapons, and I'm guessing that the gun that killed a man has your finger-prints on it," I said plainly. "Not to mention the fact that the dead man had a note in his pocket blaming you if anything went wrong this weekend."

Charlotte's brows dipped and she seemed on the verge of protesting once more before she caught the eyes of her family, their expressions clearly willing to throw her under the bus. Charlotte relented, each word crisp. "I want my lawyer."

"That can be arranged, but you're still coming with us," Charlie said.

Jill handed Charlie some handcuffs, and he pulled Charlotte's hands behind her back. Even so, she wasn't done with this crowd.

First, she looked to Will, whose face was falling into a somber expression.

Will sat up and stood to his feet, glancing at Charlotte, catching her fiery look. She was not only the other woman; she was his boss, and the trepidation in his features showed he was well aware of these facts.

"How do you even know her?" Valerie asked, her head darting back and forth between her husband and this other woman.

Will hung his head, but answered, "Through Todd. He reached out on Instagram months ago to congratulate me on the baby, and we started messaging. When I lost my job and you quit working, he told me that he had a side gig for me." Will finally looked up, studying his wife's face. What he saw must've encouraged him to continue. "That's when he introduced me to Charlotte. I was just trying to provide for our family, especially after Ollie had to stay in the hospital. Todd said that eventually I could work with the Swanson family and make enough money that you would never need to lift a finger again. I swear on Ollie's life that I had nothing to do with killing Todd. He was my friend. I would never—"

"That's enough," Valerie said, holding her head high as she absorbed the information.

Will turned to Charlotte. "Charlotte, I'm sorry. I didn't mean to..." Will couldn't seem to find the words for what he hadn't meant to do, but I thought I could fill them in for him. He hadn't meant to cheat on his wife? To trick the thieves out of their own heist? To do whatever it took to make money for his family? Will said none of these things, and his silence hung in the air.

"When Todd introduced you to me, I thought you were the real deal," Charlotte said, her voice calm at first, but steadily rising. "I thought you could help us start something bigger. I had no idea you would betray me for a few thousand dollars."

She narrowed her eyes and looked Valerie up and down, shaking her head in derision. Even before she spoke, I could see that her next words were meant to cut like a knife. "When we were in bed last night, he told me that you and your brat were just a burden hanging around his neck."

I heard gasps from the wedding attendees, especially from the bride's side. Many of them were from Aubergine and had known Valerie for her entire life.

Valerie's eyes widened, and when she looked to her husband, he quickly averted his gaze. She was realizing that Will was not only a criminal. He was also a lying, cheating husband.

Will lifted his chin, eyes darting between Charlotte and Valerie as he said weakly, "Don't talk about my family after you killed my oldest friend."

Charlotte's face suddenly contorted as if he'd struck her. "You didn't need him. I'm the only one you need."

In that one statement I saw that it wasn't just love or money at play here. It was a twisted sort of jealousy. Charlotte had not only fallen in love with Will; she'd wanted him completely to herself. Who knew what she'd planned next for the two of them?

Valerie, clearly angry but trying to remain measured, handed Ollie to Savilla's waiting arms as her eyes focused intently on Charlotte.

"That's my husband you're talking about," Valerie said, her expression a mixture of anger and betrayal as she moved toward Charlotte, helpless now in handcuffs. "Even though Will was being an idiot, he was being an idiot for us. For me and my son. As for you..." Valerie trailed off, unable to find words for what she meant. Then, she reared back and slapped Charlotte hard across the face.

Charlotte's cheek glowed red from the slap, and the redness seemed only to fuel her growing anger. She turned toward the groom's side of the ballroom, almost shouting now. "I did this for all of you, my ungrateful imbeciles." She looked straight at Patty. "Your stupid boy-toy was planning a whole other side gig this weekend. He was going to take from everything our family has worked for, and you were going to let him. You're not a true Swanson."

Bella spoke up for the first time in all of this, obviously taking Patty's side as she addressed Charlotte. "Todd betrayed all of us. He saw the chance to sell the art himself, pocket the profit, and disappear. We might steal art, but you're the real criminal here. You killed a man."

Patty inhaled deeply, but she didn't respond, silenced and willing to let another speak on her behalf. If it hadn't been because of a murderer, I would've been impressed.

Charlie and the deputy started with Charlotte back down the aisle, but I couldn't let her go without asking questions that the woman might, in her rage, answer.

"Where were you?" I demanded of Charlotte, "when you shot Todd?"

A smirk reached Charlotte's lips as her head spun around and her eyes found mine. "Wouldn't you like to know, you bitch?"

I kept my voice even, trying another question. "Why did you call Charlie right before you shot Todd Anderson? Why pretend to be an alarm company?"

I saw Charlotte mentally calculating. She was guilty, and we all knew it. We also had the murder weapon, and her fingerprints would confirm her as the killer. There wasn't much left to lose, and adrenaline was coursing through her body, making her reckless.

"If you're not gonna talk here, I'm happy to get you into the interrogation room," Charlie said gruffly, taking her upper arm in his hand.

Either his words, his touch, or his tone—or all three—sent Charlotte over the edge. She squeezed her eyes shut and attempted to yank herself from his grasp, but Charlie's fingers held on tighter.

"I wanted you there, you know," she screamed at Charlie from between clenched teeth, angry tears in her eyes. "I needed a suspect, and I picked you."

Charlie's eyes widened, surprised at the venom in her words.

Charlotte's head shook, almost violently. "I've known men like you, small-town do-gooders. You think you're God's gift to law enforcement." Her cheeks reddened as if she remembered someone from her own past. "I knew you would be in the way, looking behind locked doors and asking questions that no one needed to ask. If I could use local law enforcement as a distraction from me, all the better."

I thought of the agents who would soon be descending on Swanson, Texas, if they hadn't already. Charlotte would hate them —and us—even more when she found out. Thankfully, by then she would hopefully be behind bars.

"It was time one of you paid for trying to destroy what we are trying to build," Charlotte spat again.

"What exactly have you been building?" I asked, trying to lower my voice so as to keep her talking.

Myrtis, her expression almost proud, stood from her seat in the audience. "What will be the most lucrative art business ever—if we can get the right people in place and keep the ridiculous regulations out of our way." She sounded as if she was parroting something she'd heard many times.

"That's enough," Michael Swanson said, putting out a hand to keep any other secrets from being revealed. His tone was authoritative, fatherly even. "Why don't we all take a beat and keep our mouths shut if we know what's good for us?"

"It's too late for that," I said, hoping I sounded confident, like I was a step ahead. "We also know Bella Rivera stole this painting from the Salon upstairs."

Bella shrank in her seat as Mr. Weathers, who'd kept his head through this entire ordeal, held up the artwork so the wedding attendees could see that it was unblemished.

Onlookers mumbled from their seats, astounded. This ceremony was certainly more than they'd bargained for.

"We also know about the other six pieces that have gone missing from the Collective," Mr. Weathers added.

"And three that were stolen from my shop," Aunt DeeDee called out from the other side of the ballroom.

The entire roomed was stunned.

Charlie began leading Charlotte down the aisle, a wedding in reverse. "We'll talk more at the station," he said. As he walked, he read Charlotte the Miranda rights: "You have the right to remain silent. Anything you do or say can be held against you in..." The words continued, but I'd heard them so often, I barely noticed the singsong phrases.

Jill then began to put Will Hurt in handcuffs, giving me a curt nod as if to say I'd done well once again.

With Will's hands behind his back, he called to his wife as he was led away. "I'm sorry, Val. It was a fling. It meant—"

Valerie cut him off. "That's enough. I trusted you. I gave you my life. I gave you a son. I won't make that mistake again." Valerie turned to Jill. "Take him away."

Charlie had officers on the way, ready to round up the entire Swanson clan for questioning about their business endeavors in the art world. It would take him all day and into the night to get the information he needed—unless they called in a lawyer. Either way, he would be planted at The Rose for the foreseeable future.

Savilla and Aunt DeeDee were hugging and comforting Valerie and Baby Ollie, and I went to join them. I hated that a family would have to suffer because Will had been caught, but based on Valerie's reaction to all of this, I was hopeful that she herself would be able to tough it out.

Now, Savilla pulled the baby close and patted Valerie on the back. "I've got a hugenormous house, and you two are welcome for as long as you want to stay."

Aunt DeeDee tilted her head and looked at me, her face mirroring my own surprise. Savilla was full of hospitality, but I had no idea she would want people to live here with her.

I shook my head in wonder at her big heart, thinking that I wouldn't be surprised if I showed up to visit this summer and Savilla had taken in half the town. Maybe instead of a hotel, she would turn the house into a school of some sort, allow children to run up and down the halls all day long. Who knew what things Savilla Finch might decide to do?

As I watched Charlie organize the Swansons into rows at the front of the Primrose Ballroom, I was reminded that I still had something big to decide as well, namely whether or not I was planning to come back home to Aubergine and open my own practice after I finished school in May—or take the fellowship that would keep me away for the next four years and potentially send my career in a totally different direction.

Charlie was a big part of that decision.

"What are you thinking about, doll?" Aunt DeeDee asked, approaching me with an arm extended to pull me into a hug. Before I could answer she gently led me outside the ballroom and toward the back of the house, where we could see the Blue Ridge Mountains through the windows, the sun hovering just over the top of the ridges.

"Oh, you know," I finally said. "Just thinking about the next murder I'm going to solve."

"Let's pray that The Rose stays murder-free from here on out." Aunt DeeDee laughed, shaking her head.

I leaned against my aunt's shoulder and let out a deep sigh.

She seemed to sense I wasn't saying something. "What else is on your mind, baby girl?"

"Nothing, really. Just thinking about the future, about what comes next for me."

"You remember what your momma used to say whenever she had to decide between two options?" Aunt DeeDee asked.

I did remember, and I quoted the saying now: "'Chances are both paths end at the same mile marker at some point.'"

"That wisdom served her well." Aunt DeeDee inhaled as if she wasn't sure if she should say what was actually on her mind but then decided to proceed anyway. "You know that as soon as you were born, I was thrilled to be an auntie, but when your momma first told me she was pregnant, I thought she was crazy for all of it: for raising a baby as a single woman, for not telling anyone who the father was, for not making him be involved." She looked from me into the distance of the towering peaks that made us feel small in the best way. "I'm glad your momma was crazy in her own way, and I think as we saw tonight, she passed on a little bit of that delightful madness to you."

"Are you saying I should take the crazy-looking path?" I asked, with a soft smile.

"It'll probably be the most fun," Aunt DeeDee said simply, as we both stared into the mountains that were home to us.

EPILOGUE
FIVE MONTHS LATER

I unpacked a box with my bedding inside, tugging at the sheets until they stretched over the edge of the mattress. Next, I pulled out a blanket and pillow shams. Momma had always said that if the kitchen and bedroom were livable, a new place would look much brighter.

As I fluffed the comforter and spread it across my bed, I wondered what Momma would think of my decision to live and work here. Just as quickly, I reminded myself of what Aunt DeeDee and Momma had poured into me for more than a quarter of a century: they would both want me to direct my own life now.

"These are the last of them," Charlie said, setting three more boxes down and coming behind me with his strong arms. He reached around my body and clasped his hands together, nuzzling into my neck. "I don't know how I'm going to get any work done with you just down the road."

We were standing in the Carriage House of The Rose, where I'd decided to live upstairs while opening my practice downstairs, caring for animals of all sizes in and around Aubergine.

"I'll be busy too," I said, playfully. "And if you show up without an appointment, you'll have to wait for me like everyone else."

Charlie's expression suddenly turned serious. "I'd wait forever for you, but I'm really, really glad I don't have to."

I knew it seemed crazy to some that I'd given up the fellowship, but I'd decided that I wanted a small life. I craved to be in a place where I could know and be known, love and be loved. As Momma would have said, I knew my own mind.

Charlie kissed me in a way that continued to make my head spin, and when he pulled back, I folded myself into his chest, tears surprising me by springing to my eyes.

"Hey, you okay?" he asked, putting his chin against the top of my head.

I nodded into him, thinking of all the things and people I was so grateful for: Lacy's very small wedding ceremony this evening in the garden, my aunt begging to make her wedding cake since it would be such a small guest list this time; Savilla delighted to have me living so near; and this man who was holding me.

Momma had not only given me life—she'd given me a life here in Aubergine, tucked in between my mountains.

I kissed Charlie again, and I knew I was exactly where I wanted to be.

Thank you for reading *A Bride's Guide to Happiness and Homicide*. It's been so wonderful to explore the ongoing friendships and romances in the Blue Ridge Mountains of Virginia. If you'd like to hear about my new and upcoming releases, you can sign up for my author newsletter.

www.stormpublishing.co/kristen-bird

If you enjoyed *A Bride's Guide to Happiness and Homicide* and could spare a moment to leave a review, that would be hugely appreciated. Even a short review can make all the difference in encouraging a reader to discover my books for the first time. Thank you so much!

Writing about Lacy's wedding mishaps allowed me the opportunity to explore more of the town of Aubergine, and I adored inventing and getting to know even more citizens that populate the hamlet where Dakota Green grew up.

This past summer I traveled with my husband and three teenagers to the Biltmore Estate in Asheville, North Carolina, and it was a fresh experience coming back to the mansion that has inspired all three of Dakota's mysteries. From the Halloween room, to the pool that had to be filled—and emptied and scrubbed—by a team of servants in the days before chlorine, this real-life house allowed me not only to step back into the past but also to reimagine Dakota and Savilla roaming the halls today.

The women at the heart of this series are the real heroes, their relationships deepening the themes of sisterhood in the midst of whatever tragedy or joy life throws at them. I hope you've enjoyed spending time with Dakota, Lacy, Savilla, and Aunt DeeDee as much as I have, and I can only imagine them roaming the halls of the Rose Palace together for years to come.

Happy reading,

Kristen

instagram.com/kristenbirdwrites
facebook.com/kristen.bird.writes
x.com/kbirdwrites
linkedin.com/in/kristen-bird-b28233224